I0655604

ECHOES
OF THE FLUTE

By Mark Wildyr

STARbooks Press, Herndon, VA

Copyright © 2014 by STARbooks Press

ISBN 13: 978-1-61303-082-0

This book is a work of fiction. Names, characters, places, situations and
incidents are the product of the authors' imaginations or are used fictitiously.
Any resemblance to actual events, locales, or persons, living or dead, is purely
coincidental. All rights reserved, including the right of reproduction in whole
or in part in any form.

Published in the United States by STARbooks Press, PO Box 711612,
Herndon, VA 20171. Printed in the United States

Cover Design by Emma Aldous: www.arthousepublishing.co.uk

"Be civilized and prosper."

Yet fortune never smiles. Only wretched pain.

Warriors, forced into trousers and called by alien names.

Drums remind of yesteryear.

Flutes lament what was.

Stanza from the poem "Echoes of the Flute" by Mark Wildyr

Contents

PROLOGUE

Dakota Territory, June 1878

A mob surged across the wooden bridge like a primordial organism in search of food. Torchlight punched flickering holes in the black night as farmers and merchants and housewives and mothers churned restlessly in front of a cabin on the north bank of the crick. Moments later, a white-stockinged blue roan pulled a buckboard into their midst.

A hook-nosed man clad in black bellowed from the driver's bench, "Come out, sinners. Atone to these good people and the Lord God Almighty!" Despite a thin frame, his voice was deep and sonorous.

The cabin door opened, flooding the porch with lantern glow. A tall man walked out to face the group. "What's going on here? Why're you tromping around in my yard this time of night?"

"You are abominations in the sight of God! The judgment of *Leviticus 20:13* shall be upon you this night."

"I have sinned against no one. Your words are farts in the wind."

"Did you hear? Profanity! Yes, you *have sinned*, brother. 'Mankind shall not lie with mankind as he lieth with womankind,'" the Preacher intoned. "Confess and beg forgiveness."

"Stop acting the fool and get out of here. Go home and leave me in peace." He started back into the cabin.

"He's goin' for a gun!" someone yelled.

As the man turned to protest, a bullet caught him in the chest. He stumbled against the doorjamb. A second slug broke his shoulder and propelled him through the cabin's threshold. He managed to close the door and drop the bar to barricade it before collapsing onto the floor.

When torches hurled on the roof kindled a hungry fire, the black-frocked preacher flicked his reins and turned the rig around, scattering members of his flock.

A pinto charged out of the tree line into the pack, the rider yelling and firing his rifle into the air. After a shocked silence, the mob rushed the newcomer. Hands snatched him from the saddle before he could bring his weapon to bear.

By the time the maddened horde hoisted a rope over a cottonwood branch and left the horseman kicking and gasping his life away, the buckboard raced for Yanube City.

CHAPTER 1

Yanube City, Dakota Territory, one year earlier

The anvil clanged like the Sunday bell down at Main Street Methodist Church, spitting red-orange sparks with each blow of Timo Bowers's hammer. Made me think of a chorus of angels with fiery wings. When the blacksmith thrust tongs gripping a glowing ingot of iron into the fire pit, I applied bellows until the metal glowed. Then he placed it on the anvil and began conducting his choir all over again.

The smith's name was Timothy, but he'd held onto Timo ever since my Uncle Cut Hand slapped it on him when his family wintered at Teacher's Mead after the Sioux killed the rest of their small wagon train. Ten-year-old Timo and his little sister were terrified of Cut Hand, a pure-blood Yanube Indian, so he spent the long snowbound months easing the children's fears and becoming their best friend.

All this Timo had told me many times, usually starting with, "John, it's like he was standing here in front of me after all these years."

Better'n forty of them, I figured. The smith had to be a mite past fifty now. In the three weeks I'd been apprenticing at the forge with Timo, I'd heard the story until it was boresome. He always ended up saying how much I looked like Cut. Not my grandpa, but Cut Hand.

"Well, he *was* my grandmother's brother," I'd say.

"Finest-looking man I ever seen," Timo would come back at me.

I already knew a good deal about smithing. Crow Johnson, the Absaroka Pa'd hired to handle our forge at Teacher's Mead fifty miles to the east, had taught me a lot before he left for Crow Indian country to look after his sick father. So here I was, trying to learn all I could from the best blacksmith and farrier in the territory.

"That's enough for today, John," he said. "Let's go in and clean up. I got a pepper stew on the stove to pad our bread baskets. Something special for your last night here. You glad to be going home tomorrow?"

"Yes, sir. I miss it. But I sure learned a lot from you."

He waved away my claim as he closed the doors to the shop and turned toward his home a hippity-hop off to the east. "Wasn't much for me to do. That Crow Indian taught you pretty good."

"He gave me the basics, but you let me know the why, not just the what. Otter says knowing why the what's the what is important."

"Otter's about the smartest Indian I ever knowed." Timo unlatched the door to the house. This morning, he'd banked coals in the kitchen

3

stove to take the chill off the pots of water left on top. It was high summer, so the water didn't need much warming.

Stripping in front of other men didn't bother me any. My pa and my brother Alex and Matthew Brandt — who might as well be my brother — and me were always showing some flesh between skinny dipping in the river or spending time in the sweat lodge, a holdover from Pa's heritage. He was born half Yanube — a cousin of the Sioux.

Timo didn't have brothers and was shy about shucking his clothes in front of others. So we cleaned up at different times to preserve his modesty. After visiting the necessary, I walked into the back room he used for bathing and found two tubs of water.

"Hope it don't bother you none, but since it's your last night here, I thought we'd sit and jaw a spell."

"Fine by me." I slipped braces off my shoulders and was buff in half a minute. I stuck a toe in the water and backed off, turning away when I saw where he was looking. "Tad warm," I mumbled.

He gulped aloud. "You look just like him."

I shook my head. "Can't. He was full-blood, I'm quarter."

"He was like that, too. Never minded me looking at him nekked."

I *hadn't* minded, but I was beginning to. "That's the thing about Indians. They figure the body just needs enough cover to keep warm."

Beginning to go all goose-pimply, I stuck a foot in the tub and tried not to howl. Despite fixing to roast my acorns, I sat down.

"For somebody so young, you're … you're built like a grown man."

"Hard work, I guess."

He finished undressing and walked to the other tub. He'd had a good look at me, so I took one at him. Smithing had kept him fit as a fiddle. He had more hair than I did. I took after my pa's side of the family more than my ma's. Pa didn't have body hair anywhere except right around his privates.

As he settled into his tub, I grabbed a bar of soap and started scrubbing. Getting sweaty and grubby didn't distress me any, but it sure was a pleasure washing the grime away. At the Mead, Grandpa Billy had used gravity to bring spring water from the hill behind us right into the stone house. It felt fresher standing beneath a stream of water than sitting in your own washed-off dirt. I always used a jug of fresh water to sluice over me after tub-bathing.

That done, I wrapped myself in a big towel and sat on a stool while he kept on soaking. Didn't seem friendly to walk away when he'd hoped to do some talking, so I sat and listened to him reminisce about the old days. Inevitably, he ended up comparing me to my great uncle.

"You got his build. He was graceful like you are. Them eyes. Never seen none like them again … until you come around. Black as pure carbon with little flecks of gold."

"My pa's got eyes like that, too." Good to have something to contribute.

"You're the spitting image of him. Except …"

"Except my hair."

"That's it. First time I seen your head, I thought somebody'd took a paintbrush to it."

Worn short in the white man's way, my mop was a glossy Indian black with little strands of my ma's yellow hair sprinkled throughout it. Alexander claimed my gold-speckled head made the antelope curious, and Matthew complained it chased the deer away. I'd taken some teasing about it, so hair was a halfway touchy subject. Timo said it was pretty. Not strange, like everybody else called it, but pretty.

Figuring we'd been sociable enough, I excused myself and threw on some fresh duds before going out to the stable to check on Arrow Wind. My pony was the second war horse in the family labeled that way. Cut Hand had ridden the original and died astride his back.

After working our way through the pot of pepper stew and playing our usual game of draughts — he called it checkers — we said good night. I went to my room and shucked down to the short linen breechcloth that was my underwear. I couldn't abide long johns.

Timo didn't spend much on candle wax or coal-oil, so I couldn't read, as was my habit, before taking to bed. When Cut Hand first brought Billy Strobaw to Yanube country back in '32, he'd taught Cut and Otter and Dog Fox — that was Pa's Indian name — to read and write in English. Otter kept it up with us kids after Grandpa died.

I blew out the candle and crawled onto the feather tick mattress. The bedding was meant for winter sleeping — and this was June — so it was hot even when the night turned cool. Other than collecting heat, it was comfortable, though. When I sank down into the feathers, they snuggled me close and safe.

I came awake when Timo entered the darkened room. The puffy mattress lifted me as his weight dropped onto the other side. Lying nearly naked on the flat of my back, I froze when a calloused hand touched my arm. I probably should have got huffy, but I didn't. I remained quiet as his broad palm swept my chest, puckering my nipples and testing my flesh.

The horny hand had a curiously gentle feel. His fingers came to rest on my manhood, and heat flooded my viscera like syrupy lava. When he massaged my staff through the thin undershift, there wasn't anything I could do to keep from getting hard. In all my eighteen summers, no one had ever touched me like that.

He pulled down my loincloth, and grasped my cock. His tongue swirled around my slit. Then a warm, welcoming mouth slid halfway down my throbbing member. My legs scissored when Timo took more of me into his wet maw. A goosey, creepy, sensual feeling rode the chill bumps sweeping down my back.

My toes curled as his head rose and fell in an increasingly hypnotic rhythm. I panted into the darkness in soft puffs as my time neared. I was unable to move beyond the involuntary things. I got hotter, harder. The magma boiling inside me thickened and pulsed, seeking release. Then Timo went all the way down on me.

My body arched. I threw my hips into him as orgasm struck. The lava broke loose and spewed liquid heat into his invisible orifice. My muscles spasmed, convulsing until I danced on the mattress like bacon over fire. My seed spewed out of me so hard I grew swimmy-headed. Just when I thought it was over, his tongue swirled around my glans, and it was like coming all over again. I gushed more semen.

Finally, the night was still and quiet, except for my labored breathing. I licked dry lips and smelled sated lust and a hint of tobacco and alcohol. I grew aware of the rough texture of bed linens against my damp skin and the weight of the man on my groin. Time stretched out. Tarnation, had Timo gone to sleep with my shrunken *che* in his mouth? As I wrestled with that thought, he rose and left the room without uttering a word, leaving me to study on what had happened.

I knew one thing for sure. It wasn't me he'd done that for ... it had been for Cut Hand. His wanting of my dead uncle was so powerful I could almost feel his presence. And I'd never believed in *wah-nah-gee* ... ghosts.

# # # # #

The next morning, Timo said nothing about last night, so I didn't either. I kept looking at him, but he wouldn't meet my eyes. His goodbyes were pleasant enough, but our handshake was brief.

Bamboozled, I turned north upon leaving Yanube City instead of heading home. Arrow hadn't been ridden much during my stay at the

Bowers place, so he was frisky and ready for a workout. It didn't take us long to cover the seven miles out to Morrow Farm.

Joseph Strobaw Otter — who was known as River Otter to fellow tribesmen and Otter to my family — walked out of the cabin as I crossed the bridge over Turtle Crick and rode into the yard.

He gave the open-handed greeting. "*Hah-ue, dah-koh-zjah.*"

Otter had called all Cuthan Strobaw's kids "grandchild" for as long as I could remember. Cuthan was Pa's American name. I greeted Otter with an Indian handshake, grasping forearms instead of palms.

He looked me over. "You are becoming a man, War Eagle." He used my natural name when nobody was around. "What brings you all the way out here? Is anything wrong?"

I regarded the handsome man who'd been my grandfather's constant companion for the last two decades of his life. He had to be on the high side of fifty, but his back was straight, his hair black and lustrous, and his teeth good. He would probably die working Major Morrow's fields. The retired army officer had some sort of connection with Teacher's Mead I didn't fully understand.

After that situation with Timo Bowers last night, I'd thought of Otter. He'd always been a strong, constant guardian, and I would trust him with my life. It had always been that way.

"No, there is nothing wrong. At least, that I know about. I've been the last three weeks in Yanube City learning about blacksmithing."

"Good. A man can't know too much."

I laughed. "They called Grandpa Billy the Teacher, but that should have been your name. You're the one who taught all of us."

"I only passed on what he'd given me. There weren't any schools in the territory back then. Still, we were the fortunate ones. In other places, the white men sent our away children to schools they set up on reservations."

I'd been ignorant of my narrow escape.

He walked with me while I watered Arrow before ground tethering the pony on the shady side of the house. Then we went to the covered porch where we shared drinks from a keg of passably cool water.

We spent time catching up on events, but even after enough polite talk had gone by, I was still at a loss how to bring up the question I'd come to pose. Things of the flesh were best kept personal, but what had happened last night preyed on my mind. He saw through me and asked straight out what the problem was.

"Don't know if it is a problem." With hot, stinging cheeks, I charged straight into the thing and told him what went on in that dark room.

Otter heard me out without speaking. After I finished, he got up and went inside the house, returning with an old tome roughly bound in buffalo hide.

"It is time you read this."

He'd switched to Lakota, so this was something of importance. I opened the cover. There was no title, but I recognized my grandpa's hand. I turned to the back and read the final words.

William Joseph Strobaw, also known as Teacher and the
Red Win-tay to the People of the Yanube,
This final day of October
Year of our lord 1861, at Teacher's Mead on the Upper Yanube

"Grandpa's?"

"The story of his life written in his own hand. He was honest, so you will learn surprising secrets. It might open your eyes in this matter that bothers you. Billy was a white man, but he came to view his world with the eyes of a red man. You have both white eyes and red eyes. It is time for you to decide which to use."

"I don't understand."

"You can view what happened with shame or not. Read the pages, Eagle. Then come back and talk so we can see how it will be for you."

# # # # #

Major Morrow returned that afternoon from visiting the Tiller farm. Andre Tiller was a widowed man with a seven-year-old girl who lived a mile up Turtle Crick to the west. James — that's Major Morrow — had virtually adopted Libby as his granddaughter.

The Major had been Otter's win-tay wife, for years now. Ma's Christian Danish soul considered men lying with men shameful, not to mention sinful. Strange because she'd lived in the Strobaw house after she married Pa and had grown to love Billy and Otter. Pa and us kids just accepted their relationship for what it was.

James, a retired cavalry officer, was some older than Otter, and age had begun to show in him. His once-blond hair was taking on some snow. The ramrod spine remained, but his steps were not as steady as they once had been. Nonetheless, his mind was quick.

Overnighting at Turtle Crick seemed prudent since it was over fifty miles to Teacher's Mead. I cracked Grandpa Billy's journal that evening but starved the lantern when they went to bed. Settling into my blankets beside the stove, I thought about what I'd read.

Grandpa Billy had been a young man when he met Cut Hand on his way to Fort Wheeler. Billy had been drawn to him from first sight. The two men across the room who shared that same kind of love didn't seem monstrous or evil like folks painted people with those appetites.

# # # # #

Otter stuffed me with pork and eggs and potatoes the next morning before I started for home. He didn't mention the Timo Bowers thing again but told me to read the journal and find my own nature.

I crosscut straight for the Mead as the road was a longer way. Nonetheless, I was in no hurry. A rill and a small stand of trees beckoned at mid-day, providing an excuse to give Arrow a rest. After removing his saddle to use as a back rest, I flopped down to munch jerky and opened Grandpa Billy's journal.

His clear, reasoned thinking about the morality of the life he'd led stirred me. Raised in a strict Christian home, he was shaken by his physical longing for Cut Hand. In time, he came see it as acceptable because of the deep love they held for one another. But Grandpa decried casual liaisons without commitment as sinful. My skin prickled. I held no love for Timo Bowers.

Cut Hand had no problem with their union. He was raised with the concept of the Circle of Life, allowing individuals to live according to their nature without strictures about their choices.

Then I came to the part of the journal that almost shook me loose from my senses. Dog Fox — that's my Pa, Cuthan — wasn't Grandpa Billy's son. He was *Cut Hand's*. So Grandpa Billy wasn't my grandpa. Pa wasn't a half-breed ... I was. And Alexander and our sisters, Rachel Ann and Hannah, too.

I laid the book on my belly and stared up through the tree limbs at the blue sky above. They'd undertaken that monumental deception because Billy had willed the Mead to Cuthan, whose American name was an artifice to keep his father's name alive. No blood Indian would have been allowed to inherit the good rich earth of his own homeland. As it was, upholding Billy's will had been a narrow thing. Some who coveted the farm suggested trading it for a plot up on the Mississippi River where ground had been set aside for half-breed landowners.

Arrow's snicker roused me from an unintended nap. I scrambled to my feet and saw a squad of cavalry approach. I made no move toward my rifle, even though the army tended to look on all Indians as traitors because some of the tribes had fought for the Confederacy. They ignored the fact others raised the hatchet for the Union.

The sandy-haired young officer leading them showed no overt hostility as he gave a casual salute. "Do you require assistance?"

"No, just doing some woolgathering. I'm on my way home to Teacher's Mead."

"You'll be one of the Strobaw boys, then. Met you father once in town. You favor him. I'm Second Lieutenant Gideon Haleworthy."

When his blue eyes wandered to my black mop with gold speckles, I clamped my hat on my head. "Pleased to meet you, sir. You new to the command?"

"Been in-country for four months now. Hail from Boston originally."

"Hope you like our part of Turtle Island. Been to the Mead, yet?"

"No, sir, but I'd like to visit."

"Consider yourself invited. Ma always has an extra place set at the table."

With a fingers to the brim salute, Lt. Haleworthy led his detachment north toward Trickling Water Crick. I watched them go before throwing my saddle on Arrow and turning his nose toward home.

It was coming dark when I raised the three hills protecting the north side of the Mead. The moon was up by the time I dismounted in front of the big stone house I'd called home all my life. The forge sat across the road next to the stable and corral. Until last summer, the Mead had been the last stagecoach rest before the long run to Yanube City. There was now a rude swing station between us and town, but this remained the last opportunity for passengers to have a good meal. Ma and her helper, Jane Appleton, had become famous from Fort Ramson to Yanube City for their meals. Jane's husband, Curtis, worked the farm as a hired hand alongside Pa and Alex.

Aside from smithing, I also took care of the stagecoach teams — Matthew's job until he lit out last year. My sisters helped with cooking and taking care of stagecoach passengers on the outbound stage to Fort Ramson on Tuesdays and the inbound to Yanube City on Thursdays.

I was brushing Arrow down in the stable when Pa came in. "Getting worried about you. Expected you yesterday. This morning at the latest." A smidgen of rebuke hid in his voice.

"I stopped by to see Otter." I filled him in without owning up to what took me there in the first place. When we went to the house, Ma had a tin of food on the stove warming for me.

The family crowded around. eager for news. Rachel Ann and Hannah took seats at the table to catch every word. Alex plopped into a chair at the opposite end with a serious look — like he always wore. Matthew used to say my brother was Pa's age, not ours. I repeated what I'd told Pa as I ate. Ma puttered around in the kitchen with an ear fixed on us. She was pleased to have me home.

I understood. When one of the family was missing, it left a hole in your life. Matthew's absence did that for me. He wasn't Strobaw blood, but he might as well have been. He'd been a scared six-year-old orphan when Otter brought him to the Mead after the militia killed his mother and brother. Half Yanube and half Teton Sioux, Matthew was only a year older than I. So he was more my brother than my real brother.

Over the years, Matthew — whose other name was Little Bear — would get a bellyful of Ma not letting him to be "Indian" enough, so he'd take off to see Otter, who let him run around in a breechcloth and be Bear. Ma was just trying to see we survived in a white man's world, but that didn't keep Matthew from feeling his blood from time to time.

Spring a year ago, his pecker got him in trouble. He'd taken to hopping on Wind Rider, his roan gelding, and riding off to see the Killpennys about four miles upriver. He and Esau Killpenny, just a year older than Matthew, got along, but it was Esau's sister Minnie who got his attention. She was only sixteen, but the first time I saw her she looked like Mother Earth. She was full and ripe and luscious and didn't even know it.

Mr. Killpenny caught them sparking out in the woods. To hear Matthew tell it, he didn't actually have it in, but it was out and hunting for a warm place to call home. Anyway, he caused a hell of a stink, so Ma didn't put up a fuss when Matthew wanted to go stay with Otter for a while. About this time last year, Otter sent word Matthew had gone wandering. A month or so later, an Indian traveling from the Laramie country stopped at Otter's and delivered a message saying Matthew was going to try it on his own hook for a while.

Everybody was relieved but me. Well, I was relieved, but that man left a gaping hole in my chest. We'd played and hunted and studied lessons and worked beside one another for thirteen years, and I never thought about the time we'd go our separate ways. Everybody tells me I'm smart, but I can be a blockhead sometimes.

CHAPTER 2

There was plenty of work waiting for me the next morning. Ma needed a bigger stew pot. One of the coach horses had thrown a shoe. We were always needing horseshoes. When the coach pulled in on Thursday morning, I hitched up the new team and saw to the horses being left behind. One was limping and needed a good liniment rub.

On Saturday, I managed time to bring out Billy's journal for a read up in the barn loft. I got to know about Butterfly and Lone Eagle. Until then they'd just been headstones in the Mead's cemetery.

I put the book away and wandered down to the Yanube. A pool we used as a swimming hole started to look good, so I shucked my clothes and dived in. Swimming's fun when you've got company for horseplay. Today, the water tickling my privates wasn't doing the job for me. So I settled for taking a bath.

Standing bare-assed in the water washing away the day's grime, I caught a glimpse of someone out of the corner of my eye. Before I had a chance to react, a naked form leapt from the riverbank and tumbled me over into the water. I shrugged him off and came up fighting.

Matthew, laughing like a ten-year-old, splashed water in my face. "Hah, you would be a dead man if I was *doh-kah*."

My fear turned to delight. I rubbed the water out of my eyes and shook my head. "You're not a hostile. You're just a skinny tepee Indian living in the past."

"Tell that to the *ah-kee-chee-dah* at Greasy Grass."

"What do the soldiers at Little Big Horn know about you?"

His naked chest swelled. "I was there."

"You were at Little Big Horn? At the Custer battle?"

Excitement burned in his dark eyes. "I was there."

"That's a big one."

"If you're talking about my pipe, you're right, but I was there fighting blue coats."

"You're full of it. How many did you kill?"

He sobered. "One. Maybe two."

"Seems like a warrior would know how many he killed."

His chin went up. "There speaks a man who's never seen the elephant or fired a shot in anger. Things get all mixed up in battle. You never know what's going on. Not even ..." His voice dried up. "Not even exactly what you're doing."

Bear wasn't pulling my dink. He was serious. I didn't know what to say, so I asked him when he got back.

"Half an hour back. After we said hello, Ma told me to go put on some decent clothes."

Ma didn't permit breechclouts at the Mead. She considered them uncivilized.

"Rachel Ann told me you'd walked down the river, so I came here instead of putting on pants."

"You back for good?"

He shrugged. His shoulders had filled out, but the part about being skinny was true. He'd lost weight. He was leaner but harder.

"Might stay a while," he answered. "But who knows when I'll have a hankering to move on again."

"Good. One of the coach horses that pulled in Thursday's still limping. You can doctor him."

"That wasn't the only place I was." Something in his voice made me look at him. "I fought at the Rosebud with Crazy Horse. He's a great man, Eagle. Never seen a man fight like him. We beat the War Chief Crook at Rosebud Creek." He spoke as if remembering was reliving. "After riding all night to get there, we fought for six hours. Crazy Horse was everywhere. He talked to me — more than once. Said he was proud of me. We made the Americans turn back at Rosebud, so they weren't there to fight with Custer at Greasy Grass eight days later."

Greasy Grass was what the warriors called Little Bighorn. I held my tongue, afraid of drawing him back from wherever he was.

"I was with still with Crazy Horse in the Tongue River Valley in January of this year after what was left of Dull Knife's band straggled in to join us. The soldiers had snuck up on his village while everybody was asleep and killed a lot of Cheyenne. Slit the throats of most of their horses and destroyed their supplies.

"After talking to Dull Knife, Crazy Horse decided to palaver with the Americans. But Star Chief Miles's Crow scouts murdered our delegation." A shiver when through Matthew … Bear. "I was supposed to be one of them, but Crazy Horse replaced me with an older warrior at the last minute."

Matthew looked at me, back in the present now. "Wolf Mountain wasn't so good. Miles had artillery on the high ground and pounded us. When the weather turned bad, Crazy Horse withdrew. After that, some of the warriors went back to the reservations to get allotments for their families."

A frown tugged at the corners of his broad mouth. "That's what the army's doing now. Pushing the tribes onto reservations and hoping we'll just lie down and die when we can't roam free anymore."

"Is that when you left?"

He shook his head. Leaning against the pressure of the current, Matthew told me he'd stayed with Crazy Horse until May. "Then the Shirt Wearer decided to take what was left of his people to Camp Robinson in Nebraska to surrender. Crazy Horse knew I had a home to go to, so he sent me away," Matthew finished.

"If that's what the army is doing, it's good you came back. The Mead's a safe place for us. A good spirit home."

He stared at my left earlobe and snorted. "It's nothing but a little reservation."

"Don't look at it like that. We're free to do whatever we want."

"It's better than some of the places they're putting us. But we're still Indians. You forget that sometimes, John. One of these days they'll make you face up to it. Just wait and see."

His words put an ache in my heart. "Don't you understand the warrior's road is about gone. All of that's come to an end."

"You don't know what you're talking about. Sitting Bull was called to the Sun Dance last year. While he was dancing, he saw things and predicted a great victory. And it happened, too. We whipped the whites good at Greasy Grass."

"Seems to me like you just made them mad. Got them all stirred up. I hear Sitting Bull's gone to Canada."

"To regroup. He'll make medicine and plan things out. He and Crazy Horse will ride again, you'll see."

I swallowed hard and tried to think of something to say. What came out surprised even me. "I hear Crazy Horse has a win-tay wife."

He met my eyes just like a white man. Uncomfortable, I turned away. He was on me instantly, wrestling like we did as kids. His arms gripped me from behind and pressed me to him. I managed to twist around to face him, intending to tumble us into the current. If he wanted horseplay, he'd get it. I froze. His lips were close to mine. His eyes looked deep down inside me.

"I thought about you." His voice was a scratchy growl in his throat. His Adam's apple bobbed. "I wondered if I'd live to see you again."

Then he pressed his lips to mine. I froze, thinking of Timo and what he'd done and how I still didn't know how to handle it. But now ... now, I didn't want to deny Bear. He was handsome and desirable and young and my friend.

His tongue pushed into my mouth. The heat of his kiss flowed down into my belly and my vitals. His yard rose and pressed between my legs.

I shoved him away. "What are you doing?"

"What we both want."

"You, maybe. But ... but not me."

He grabbed my thickening cock. "That's not what this says."

His touch was almost too much for me, but I squirmed from his grasp. "I'm not just a prick. I have a mind and a heart."

"Yes, but they tell the prick what to do. You want me, Eagle."

Thoughtless, panicky words spewed out of my mouth. "Maybe I'll give you my cock, but I won't take yours. I won't be your win-tay. You just want one because Crazy Horse has one."

He stared at me for a long moment before wading to the shore where he wrung water from his long, flowing mane. His cock stood hard and proud, reaching for the sky, throbbing against his flat belly at times. It was big and strong and straight.

I wished to call back my words.

"So be it," He reached for his loincloth draped over a tree limb.

I stepped forward, my legs slow and leaden in the current. "Wait!"

"Why? Have you changed your mind?"

I clamped my mouth shut, uncertain of what to say.

He spoke in Lakota. "I thought not. Goodbye, Brother."

He turned and strode away, his manly form robbing me of my wits. I cried out in pain. "If you go, don't ever come back!"

He disappeared into the thin forest hugging the banks of the river. When he rode away with a pounding of hooves, my gut shriveled. A weakness came over me, collapsing my legs. With no control over my paralyzed muscles, I was swept downstream, pulling me farther and farther from him. Finally regaining my wits, I clawed my way to the shore and hung onto a stone overhang as the current sought to drag me away. To my surprise, I wept.

# # # # #

The incident at the river shook me right down to my heels. My response to Matthew left me doubting my horse sense. The shadow of his lips on mine haunted me. I'd never been moved by a kiss like that

16

before. Hell, I'd never been *kissed* before. Maybe I ought to go find a girl while it was fresh on my mind. You know, to compare. But there weren't any girls around except Rachel Ann and Hannah, and I wasn't about to kiss my own sisters. Well, that wasn't exactly true. Minnie Killpenny lived just a few miles up the river.

Then there was that other thing. I got hard remembering Matthew's hand on my rod. I might be able to snatch a kiss from Minnie, but could I finagle her into groping me, too?

When I had some free time the following Saturday, I hogged the bathing room until Rachel Ann banged on the door wanting in. I told her to use one of the necessaries for the coach passengers.

Squeaky clean, I pointed Arrow's nose north instead of heading upriver. Matthew had set up camp on the north side of the hills along Strobaw's Crick, but nobody had seen or heard from him since he went racing away from the swimming hole. I found his camp, but there was no sign of him or Wind Rider. His tracks led up the creek. It looked like he was out hunting, so I gave up and headed for Killpenny Farm.

I'd wasted a good bath by the time I got there. Sweaty from the sun, I kinda smelled like Arrow Wind. What kind of reception would the farmer give me after Matthew's stunt last year?

Mr. Killpenny made me welcome and took time to sip water with me on his front porch. He offered spirits, but despite craving alcohol to bolster my intent to kiss his daughter, I declined.

The Killpennys were plain folks, but their fry came out fairer than the parents. Esau was Alex's age — twenty — and my height — about five-ten. But he outweighed me by twenty pounds. Blue-eyed, he was pleasant to look at and friendly as long as you'd talk hunting with him.

Minnie — she liked to be called Min — was shy and easy to look at. Ma was fond of saying she wasn't yet seventeen and looked twenty. She was blonde and green-eyed. Pretty as all get out. But shy. How in the hell had Matthew gotten her out in the trees last year?

The Killpennys must have been wondering that, as well, because they stuck real close while Min and I sat on the porch and talked.

After I figured I'd worn out my welcome, I said my goodbyes and went to get Arrow. I'd ground hitched him, but he'd followed the vegetation around behind the barn as he grazed. Min came along with me when I walked out to get him.

As soon as we were out of sight, I grabbed her. She must have thought a wild Indian was attacking her, but she didn't do anything except give a grunt when I planted my lips on hers. Had to ... or I'd have lost my nerve. After about thirty seconds, I came up for air, muttered something — not sure what — before vaulting aboard Arrow and laying heels to his flanks.

Half a mile later, I reined my gelding to a walk and considered things. The two kisses didn't even compare. Min's was soft and sweet … and kinda like kissing my sisters. Matthew's had reached right down inside me and yanked on my innards.

I headed straight for Matthew's camp again, but it wasn't there anymore. The earth had been wiped clear of any sign of him. He'd come back and seen my tracks and wanted no part of me. I must have hurt him awful bad that day at the swimming hole.

I could have ridden in a big circle and picked up his trail, but this made it plain he was through with me. Arrow turned down the crick and took me home with the hole Matthew always left in my chest back in place — except bigger this time.

# # # # #

I don't have a stoic Indian face like my pa, and he picked up on my mood. Wednesday, he caught me at the end of the day and led the way to the hills behind the Mead. As he always did when he wanted to talk privately, he walked right up the side of the hollow hill, the tallest of our three guardians.

As Pa sat cross-legged on the ground, I took a good look at him. You know, a *real* look. You see people every day and know it's them, but you never really look at them. Cuthan Strobaw wore his hair in the white man's way, and there wasn't a strand of gray in it. Heck, he did most things in the white man's way. And that made my talk harder.

"I never get tired of the view from up here," he said in his deep voice. "Sometimes I get so busy I forget to really look at things."

Him speaking my very thoughts almost spooked me. Sometimes I suspected he was a secret shaman. He looked at me through those eyes Otter said belonged to Cut Hand — and me. I might share my eyes with those two, but nobody had my hair. The yellow scattered all through it was unique to me. Once people saw it, they never forgot me.

Pa was the most patient man I'd ever known, but if I didn't stop dawdling and get to it, he'd ask me straight out what was the matter. Yet I didn't know how to cut this catfish open.

He beat me to it. "What's bothering you, John?"

"Have you read Grandpa Billy's journal?"

His eyebrows shot up. "Have you?"

18

"Uh huh. Otter gave it to me when I ... Well, when I told him what happened the night before I left Timo's. He said I needed to know a few things."

Out of the corner of my eye, I saw Pa's mouth grow tight. "What happened before you left Timo's?"

"I don't wanna to get anybody in trouble."

"Should somebody be in trouble?"

When I blush, I go almost as dark as those Buffalo Soldiers I'd seen after the war. "I don't know, but Timo ... " I swallowed hard. "He came into my room the last night I was there. And ... and he put his mouth on me." I couldn't look at Pa, but I have good peripheral vision. He fooled me. There was no outrage on his face.

"And you told Otter?"

"I needed to talk to someone, and he was only seven miles away. You were fifty."

"What did you think about what Timo did?"

"I don't know." That sounded like a jackass braying.

"Were you ashamed?"

I blinked. "Ashamed? Why would I be ashamed? Grandpa Billy and Cut Hand, I mean, your pa and Billy did things like that, and I don't think they were ashamed."

"Customs were different back then."

"I know. Win-tays weren't looked down on in those days."

"Do you know why they weren't?"

"The Circle of Life thing, I guess. That makes a lot of sense to me. It's a way of thinking that doesn't try to force a fellow to be what he isn't. It just lets him be what he naturally is."

He nodded. "Cut Hand and Billy were just being who they were."

"That's it, Pa. How do I be who I am when I don't know who I am?"

He picked up a stick and scratched a big circle in the ground. He was sorting things out in his mind. At length, he drew a line through the wheel so it looked like the old Greek letter, Theta.

"John ... No, not John. This is Dog Fox talking to War Eagle, and that's important. If I was Cuthan Strobaw speaking to John Strobaw, I'm not sure I could say what I'm about to. Do you understand me?"

"You're saying if you had to talk to me like a white man, your words would be different."

"Yes, that's right." He switched to the Lakota tongue. "Son, you've heard us speak of an Indian grandmother laying out a doll and a knife for her grandson, haven't you?"

"I've heard that if he picked up a knife, he'd grow up to be a man. But if I picked up a doll ..."

"I think you would have picked up the knife."

"Me, too. But if that's right, then why did I lie there and let Timo do that to me?"

"Why did my father permit Billy's touch? Under the Old Way, a man could lie with a win-tay, and it would not be wrong."

I snickered. "It's hard for me to see Timo Bowers picking up a doll."

Pa laughed. "Yes, but a win-tay does not have to act womanly. No one accused Billy of that. When I was young, some of the win-tays dressed as women and acted as women because that fit their nature. Others dressed as men and acted as men, yet chose to lie with men because that was theirs."

"According to Grandpa ... uh, Billy's ..."

"It's all right to call him grandpa. He was my father in all but blood from the time I was fifteen years old. He deserves the title."

"His journal says it's all right for a man to lie with a win-tay but not to lie with another man. How do you know the difference?"

He thought that one over so long I started to get nervous. Finally, he cleared his throat. "Eagle, you and your brother must have thought about measuring yourselves against one another when you were growing up. That kind of curiosity is natural. You might even have abused yourselves together. That is not a good example because the nature of the thing would have been wrong. You are blood brothers, which would be incest. But let's take Matthew for example."

Should I hide my head or run away? This was getting too close to where I lived.

"It is likely you've been curious with him, as well. That is natural. But if you've wanted to take it further, then you must consider your nature."

My mind stood still.

"Son, are you all right?"

"Huh? Uh, sure. I'm just trying to wrap my head around what you said. So Cut Hand accepted Billy's touch because he was the man in their relationship?"

"I believe so. My father was happy with Billy. It gave him everything he needed except for one."

"You," I said.

"Yes. He had an urge … nay, a need to father children. In the end, that was what drove them apart as lovers, although they remained friends until the end."

"That's what got between Billy and Lone Eagle, too." I rubbed the side of my nose to quell an itch. "Then why didn't Billy or Otter feel the need?"

"I cannot answer that except to say it was their nature."

"So you don't see anything wrong with that kind of thing?"

He was quiet again for a long time. My pa is an active man, so he was grappling for an answer.

"Not a lot of our people led that kind of life. They were rare, but they were accepted. Oh, some laughed at them and mimicked them. Even so, some win-tays were honored as inward looking people who could see the world with the eyes of both a man and a woman. My heritage says there is nothing wrong with it. But it is no longer my world we are living in."

"It's Ma's," I said. "We're living in the white man's world now."

"Just so. You've read the Holy Bible, so you know what it says about such things."

"That doesn't mean I understand it. Not all of it, anyway."

"Nor do I. But the whites believe every word is God-given; therefore, it must be true."

I shook my head. "They just fought a big war over black slaves. The North won and said slavery was illegal. But the Bible talks about slaves being all right and tells you not to eat certain things, and it has wars."

Pa held up his hand. "The Holy Book is divided into two parts. The first contains all of those strictures. The second is about the coming of the Messiah and his lessons for us. How he takes the sin from our shoulders and accepts it as his own."

"If that's true, why can't I can go sinning all over the place and let Him take it all on Himself."

"Have you known very many white men who are so patient? It would be risky to test Him that much." Pa straightened his back, struck his knees with the palms of his hands, and switched to English. "Has our talk helped?"

"It's given me a lot to think about."

"I … uh … wouldn't mention this talk to your mother. Not until things are settled in your mind."

"No, sir. I won't."

"Son, once you come to grips with this thing, you must be very careful should you decide in a certain way. The white men fear what they consider unnatural deviancy so much they kill when they confront it.

CHAPTER 3

The talk with Pa didn't leave me feeling any easier. Maybe I ought to take another trip to the Killpennys and get a spark going with Minnie … uh, Min. That idea didn't raise much interest, so I decided to wait until the next time we met at church. That probably wouldn't be until November when we'd celebrate Thanksgiving Day. The fact that was another five months down the road didn't rankle any.

Turned out the wait wasn't that long. Ma wanted to have her brothers over for Independence Day. Pa decided to make it a real party when we got word Otter and James were coming for a visit, so he invited the Killpennys. Our hundred-and-first national birthday fell on Wednesday. The day between the inbound outbound stages was a day we could afford to take off.

Ma put Otter and James in the little cabin that had been Otter's home before he moved to Morrow Farm. Crow Johnson had lived there, but he was gone now. I'd considered asking for it, but Alex, as the eldest, was entitled, even though he didn't show any interest.

After the evening meal on the day James and Otter arrived, I moseyed along with them to the cabin. James went on inside, but Otter and I sat a spell on the porch. My legs hit the ground solider than his. Dang, I was taller than he was. He waited me out.

"I read Grandpa's journal. I learned a lot from reading it but …"

"But you didn't find your own answers. You're feeling like Billy when he first set eyes on Cut Hand. Yearning … but not certain."

Semi-darkness made talking easier. "And it's got worse now." I told him about Matthew and me at the river.

Otter nodded his head. "Now I understand. After Bear left here, he stopped by our place for a spell. I felt like he wanted to talk. We even sat and soaked in Turtle Crick like we used to do. Thought it would loosen his tongue. It did, but he talked of other things. Dangerous things."

"The Little Bighorn?"

"And others. Now I know what he really wanted to talk about."

"I didn't find it hard to tell you."

Otter was silent for a moment. "It wasn't ripe yet, else he would have. He knows he can trust me. Eagle, what would have happened if he'd been at his camp when you returned from the Killpenny Farm?"

The falling night cloaked my shrug. "We'd have fought or fucked, maybe both." I flushed at my crass language. "I don't know. I want to ... touch him. But I don't know if I'm ready to do the things he wants."

Otter switched to Lakota and called me grandson. "*Dah-koh-zjah,* you are your own man now. When it is time, you will decide your nature. When it reveals itself to you, do not let anyone push you into one thing when you are the other. To do so will cripple your mind."

I'd been hoping Otter, who had lived the life, would decide for me. All he could do was to tell me I was free to make my own decisions. I leaned back on my arms with my palms flat on the planking. "How long did Matthew stay with you?"

"Two days. Then he took off without saying where he was going."

"Fort Robinson," I said. "He's gone to Crazy Horse."

"That is probably true. He is taken with the man. And in truth, Crazy Horse is the greatest warrior we've seen in many a year. If I were Bear's age, I would likely do the same."

"I'm afraid for him."

"Justifiably so. This thing cannot end well. This — what did they call it? The Black Hills War? — has weakened the tribes. It must be clear to everyone we'll never throw off the yoke of the white man."

Moonlight caught in his eyes as he turned toward me. "But all of this cannot mean much to you. Thanks to your mother, you've lived as a white man. Don't misunderstand. I do not demean her. She saw more clearly than any of us you had to become white in order to survive. And she was right." He paused. "But what is teasing your mind will find more comfort in your red blood than in her white blood. But even among the tribes, it is not as well accepted as it once was."

# # # # #

My uncles — Ma's brothers, Jacob and Christian Jacobsen — were the first to arrive the next day. Grandpa Hans had died two years ago, and the brothers now ran the farm a mile to the east of us. Jacob, a stick-in-the-mud, had married a woman from Fort Ramson named Matilda, but called Matty, five years back and had three fry. Aside from siring children, the only thing he was interested in was farming. He and Alex got along well. Not over the fornicating but the farming. My brother got as excited over a new turnip pushing up out of the ground as I did about ... well, about Matthew. I snickered while imagining him up in the hayloft jerking his *che* while he ate the blessed turnip.

Even though he was somewhere around forty, Christian was easy to look at and churk — that is, a lot more fun than his older brother. He'd wrestle and footrace and play mumbly-peg all day long. Today, he brought along a ball he'd made out of cow leather and a bat carved from an ash limb. Christian organized a game of round ball anytime he could. He'd gotten even more rabid about it after they organized the National League back east and started calling it baseball.

The Killpennys didn't show up until almost high noon, arriving in a buckboard pulled by a brace of brevet horses. That's what folks around here called mules. Esau rode a good-looking buckskin. After the women unloaded the dishes, we men set up boards on sawhorses to make a long table. Then the women started bringing out steaming pots of this and smoldering plates of that. Pa'd slaughtered one of our piglets. Esau contributed some gamey deer, and I'd bagged a wild turkey for the feast. Of course, Ma and Jane Appleton and the girls had cooked up a mess of every vegetable I'd ever heard about.

During talk around the table, we learned Killpenny had been a Pikes Peaker in the Colorado gold rush of '49. Then he'd worked for a railroad until the Panic of '73, when a bunch of them went bankrupt. He'd joined the huge unemployed workforce until he decided to come out here and file for some land.

Mr. Killpenny told us how things were changing back east. Everything was "industrialization" now. That's how the North had won the war, he claimed. They had the factories, so they produced the guns and ammunition ... ergo, they won the war. Seemed like simple-minded reasoning to me, but that's what Billy had predicted in his journal, so maybe there was something to it, after all.

This was supposed to be the Gilded Age, yet they told us we were in the Long Depression. I mentally shook my head. Crop prices were decent, so the Mead was prospering, as was the Jacobsen's Farm.

Pa and Alex cut watermelons that had been cooling in the crick, and I was close to splitting a gut by the time Christian promoted a watermelon seed spitting contest. He was the champ. I came in second.

Mr. Killpenny hauled out a jug of Red Eye he'd brought, but we went light on it except for the white men. Everybody was always talking about drunk Indians, but I'd never seen Pa or Otter roostered. Funny thing about alcohol. It affected everyone differently. James seemed to get wiser. Mr. Killpenny got rosier in the face and turned into a pettifogger. Jacob got sterner, and Christian was up for more high-jinks. Like Pa, Curtis didn't drink much. The women didn't imbibe, of course. Shame, I'd like to have seen if chubby Mrs. Killpenny loosened up any or if Jane Appleton lost her pinched look.

I'd got tight once when Matthew brought back some bark juice from one of his forays to wherever. Didn't like it. It felt good during ... but was hell after.

The liquor loosened Mr. Killpenny's tongue enough to ask about something obviously weighing on his mind. "You hear about them Nez Perces whipping the U.S. Cavalry?"

"You talking about White Bird Canyon?" Christian's good-looking face was flushed red. He'd likely end up sick tomorrow and be miserable doing the chores.

Mr. Killpenny wasn't much better off. "That's the one."

"What about it?" Jacob didn't seem snockered like his brother.

Esau's eyes looked like they were having trouble focusing. "He's worried about the news stirring up our local Indians."

"We got anything to worry about?" his father asked.

I caught the gleam in Otter's eye before he spoke up. "The Pierced Noses whipping some white soldiers isn't going to raise my blood any. Probably won't stir up Cuthan and Alex and John much either."

"And they're about all the savages left in this part of the territory." Christian looked as if he was going to bust out laughing.

"I didn't mean no offense."

"And you gave none, Mr. Killpenny," Pa said. "But what Christian said is true. There are few tribesmen left between Fort Ramson and Yanube City. If there's trouble, it'll come from a few renegades passing through, or highwaymen seeking illicit profit. And that hasn't happened in quite a spell."

By this time, Mr. Killpenny's vivid complexion warned of apoplexy.

Midafternoon, I noticed Min hanging around me. Well, I'd noticed before, but I was too busy playing ball or spitting watermelon seeds or pitching horseshoes to pay her any mind. When I plopped down on the edge of the porch, she came over to sit beside me and dimple prettily.

"You sure do play good town ball." That's probably what they called round ball where she came from. Of course, it was baseball now. I'd hit a couple of pitches and managed to slide home once.

"Thanks. Just takes a good eye." Uh oh. Shouldn't have said that. Now she'd talk about my eyes. Then it'd be my hair.

"You sure do have nice ones." Her cheeks turned as red as our tom turkey's beard. "I mean, strange ones. But they're pretty, too."

"Somebody's always talking about my weird eyes."

26

She made a moue with her lips. "They're not weird. They're … well, pretty. All that gold in them." Then her gaze moved upward. "And that hair." Her hand fluttered.

"It's all right. You can touch it."

She reached out and tousled my locks before snatching her hand away and glancing around to see if anyone had noticed. Then she snickered. "I thought at first you'd painted it."

"That's what everybody thinks. Nope. The Good Lord did that."

I got up and stretched, giving her a look. As I walked around the edge of the house, she stood and followed me. We had to go clear round the back before everyone else was out of sight. I didn't grab her this time, I just put my hands on her shoulders, and we leaned into one another. She opened her lips, and I gave her my tongue.

I might have gotten a little bolder except when I opened my eyes, Rachel Ann was standing there as big as life. Her face got a smart aleck smirk on it before she darted away. Would she tell everyone Minnie and me were canoodling back behind the house?

"What is it?" Min asked.

"Thought somebody was there."

Her pink lips opened. Her eyes darted around. "I'd better go back. Be best if I go the way we came, and you go round the other way."

After she left, I leaned against the warm stones of the house. The kiss had been better. Maybe because it wasn't so rushed. I'd felt *something* when I kissed her, but my thing didn't get hard like it did with Matthew. Of course that had been better'n a month ago, so maybe I'd just built it up in my mind.

Horse apples! I was more confused than ever.

# # # # #

We paid for our excesses the next day when the Yanube City stage came in. Stagecoach day was always a busy one. The womenfolk saw to the passengers and coachmen while Pa lent me a hand harnessing a fresh team of big horses. Curtis and Alex kept on working the farm.

Even when the carriage was on the road south of the river heading toward Yanube City, we still had things to do. Cleaning up and caring for the incoming horses made for a long day. The eats were pretty good because Ma always cooked more than the passengers ate. Ordinarily that would have been a bonus, but after yesterday's binge, I couldn't look at a fried chicken leg.

Things settled back to normal, but I worked with an ache in my chest. Was I missing my brother Matthew, or was I longing for the handsome man who'd kissed me and held onto my puffed up penis at the river? Whatever the reason, I was worried about him.

Over the next few weeks, stagecoaches brought word of railroad troubles that sounded like near insurrection. A strike by the rail workers started in West Virginia about ten days after our nation's birthday and spread so fast to Maryland and Pennsylvania and Illinois that the National Guard was called in to shoot and bayonet workers at will. Something like fifty or so dead. It didn't end until President Hayes called out federal troops. Hayes was the man some claimed had scooted into the White House backwards when more people voted for the Democratic governor of New York, Samuel J. Tilden, than for him.

We got wind of the Battle of Big Hole up in Montana where the army whipped the Nez Perce. Later, more details made it look more like a draw. I didn't worry about the Big Hole Basin fight because Matthew — or Bear as he'd be calling himself now — wouldn't be riding with the Pierced Noses. He'd be with Crazy Horse's Oglala.

The Thursday stage from Fort Ramson came in right on schedule. Dusty Skediver had the best reputation in the company for getting his passengers where they were going on time. When I brought the brace of fresh horses from the corral, Rachel Ann was standing there with her mouth open. That wasn't like her. She was usually flying around helping the ladies in the coach get fed and comfortable.

"Did you hear?" Her voice had a quiver in it.

"All I heard was a grouchy driver wanting his fresh team."

"It's Crazy Horse. They killed Crazy Horse."

My blood drained down below my waistline. "What happened?" My words sounded like they were coming from somewhere else.

"They said he tried to break out of the Red Cloud Agency. Matthew'll be with him, won't he?"

I dropped the reins and rushed to where Pa was talking to the driver.

Dusty spat a wad of tobacco juice. "One less killer, I say. He was planning a big uprising. Got him just in time." The stagecoach driver wasn't a bad egg, but Crazy Horse scared all whites stupid.

My father's jaw clenched before he spoke. "Was anyone else killed besides His-Horse-is-Spirited?

"Who?" Dusty reared back and blinked like he'd just realized he was talking to two Indians.

"Crazy Horse," I said. "That's his real name."

"Be damned. Never heard that. But I guess you'd know. News ain't too clear yet. Just happened last week." Dusty scratched his bristly chin. "Oughta deal with that other snake and be rid of them both."

He meant Sitting Bull, of course. I was tempted to hook up his team wrong, but there were too many passengers who might get hurt.

I went back and put the horses in harness, gritting my teeth until the coach cleared the bridge across the Yanube. Then I hunted up Pa and found him talking to my mother and Alex.

"I gotta know, Pa." I interrupted him. "I'm going to the fort and see if I can find out anything."

"We're all worried about Matthew. Ride for Morrow Farm and get James to take you to the fort. He'll get a better reception."

Ma put a hand to his shoulder. "Are we sure Matthew was there?"

"Crazy Horse was his hero," I said. "He'll be as close to the Shirt Wearer as he can. And he won't be Matthew now. He'll be Bear unless he's earned a fighting name."

Her blue eyes widened. "What fighting?"

Pa saved my bacon. "He's been with some of the bands when they've had skirmishes, that's all."

"I'll crosscut to the farm. Make better time that way."

"Maybe we should wait for more word," she said.

I gave her my best white man's stare. "He's my brother, Ma."

She flushed. "Yes, and he's my son, young man. Do you think I love him any less?"

The word love threw me for a minute. She was talking about a different love, but it brought everything clear in my mind.

"I'm going."

"Go get some clean clothes, and I'll fix you some bait for the road."

"Jerky and a couple of airtights of peaches ought to be enough."

She hurried for the house.

"Take a spare horse so you can spell Arrow." Pa said.

In half an hour, my pony was skirting the western hill behind Teacher's Mead with a pinto tied to his tail. I put the horses into a single foot, a fast comfortable gait that covered ground but didn't push them too hard. Even so, I switched from horseback to horseback often. Deep in the night, I crossed the wooden bridge over Turtle Crick and pulled up in the farmyard. As I dismounted, someone was standing on the porch. A rifle barrel glinted in the moonlight.

"Otter, it's me ... John."

"Eagle, what's wrong?"

Before I finished spilling out my story, James was standing beside us on the porch. When I shut up, he took charge.

"We'll go to the fort in the morning. They're bound to have more accurate news over the grapevine by now. Damnation, I usually go to town at least once a week, but I kept putting it off."

"Let's take care of your animals," Otter said. "Are you hungry?"

"No, sir. Ma sent victuals."

James returned to the cabin to prepare a pallet for my bed while Otter helped me rub down the two horses. As we worked, I expected him to ask about what we had discussed the last time I was here. Instead, he wanted to know if I had been on my *hemblecha* yet.

I looked over Arrow's broad back and watched him curry the pinto. "A Vision Quest? I never considered it."

"Think about it. You might find the answer to the question you're seeking."

"I thought it was to learn about your future."

He turned to face me. "Is that not your future?"

Before returning to the house, I took Billy's journal from my saddlebags and returned it to Otter. He hugged it to his chest, so I knew it was precious to him.

James had heated water for me, so I washed up before taking to my blankets. I'd planned on thinking matters over, but the next thing I knew, Otter was shaking my shoulder. He remained at the farm while James and I rode for the post.

#####

Fort Yanube had once been a place such as I imagined a fortress to be, hiding itself behind a palisade with ramparts for defending against hostiles ... or at least that's what my pa and Otter had told me. I hadn't been on a military post since I was a kid. Now the fort was an open place with little in the way of fencing and nothing of the walls remaining. Barracks and other military buildings surrounded a two-storied headquarters at the end of a grass parade ground.

James was not acquainted with the new commandant, but his rank and reputation gained us entry. After dismounting, we hitched our horses and climbed the steps. A man with sergeant's stripes stood and came to attention when James identified himself. Then he scurried away to find the adjutant, a curly-haired captain who looked to be in the middle of his thirties.

The adjutant went stiff and saluted. James returned the courtesy and then made himself comfortable on a bench until we were invited up to the commandant's office. As we started up the stairs, a man with yellow bars on his shoulder was coming down.

"Mr. Strobaw? Good to see you again."

I recognized Lt. Haleworthy and introduced James before we went on up the stairs. Major Dabney Irons was older than I thought he would be, probably close onto fifty. But he was still a man of vigor. His hair was cut close to his scalp and was as gray as a lead ingot. He seemed of a gruff nature but was courteous enough to James. After introductions, they fell into a discussion of military affairs and went about identifying mutual friends in the service. Only after this ran down did Irons inquire after our interest.

The Major gave us his version of the death of Crazy Horse, although there were still some details in question. When the war leader brought his people into the Red Cloud Agency, he established a village a short distance removed.

After Chief Joseph and his Nez Perce broke out in Idaho and headed north toward Canada, the army asked Crazy horse and a leader of the Miniconjou, Touch the Clouds, to join them against the renegades. The two leaders objected, saying they were committed to peace. Pressed to reconsider, Crazy Horse said if he must go to war, he would fight until all the white men were dead. Upon hearing this, General George Crook ordered his arrest.

The following morning two columns moved on Crazy Horse's village, but the wily chief had dispersed his people and fled with his sick wife to the Spotted Tail Agency. The army brought him back and put him in the guardhouse at Red Cloud. He was bayonetted by one of his guards when he tried to escape on September 5 of this year — 1877. Crazy Horse died that night of his wound. Little Big Man was there and bore witness to these facts.

James cleared his throat once the Major had finished his tale. "Were there other casualties? We've heard rumors ranging from ten to twenty to wholesale slaughter."

"I can tell you with reasonable certainty that Crazy Horse was the sole casualty."

James stood and expressed his appreciation for the Major's time and courtesy. It was all I could do to remain civil.

"I don't believe it." The words spilled out of my mouth as soon as we were mounted and headed for the sentry box.

"I don't doubt the basic facts," James said. "Just the details."

Once we arrived back at the farm, we huddled with Otter and repeated the Major's story. It left a bitter taste in Otter's mouth, too.

"If Crazy Horse planned on going out, he wouldn't declare he'd kill all the whites. Not unless it was said in the heat of anger, but that doesn't appear to be the case. Sending his people on ahead of him sounds right. He'd have joined them after he left his wife with the doctor at Spotted Tail. But the rest of the story is sour to me. This is the way the army wants it to be, nothing more."

He turned to me. "As tragic as it was, at least we know Bear didn't die with Crazy Horse. Now if he has sense enough to stay out of trouble, he will survive this."

# # # # #

Otter's question of the previous night had got me to thinking. I'd never even considered undertaking a Vision Quest. Maybe I'd been wrong. If I was truly seeking the key to my nature, what better way to find it than a dream vision? After James went to visit the Tillers later that day, I broached the subject with Otter.

"Are you certain you wish to do this? It is a hard journey."

"I don't care. I want to do it. Need to do it. Will you be my guide?"

"Aye. I will help, but you must do the suffering. Eat well tonight, because you'll have nothing during your Crying for a Vision. Sometimes that takes four or five days. The Comanche Moon is already upon us, so the weather might not hold."

I took his words to heart and made a pig of myself at supper. James, of course, knew what was going on. The ease with which these two shared things made an impression on me. They came out of two different cultures, yet their understanding of one another seemed perfect.

CHAPTER 4

Early the next morning, Otter led me across the bridge to his *okinare*, his medicine lodge. Steam swirled around the interior of the small enclosure as we stripped and took our seats. He poured more water on the glowing stones, and waves of heat opened my pores. Sweat streamed in rivulets, leaving me giddy. I bowed my head as Otter asked *Wakan Tanka* to walk with me on my quest. He prayed for my body and my soul and my mind. I sang the song I'd composed last night begging for enlightenment.

At length, Otter beckoned me outside to plunge into the bracing waters of Turtle Crick. The shock gave me an erection, but my heart was pure. I felt no embarrassment. As we climbed out of the water on the cabin side of the crick and dried off, three mounted men watched from a distance. I donned a breechclout and moccasins, my erection fading under such foreign scrutiny.

I turned my back on the strangers to accept the treasure Otter placed in my hands — a red Calinite calumet that had belonged to our *tiospaye*, our band. It was older than I knew how to count and sacred to our people. He also handed over a bag of tobacco, a worn buffalo robe, and four tatters of cloth, each dyed a different hue: white, green, yellow, and black, representing the cardinal directions. He gave me a burlap bag filled with sage. Then Otter placed a soft leather pouch strung on deer sinew around my neck. A medicine bag filled with small things from my past. A bit of my life cord and small totems.

"If your Crying for a Vision is successful, *Wakan Tanka* will send a messenger. A buffalo for the north. A mouse for the south. An eagle for the east, and a bear for the west. Do not eat or drink until your vision appears. Where you will go to seek your message?"

I nodded to the north. "Not far. To a place that has meaning for both of us." My trek would take me to the glen where Matthew's mother and brother rested.

"Then go in peace and return in wisdom."

Ignoring the intruders south of the crick, I mounted the hill behind the cabin and crossed the savannah to a clearing in a small grove of pines. After selecting a spot, I scratched a square in the dirt with my knife, careful that each side was flush with a cardinal direction. I secured each bit of cloth on its appropriate side of the square with a rock. The bag of sage would serve as my bed. Ready now, I shucked both apron and moccasins to sit on the buffalo robe, facing east — the First Direction.

Doubt struck me like a body blow. Why was I naked on an old buffalo robe in the chill of an autumn day staring through a thin line of trees out onto the rolling prairie? Why was I not concerned I had displayed an erection to strangers? Was this me? Who was I, anyway?

I closed my eyes, lifted my arms — palms up — and spoke to Him who claimed the Cross and Him who claimed the White Buffalo. "Oh, Great Father, help me. I don't know what to do. One part of me calls you God. The other, *Wakan Tanka*. Does it matter so long as I show respect? Now I pray, beseech, *beg* you to show me the way."

I sang, sometimes clearly, cogently, and sometimes spouting nonsense. I chanted in English and in Lakota and saw things never before seen. My eyesight made out minute details on thick-barked pines boles, pliable green needles, and discovered the intricate beauty of cones. Veined leaves of a blackberry bush came into clear focus, and I somehow knew Dew Drop and Standing Rock rested beneath its sturdy roots.

The smell of resin left a bitter taste on my raspy tongue. A chill breeze raised the hair from my forehead. I imagined a thousand yellow hairs on my scalp reflecting golden sunlight back to the God who had sent it. Peace settled over me, a sensation so sensual I achieved an erection again, without shame, without desire — simply because I was a man. And I had my answer. My Wishing for a Vision was right and good and proper for me ... for John Strobaw ... for War Eagle.

I lifted the holy red calumet and offered medicine smoke to the four directions and then to Father Sky and Mother Earth. Afterward, I put the pipe away in its fringed sheath and took a series of deep breaths to clear my mind. I sat still — sometimes with my eyes open, sometimes with them closed. I was silent for long periods before praying for hours as the sun ascended to its zenith, passed, and began to drop. I left the square only to eliminate bodily wastes. Otherwise, I sat or knelt on the buffalo robe in its center. My belly rumbled. My throat dried up.

When night arrived, I pulled the buffalo robe around me and lay upon the sacred sage bed, but sleep was slow to come. Night voices intruded upon my consciousness. Fool coyote yipped in the distance. A mate answered from the other side of the earth. Then, from far to the north came the deeper howl of wolves. They were early this year. Munching noises warned of deer or antelope in the glade. The Great Spirit had made me invisible to them. I would have my vision.

I slept fitfully and was up to watch the sun tint the sky as pink as one of Ma's roses. I took another ritual smoke. That day passed as had the former, except I was hungrier and more dehydrated. I had difficulty working up saliva. Still no messenger, no supernatural came to reveal itself. I shivered on my bed of sage. Even the buffalo robe could not still the tremors. Cold? Fear? Awe?

The sun was slow to rise on the third day. Unsteady on my feet, I urinated a pitiful, dark yellow stream. Once back on the robe, I fell to my knees as an anxious, mish-mash of blather — half-prayer, half nonsense — struggled to get past my parched voice box.

To my anguish, that day ended and the next began with nothing to show for my suffering. Was it because I had forgotten to medicine smoke yesterday? Had I ruined the whole thing? Unable to remain upright, my torso teetered back and forth like a spent top trying to decide which way to topple.

I do not know when or how it happened, but there came a moment I no longer sat on a worn robe. I soared above the earth on the wings of a golden eagle, my namesake. My earth name was fit and proper.

Vast areas passed beneath me. Ugly lines of steel marred the countryside. A black wagon belching smoke crawled over them like a huge serpent. I had never seen a railroad, but without question the monster was a train. White piles alongside the tracks became bleached buffalo bones. Herds of the living beasts seemed few and far between.

My heart lurched as a great shambling bear made its way across a valley with a pack of howling coyotes on his trail. I became so confused my wings almost failed me. Could that be Matthew ... Bear?

I flew onward — now through time rather than space — and came upon a scene of colossal excitement. Dancers raised a great noise and made good medicine as they shuffled around a holy man. Then they swelled into a tribe of dancers, and increased yet again to become nations of celebrants. Joy and jubilation filled the air. The tumult — greater even than the Sun Dance — rose up to fill me with rapture.

The high spirits vanished with the death — murder — of an important man. Who had died? Crazy Horse? No, his killing lay in the past. The Spirit Dream was of the future. Another great man, a chief, a medicine man, was yet to be butchered.

Next, I came upon a battle. Nay, not a battle, but a slaughter. Warriors and women and children lay frozen in grotesque poses across a field of bloody snow. Grief-stricken, I folded my wings to clutch my aching breast and fell. I woke flat of my back on the buffalo robe.

I lay there confused and uncomprehending. What did it all mean? If Eagle and East represented Illumination, the dream was a bust. Yet, there had been a vision. I needed guidance. Otter had explained I was free to discuss my vision with my guide but could reveal it to no one else for three days. Hah! It would take longer than that to figure it out.

I rose and promptly fell on my face. It was going to be a long mile back to the farmhouse. I struggled to my feet again and took up the calumet, leaving everything else behind. Staggering like a drunken sot, I skirted the stubby hill behind the house because my legs weren't strong enough to carry me over it. Otter and James rushed from the fields when my uncertain steps carried me as far as the porch. Otter's first words revived me.

"I can see you were successful."

I strove to speak formally, but it came out in a strangled squawk. "Honored Elder, I need your guidance."

"After you've had something to eat and drink." James handed over a jug of cool water. It tasted like honey until I got greedy and choked.

They fed me like they gave me drink, slowly and sparingly. Then Otter lent me his arm to the top of the hill behind the cabin where we sat and looked south where it seemed I could see all the way to Yanube City, seven miles distant. I couldn't, of course. I'd lost that ability by folding my eagle's wings and plunging to Mother Earth.

Otter agreed my Spirit Dream foretold a bloody conflagration yet to come, but the joy and the dancing puzzled him. He looked out over the prairie beyond Turtle Crick for a long moment without speaking.

"I know of only one thing such as what you speak. But it was in the past, so it cannot be a part of your forward-looking vision."

He spoke of a Northern Paiute prophet named Hawthorne Wodziwob on the Walker River Reservation in a place called Nevada. After typhoid and drought and starvation devastated the region, this self-proclaimed shaman, also called Fish Lake Joe, began showing up at Round Dance and Cry Dance celebrations to reveal his vision.

Wodziwob, whose name meant Gray Hair or White Hair, claimed to have traveled to the land of the dead and talked with the spirits of the recently deceased. They promised to return to their loved ones within a few years if people would help them on their journey.

"Dance … dance!" Wodziwob had preached. "Dance and your mothers and fathers and sons and daughters will come back to you. Things will get better. We'll all be happy, and there won't be no differences between us and the whites. Dance … dance!"

I interrupted. "The dead are omens of disease and death to every Indian I've ever known."

"That was a problem. But he claimed they would come back as whole human beings to join their loved ones again."

"So everyone was supposed to Round Dance?"

"He called it the Ghost Dance."

"So what happened?"

"Nothing. The Paiutes and some other tribes danced for three or four years. Last I heard, everybody'd lost faith, and the dancing stopped about five years back. In '72, if I remember right."

"What happened to Wodziwob?"

"Some say he died that year, but some claim he's still alive."

"Could that be what I saw?"

"I don't think so. Your Spirit Dream was of things yet to come. So we will have to wait and see. You'll have to live your dream, Eagle. In time, you will learn to interpret what you saw in the vision."

I made a face and asked what good was a Spirit Dream if you had to wait until it happened to understand it? He countered that I had been warned of the future, and forewarned was forearmed.

Otter found solace in one part of my dream. He was convinced the bear I had seen crossing the valley was Matthew. The coyotes on his trail were likely soldiers. Hurry, Matthew. Hurry!

"What will you do now?"

"Go looking for Matthew," I said without hesitation.

"If that is your will, then that is what you must do. But consider this. When you go searching for him, there are countless places to look. If you are but one valley off, you will pass one another unnoticed. But if he is coming home, there is only one destination."

"Two," I said. "Here and the Mead."

"Aye. Yet are not two better than a thousand?"

"You're saying it's a fool's mission."

"Nay. Not a fool's mission, but a difficult one."

"So you think I should go home and wait for him to show up."

"That is not for me to say. You will follow your own will. But I know the intelligence that hides beneath that gold speckled mop of yours, John. You will make the right decision."

John, not War Eagle. He was telling me to behave like a white man. Go home and work the forge and wait. Did I have that much patience? A flash of light down on the prairie floor caught my attention. I saw Otter had noticed it, as well.

Mark Wildyr

Lines etched his face as he gave a wan smile. "Lenses from a pair of binoculars catching sunlight. The farm is being watched. They may have been at the glen as well."

I struggled to my feet. "Spying on my Quest? Why?"

"Who knows? Hatred of our blood. There is a lot of that around. Envy because we have made a success of the farm while others flounder. Times are hard, and many go hungry."

"Those men who were watching us when we came out of the sweat lodge, were they part of this?"

"Likely. And speaking of the medicine lodge. It is time for you to purify your body. I'll prepare the rocks while you eat something more. Not too much. Just enough to make a comfortable belly."

"Will you join me?"

"No. This time is for you. Perhaps you will discover something new about your vision if you are alone."

I went into the house to a lunch of stew and sour milk and an onion so sweet I could have eaten it whole. After finishing my meal, I stripped and waded across Turtle Crick for my medicine bath. I ducked through the hut's small opening and ladled water from a bucket onto glowing stones. Breathing hot steam made me giddy. Yet no new revelations came as I sat in that silent semi-darkness.

Finally, I emerged from the tiny hut of brush and canvas and sat in the bathing place Otter and the Brandt boys and I had once shared. The cold water closed my pores. Invigorated, I climbed the bank, took the towel Otter had left for me, and dried off. I glanced around as I fastened the cloth around my waist. Two men stood in plain view on the far side of the crick.

# # # # #

I worked alongside James and Otter in the fields for a day. Then early the following morning, I mounted Arrow and headed home, leading the pinto, now packed with a dressed antelope carcass.

Less than a league from Morrow Farm, a group of horsemen approached. One sported a five-pointed star pinned to his shirt. They looked like the militia that once terrorized the countryside. Quelling an impulse to run, I pulled up and waited.

When they halted of me, the law dog spoke. "What was you doing over at Morrow Farm?"

"Why does me visiting my grandpa raise your interest?"

"Don't get sassy with me, boy. I'm Sheriff Charles Landreth, and you show some respect. What's your name?"

38

The Sheriff was a big-boned man with a thick moustache flowing out of his nostrils and hiding his upper lip. He had the veined nose of a tavern crawler. The badge and a six-gun on his hip lent him authority.

"I'm John Strobaw from Teacher's Mead. Been visiting Joseph Strobaw Otter and Major Morrow for the past few days."

"You always run around naked for everbody to see?"

The question tested my resolve to remain calm. "I am usually naked when I bathe." The man bristled. "As far as everyone seeing. I expected some privacy on Major Morrow's property."

A man on a black horse with one white stocking came forward. A long nose hooked over his mouth so far he must have had trouble getting a spoon past it. The Reverend Jeremiah Berglund of the City on the Hill Church. I'd seen him on the streets of Yanube City when I was a kid.

"What's in those packs?"

"Bait for my family."

"Is that their bribe to you?"

I blinked, uncertain over his meaning. "I'm packing game the Major sent home to my family."

The lawman spoke up. "You go on and stay out of trouble."

"I don't get into trouble, Sheriff. I do my work and mind my own business." With that, I kicked Arrow's sides so hard he grunted and took off at a gallop, almost jerking the reins of the pinto out of my hand. I brought him under control and proceeded toward the Mead at a dignified pace. The back of my neck itched for the better part of a mile, but I saw no more of the sheriff's posse.

When I arrived at the Mead, Ma was miffed because I'd been gone so long without sending back news of Matthew. She softened enough to feed me when she learned he hadn't died with Crazy Horse.

Pa and I climbed the hollow hill for a talk after my meal. Once he was finished probing for more details of Crazy Horse's murder, I confessed my *hemblecha* and recited my Spirit Dream.

"Son, you feel your red blood more than your brother and sisters. Except for Matthew. Your Ma ... and I ... have worked to make the Americans see you as white. It has been hard because you have more of me in you than your mother. Her blood shows in Alex and the girls but not in you. That means you are at greater risk than they are. You must be careful."

Swallowing disappointment over his disinterest in my vision, I stared at the ground. There was silence between us until I mentioned the men watching the Morrow farm and my confrontation with Sheriff Landreth.

His interest piqued, he asked me to repeat what the Sheriff and the Rev. Berglund had said. Then he breathed what seemed to be a prayer. "I hope James and Otter are careful."

With those words, I saw what I had been blind to before and blushed.

# # # # #

I resumed life as a blacksmith and horse tender as if nothing had happened. But it had, and I was a changed man for it. I worked with the air of one waiting for Shambling Bear. That's the way I thought of Matthew now. If I understood anything at all about my Spirit Dream, it was that he was on his way home to us ... to me.

I rose each morning and went to work trying to get my chores done so I would have time for him when he arrived. My faith faltered when the first blue norther roared down out of Canada and blanketed the countryside in white. Soon Christmas and New Year's Day were behind us. Aching for my missing heart, I often thought of Otter and James snowbound in their farmhouse on Turtle Crick, secure in one another's presence ... and longed for such confinement with Matthew.

As the winter progressed, I lost those naïve ideas and silently railed against him for depriving me of his comfort. He should have come home ... stayed home ... never left It was easier to be cross with him than to mourn his absence.

Trudging daily through the snow from the house to the forge and stable, the only places on the Mead I went during snow-blind time, began to chafe. In time, restlessness overcame me, so I pulled out my snowshoes and loaded myself down with rifle and scattergun for short excursions over the frozen landscape. Pa and Alex went with me sometimes. They were decent company, but I preferred to be alone. Yet, I could hardly make my druthers known. As the winter deepened, wolves became a problem, but I didn't let them keep me inside.

I masturbated more in the wintertime than in other seasons, probably because I was out doing things when it was warmer, but on those short, cold, gray days, I'd get to thinking about Matthew and me in the river. I could almost feel his touch on my cock. It was warmer in the forge but safer in the loft for such private enterprise.

Today, I made a place in the hay, covered it with a blanket and shucked my britches and flap down around my ankles. When I closed my eyes and tucked a blanket between my legs, Matthew appeared, standing on the riverbank wringing water out of his glossy hair. His long penis pulsed in the air. I only had to skin my manhood back once to make it stand up straight and tall.

I knew it was big. Like Pa had guessed, we'd done some measuring. Mathew's was biggest, but mine came in second, beating out Alex by a tad, but I was lots thicker around. Maybe even more than Matthew. I closed my eyes and rubbed a hand over my belly. I tweaked a tit and felt it in my nuts. Ready now, I grasped my hard prick and found a rhythm, taking the foreskin with me on each stroke. There was a Jewish family in Yanube City, and I'd met one of their kids once. How did he do this without a foreskin? Same way, I guess, but it sure would be different without that hood sliding up and down, up and down.

I beat myself harder and forgot all about Jewish boys. Matthew reappeared. Hard cock, tight butt, slab belly, flat pecks, dark nipples. Oh, shit! Oh, shit! It was more than I could stand. Orgasm struck. My innards turned to jelly. My balls sent shockwaves clear through me. Groans echoed around the loft as cum shot out of me and splattered my chest and belly. I slowed, but didn't stop, not till the last pearl drop oozed out of my softening rod. I lay panting as puddles of sperm turning cold on my skin.

CHAPTER 5

The oppressive winter of 1877-78 finally passed. A late freeze had pinched out premature buds on trees and bushes, but now the cold was truly behind us. The Goose Moon ushered in a busy time on the farm. I'd worked hard over the winter months to hone the plow blades and repair on our equipment because this was the one time of year when my back was required in the fields. We had 360 acres planted with crops ranging from wheat and corn to beans and peas.

Stagecoaches from Fort Ramson supplied news from the big "out there," and the outgoing stages kept us up to date on the goings-on in Yanube City. From the Fort Ramson coaches, we heard talk of the stubborn depression. Otter had tried to pound theories of economics into my head, but not much had taken root. How could we be in the middle of a big Industrial Revolution during the Gilded Age, and still suffer an economic hardship that reached back as far as I could remember?

Now the news was of yellow fever tearing through Cuba. On the twenty-sixth of last month — May, that is — President Hayes signed the Quarantine Act allowing the Marine Hospital Service to set up a station on the Mississippi south of New Orleans to stop the deadly disease from reaching the mainland.

The first outgoing stage in June turned our world upside down. I was leading the fresh team of trace horses from the corral when Hannah ran up and said Pa wanted me right now. I handed her the reins of the lead horse and trotted over to where Pa was engaged with Dusty Skediver. Dusty wasn't much older than I was, which made me wonder why I couldn't drive a stage and see the world.

Pa wore a deep frown. "Bad news. I don't know how to say this without just coming out with it. Otter and James are dead."

I reeled backwards as if he'd slapped my face. "What? How?"

Dusty took over. "Mob killed them. Shot the Major and burned him up in his cabin, and then they strung up Otter."

My knees went weak. I held myself upright by sheer will. Otter ... hanged? The worst death there was for an Indian. I heard Pa speaking from the bottom of a deep well.

"Why, for God's sake?"

"Been rumors about them two for years," Dusty said. "Last year some hunters seen this big kid cavorting around necked with them."

I almost moaned aloud. Dusty didn't seem to notice, but Pa did.

"Then two weeks back, the Salman kid confessed they took him out to the farm and done bad things to him."

"I don't believe it!"

Pa interrupted with more practical matters. "Where are the bodies?"

"The army saw to it the Major was buried. The Indian … uh, Otter, they wouldn't take. Hear tell, he's still at the fort's medical unit."

"I gotta go to him, Pa," My voice sounded like someone else's. I was about to throw up. They'd used my sweat bath with Otter to condemn him for things he never did. I went swoony-headed.

Pa laid a hand on my shoulder. "Let's get the stage out of here, and then make plans."

I harnessed the horses while Dusty, his shotgun, and their passengers ate. When the driver began hustling people aboard the coach, I managed to worm a few more details out of him. The Rev. Jeremiah Berglund had denounced Otter and James from the pulpit. Aaron Salman was a big kid in his teens who did work around town, usually at the livery stable.

After the stage pulled out for Fort Ramson, we had a family meeting that set the girls — and Ma — to crying. My eyes were pooling, but I blinked back tears. Wouldn't do for a nineteen-year-old man to bawl even if he was feeling as low as a snake's belly. Pa was needed at the Mead, and Alex was knee deep in taking care of freshly planted fields, so that left me to go settle Otter's affairs. That suited me just fine.

There wasn't just the body to be taken care of. He'd kept some of his silver and gold pieces in a hidey-hole under the cabin. That was likely where the deed to the farmland was, too. And perhaps a piece of paper that told what happened to things after the Major died. From what Dusty had told us, the farmhouse was burned down, but perhaps the outhouse still stood. Wouldn't be the first time I'd slept in a barn.

Pa took me up on the hollow hill while Ma outfitted me for a week's stay. He was worried about how I'd handle myself. I promised him to be careful and not go around half-cocked. That reminded me to dig out my handgun. I'd have to hide it in my saddlebags or Ma'd have a conniption fit. Pistols meant gunslingers to her.

I started for Morrow Farm right away and planned on getting there in the early morning hours, after snatching a nap on the way. At the rill where I had stopped to read Grandpa Billy's journal, I dismounted and wrapped myself in a poncho to nap, but images of me running around with an erection being the spark that resulted in Otter's and James's deaths rendered me wide awake.

In the midst of my misery ... it hit me. If Billy's journal to fell into the wrong hands, everything would come a cropper. That was proof Pa was a blood Indian. There'd be plenty of scalawags who'd raise Cain to get their hands on the Mead.

Thoughts of sleep gone, I got underway again. It was blackest night when Arrow crossed the bridge at the farm. The cabin raised a ragged silhouette, so some of the double walls were still standing. The outhouse seemed okay. I lit a candle and saw the barn door had been forced. No animals inside. No hay in the loft.

I threw down blankets upstairs and slept with one eye open. It was breaking light when I got up and went down to relieve myself. The sight of the charred timbers set my guts to rolling, but a hacked off length of rope tied to a sturdy cottonwood branch almost robbed me of my sanity. I sat down in the dirt and stared at the hemp.

Otter had died right there at the end of that rope. My blood rose, taking my pulse with it. Sweat broke out on my lip and forehead. My mind went to the sidearm in my saddlebags. But the journal and gold had to be recovered before anything else.

After scouting the area to make sure no strange eyes watched, I changed to a loincloth to keep from getting soot all over my white man's clothes. I'd been fearful the heavy stove had broken through the floor and either exposed the hiding place or blocked my entry to it. But the scavengers had hauled away the heavy piece of iron. Not much of anything had survived. One area in the corner opposite the doorway brought a chill to my blood. An unburned section of the flooring made the perfect outline of a man's body. James had died there.

"Come out of there, you thieving dog!"

The voice startled me to the point I'd have gone for my handgun had it been strapped around my waist. I whirled empty-handed to face Andre Tiller holding a scattergun leveled at my chest.

"Don't shoot, Mr. Tiller. I'm John Strobaw. From Teacher's Mead.

He jerked the gun barrel to the sky. "Sorry. Thieves been picking the place clean since ... since ..."

The sadness etched on Andre's handsome features pleased me. Someone else cared for my friends. "I was looking for the place they hid their valuables."

"I already emptied it out. Everything's at my cabin. Afraid those whoresons would get it. You can have them anytime you want. There was quite a bit of gold and silver."

"Was there a book bound in buffalo hide?"

"Your grandfather's journal? I got it hid away."

"Good. Leave it where it is. I'll pick it up later. Right now, I have to go take care of Otter's body."

Andre, a man in his mid-thirties, said he'd already done that. "I couldn't let him just lie there. I claimed him and buried him where I know he'd want to be buried. I can show you."

Some emotion I didn't recognize choked me up. "I know where. In the glen north of here. With Dew Drop and Standing Rock. You did right, Mr. Tiller."

"Andre. I'm Andre. That's where I buried him, all right. Don't know where the other two were laid, but I did the best I could."

"It was enough. Can you tell me what happened?"

He gave me the same version Dusty had, but he put a finish to it. "I came as soon as I heard shots. Otter had just left my place after dropping off some venison. I told Libby to stay in the house and ran for my horse. By the time I got here, Otter was already dead, and the mob was headed down the road to town. Must have been a baker's dozen of them. I didn't know the Major was burning up in the house."

"Was Berglund with the mob?"

"You mean that creepy preacher? Didn't see him, but I heard later he left soon as the shooting started."

"Do you know the fellow who denounced them? Name of Salman."

"I've seen him around town a few times. But I know he was lying. Otter and James might have loved one another, but they'd never debauch anyone."

I nodded. "They were true to one another." My words put pain lines on his face. There was a story here, but there wasn't time to draw it out. "Mr. Tiller … Andre, I've got to go to town, but we'll talk later. Guard those things from the hidey-hole, will you?"

"Be pleased to. There's a piece of paper in there that says it's yours now."

"What's mine?"

"Everything. They wanted you to have the farm. All 240 acres."

"Two-forty? I thought they just had their homestead."

"They added another eighty acres over the years. According to that piece of paper, the Major left his funds to my girl, Libby. He's been like

46

a grandpa to her since she was born. He had a right smart of money from the sale of his Virginia plantation after the war. The rest, they left to you."

"To me, not my pa?"

"You're John, aren't you?" I nodded. "Well, it's spelled out clear and in legal talk. These fields belong to you now. As well as the things in the hidey hole. Those two men helped me build my place, and I'll help you rebuild yours."

"Thanks, but I can't think about that now. We'll talk it over later."

"Any time you're ready. I didn't put up a marker in the glen, but you'll see where the earth's been turned."

"Who came when the call went out? The army or the sheriff's office?"

"Army. They generally come when there's a fire. You know, to look for renegades. Haven't seen the sheriff, but he coulda come when I was working my fields."

I thanked him again and dressed before riding across the bridge Otter had built with his own hands. I didn't know many people in Yanube City, but the two I did know would have some answers.

Timo Bowers wouldn't meet my eye as he told me what he knew about Otter's death, mostly a repeat of what I'd already heard. But he added that Berglund had been preaching on pederasts to his City on the Hill flock. Claimed they had two living right amongst them. When Caleb Brown confirmed Timo's facts, I had all I needed.

My carelessness at the medicine lodge might have lit the spark, but Aaron Salmon's lie had let Berglund fan the flames and destroy my friends. As soon as I cast eyes on him, I put him out of my mind. He was one of those simpletons who grow big even when they're young. He was sixteen or so, but the vacant eyes and slack jaw argued his mind was younger than that. He didn't come up with those lies. Berglund had told him what to say, and the poor fellow believed the words the minute they came out of his mouth. I'd take no satisfaction in extracting justice from him. Hell, it wouldn't have been justice.

I needed Berglund. I could march into his church and shoot him in the head like the pig he was, but that would likely be the end of me. That's the last thing Otter would have wanted.

After looking around the City on the Hill on South Main. I noticed a large piece of vacant land clogged with a few trees and a lot of brush diagonally across the street. Brown's Emporium sold me a water bag. After filling it, I rode back down Main, circling around and entering the vacant lot from the west. No one would notice me that way. There was plenty of grass for Arrow and a well-screened spot gave me a view of the front of the church and a small door on the north side. My saddlebags held the bait Ma'd packed for me, so I settled down to watch for an opportunity to isolate the preacher.

Just as on my *hemblecha*, time and space began to alter as I stared at the white wooden building. Berglund came and went. He was a regular person, but I was waiting for a variation in his schedule.

Four days passed before I got what I was looking for. A little before dusk, the reverend showed up at his side door and ushered a diminutive figure inside. The urgency of his actions caught my interest. Because a number of people still roamed the streets, I circled around to leave the vacant lot from the back side.

I hadn't bathed since leaving the Mead, but after brushing my clothes free of dust and running a hand through my hair before putting my hat back on, chances were I looked presentable.

I crossed the street and approached a man and his wife taking their ease in the shade of their front porch. They had no view of the building's north door and professed not to know when the reverend would be at the church. Well aware their eyes were on me, I walked to the City on the Hill and tried the door. It was locked, but the hardware was cheap. The mechanism gave way when I applied a little pressure, allowing me to march inside like a faithful member of the flock.

The interior was a plain affair. Ten-foot ceiling. Stark whitewashed walls. An altar cloth thrown across a table. I headed straight for a small door to the side of the pulpit, twisted the handle, and slipped through.

Berglund stood behind a little girl bent over a table with her dress bunched at her haunches. He was naked from the waist down. Coarse black hair on his legs and buttocks made him bestial. A forked tail wouldn't have surprised me. The girl, who couldn't have been more than thirteen or fourteen had a rag in her mouth to muffle her cries of pain. His humping and grunting covered the sound of my entry.

When I shouted "Rape!" at the top of my lungs, he whirled, revealing a swollen red member. He tripped on the trousers bunched around his ankles and went over on his butt. I grabbed the girl's hand and dragged her out the side door, shouting to attract attention. In moments, a small crowd had gathered. One woman gasped and pointed at a trickle of blood running down the girl's leg.

"It's the little Jones girl," someone said.

"Did this man hurt you," a woman asked.

Berglund chose that moment to appear at the door with his clothing restored. His eyes went wide when he saw the group standing there.

The child pointed at the preacher. "He did. He hurt me!"

Not a sound came from the group as they turned to stare at Berglund. He stammered a couple of times before protesting. He tried to claim I'd done it, but the family from across the street said they'd seen me enter the church just minutes before.

Berglund resorted to what had always served him best. Oratory. "It's a conspiracy," he bellowed in his church tones. "Red men hate me because I call them out for what they are … sinners, apostates, drunkards! You can't believe this man."

The girl clutched the woman who'd called her by name and began sobbing. And just like that, Berglund failed.

"Fornicator!" a bluff, red-faced man yelled.

"Pederast!" This from a woman with the look of a church goer.

"Somebody get the law!"

"Let's get 'im, boys!" The red-faced man started forward.

Berglund jumped back and slammed the door behind him. As the crowd rushed the church, I left the poor child to the mercies of the woman comforting her and raced across the street for Arrow. He was no sooner saddled than Berglund cleared the rear of the building in a buckboard and charged through the growing crowd. A few men gave chase, but they didn't have the motivation I had. They gave up when he took the wagon trace on the north bank of the river.

I headed toward Turtle Crick for a distance, then cut east at a canter. Berglund's black wouldn't go far at an all-out run while harnessed to the buckboard. There was always the danger the preacher would abandon the wagon and take to the horse's back, but he likely had his most prized possessions with him in the wagon.

Once I judged Arrow was far enough ahead of the fleeing man, I headed due south to intersect the wagon trace. Finding no fresh tracks in the dirt, I pulled up in the middle of the road to listen for the sound of an approaching wagon. My handgun was held out of sight behind the saddle pommel by the time Berglund came into view. He sawed the reins and came to a stop.

"You!" he yelled. "Get out of my way." He blinked when he saw my pistol leveled at him.

"Turn off into the tree line. Now, Preacher."

Berglund's massive Adam's apple bobbled. "I don't know what you think you're doing, but it's all a big mistake. That girl, she wanted …"

"One more word, and I'll shoot you right here."

He flipped his reins, but I sent Arrow crashing into his horse. Berglund clawed for something on the running board as I raced around the side of the wagon and shot an elbow into his throat. He gagged and slumped back on the seat. A black six-shooter fell from his hand. I tucked it into my waistband, grabbed a hame ring, and led the black off the road into the trees.

Berglund made a few gurgling noises, but he was more or less comatose as I halted beneath a large cottonwood and cut one of the reins loose with my knife. He came alive and started to make a fight of it when I looped one end around his neck, but it was too late. I snugged it against his throat and tied the loop with a knot.

He nearly jumped from the wagon when I tossed the free end over a limb, but by then he was dancing on his tiptoes. As I tied the other end of the leather to the bole of a stout sapling nearby, he made terrible coughing and gagging noises, almost unnerving me. But the thought of those same sounds issuing from Otter and the memory of how this blackguard had used me to destroy my friends hardened my heart.

When the wagon passed from beneath his feet, I feared I'd made a mistake. The cottonwood limb bent so that the toes of his boots scraped the ground. But he could only get enough purchase to prolong his agony.

After he hung limp and lifeless, I found his knife and dropped the blade in the bed of the wagon as if it had fallen from his hand after cutting the rein. No sign I had been in the area remained when I slapped the black on his rump, sending him down the trail toward Yanube City. The horse would go back to familiar territory and set off a search for the preacher. With any luck, the law would conclude, he couldn't deal with the scandal and had hanged himself like the Judas he was.

Then I rode straight for Morrow Farm.

CHAPTER 6

The sweat lodge still stood, and the Lord knew I needed purifying. Using charred timbers from the cabin for firewood and the earthen jug sitting on what was left of the front porch to carry water, I soon had a few rocks glowing. I used Otter's tongs to carry them inside the little hut.

I stripped and ducked through the opening to spend the next hour ladling water over hot stones, breathing thick steam, and praying. I sang to both the Christian God and *Wakan Tonka*, begging forgiveness even as the despicable preacher's dying rale echoed in my mind. I'd been surprised by the voided bladder and loose bowels, and they made me ashamed. Not for that coyote, but for Otter, who had probably done the same in front of a mob of whites.

Seeking relief from mental turmoil, I tried to call up scraps of conversations I'd heard in town. Anything to distract me. Edison, that famous inventor back east, had made something called a phonograph that captured noises and played them back like echoes of the real thing. What would music sound like on something like that?

A traveling photographer in town had offered to take my image for a quarter. A lot of money just to cast an eye on yourself. What would my image show? Not angel's wings, that's for sure. Devil's horns? Maybe not. My sole aim was to get justice for two of the finest men God ever created. Justice they'd never get from Sheriff Landreth and his ilk. Berglund's dead leg gave a final jerk in my mind's eye, threatening to draw me back into the pit of murder and remorse.

By the time the water was exhausted and the stones cooled, I hadn't suffocated the way I'd hoped, but at least the steam had scoured away the worst of my thoughts and achieved a tentative sort of peace. I crawled through the entryway to immerse myself in the cold, clear waters of Turtle Crick for the final phase of my catharsis. Dressed in fresh clothing from my saddlebags and feeling clean — at least on the outside — I went looking for Andre Tiller.

He stood on his porch and watched with friendly blue eyes as I dismounted and put a false bounce in my step. This was a good man. No need to burden him with the stain on my soul.

After a cordial greeting, I asked for the journal. My own thoughtless actions had made this a dangerous weapon against my family. With a leaden heart, I fed pages from the tome to the flames in Andre's cook stove. As my cultural heritage curled into black soot, I resolved to tell my brother and sisters nothing of the book. Why place them at risk with such dangerous knowledge?

Andre must have seen my anguish because he handed over a bottle of whiskey before disappearing into his bathing room to clean up after a day in the fields. I had fed the last of the journal to the flames before I noticed a little girl sitting at the table with a book and paper spread out before her.

"It's Libby, isn't it?"

"Yes, sir. You're Mr. Strobaw. I've seen you before … over at Grandpa James's and Uncle Otter's."

"I'm John. Can you call me John?"

"No, sir. But I can call you Mr. John."

"That's fine. What are you studying?"

"Arithmetic. My father makes me study every evening before I go to bed." Although she was no more than eight, there was something of the adult about her. Her dark blonde curls carried an auburn tint.

She glanced up. "You have strange hair. But I expect you know that."

"Since I was your age." Hiding the bottle in my left hand behind my leg, I looked over the neat columns she had written down.

"Do you cypher?" She craned her neck to look up at me over her shoulder.

"As a matter of fact, I do."

"Can you check my answers? Papa does it for me, but sometimes we both make an error."

I was calculating her answer to the last problem when Andre came into the room, shirtless but in fresh trousers. His chest was startlingly white, considering his arms and face were almost as bronze as mine.

"Are you finished?" He gave his daughter an indulgent smile.

"She is, and they're all correct," I said. "Smart girl."

"You checked them? Thanks. Sometimes I don't do a good job of it."

I accepted a bowl of stew left over from their supper, and we talked about farming and the weather and little bits of nothing until Libby said goodnight and went to her room. After she shut the door behind her, I told Andre what had happened in town this morning — although it was a less than forthright telling. In my version, I headed straight for the Morrow farm and a good sweat bath after the reverend fled the church ahead of an angry mob.

Andre got two pewter cups for the bottle I'd not yet uncorked. I'm not much of a drinker. Pa always warned that our people had a weakness in the blood for alcohol, so he'd pretty well scared us off the stuff. But I took a healthy swig and managed to keep it down. Andre started talking about Otter and the Major. That's the way he labeled James — the Major. The more he talked, the easier the stuff went down. We were laughing and hiccupping over remembrances of the two when a stern-faced little girl came in and complained she couldn't get any sleep.

"If you're going to drink that stuff, go to the barn."

Andre beamed at his daughter. "Good idea, honey. Come on, John."

We staggered outside into the night. He carried the bottle, leaving the cups to me. I had the presence of mind to unsaddle and stall Arrow since I was apt to finish the night here. By the time I got to the ladder with my saddlebags, Andre was halfway up, but running into some difficulty. I butted him with my shoulder, sending him barreling up through the opening. I followed and fumbled a candle from my pack.

By the time it was lit, Andre sat on the hay swigging from the bottle, which was three-quarters gone by now. He held it out to me, but I'd had enough. I spread my bedroll beside the bale he was sitting on, and stretched out on the blankets. Andre lay back on the hay.

"Lord, I'm drunk. Pay for it tomorrow." His bottle went glug.

"I got a snoot full, too."

"They were fine men. Otter saved my life. Treated some bad wolf bites. Moved Bella and me — that was my wife — right in his cabin in the middle of winter."

He went on, telling how he and his wife hadn't been prepared for the long, cold Dakota winters. He suffered again the murder of his wife and two small sons by a Sioux named Dull Lance. Then he went quiet. I thought he'd fallen asleep until he said something that snagged my attention. I eased up into a sitting position.

"What?"

"I almost got between them once. Came near to breaking them up. I felt awful."

"How'd you do that?"

"I didn't know they were together. You know what I mean? *Together.* I'd heard stories about that Red Win-tay man Otter lived with until he died. One night, Otter heard Bella and me making love while we were staying with him. I thought because his ... man ... wasn't around anymore that maybe we'd got him worked up. The Major was wintering with his troops at the fort. So … so …"

"What, Andre. What happened?"

"I did it for him," he said in a quiet voice that made him sound about fifteen-years-old. And later he gave himself to me when I went off the deep end after Bella … and the boys …" He put his head in his hands. Candle light caught in his brown locks. His shoulders shook. "God, I loved him."

He'd loved Otter. Like Billy loved Otter. Like James did. Even so, the words that came out of my mouth shocked me. "Andre, do you want to come down here?"

Without answering, he slipped from the bale and rested his head on my outstretched arm. He turned so his hair was in my face. It smelled of soap from his bath. I pulled him to me. That's all I'd intended, but he nuzzled my neck and pushed up my shirt. His tongue was warm and moist. He found a nipple and suckled. My rod ballooned.

He peered through the flickering light. His fingers caressed my cheeks, my lips, my eyes. He leaned forward and teased my lips with his, moving back and forth over mine gently, barely touching. Then his tongue traced my lips before forcing them apart. He kissed me, and for one brief moment in that darkened hayloft, Matthew was back. Then he shattered the illusion by speaking in a husky voice.

"You are a handsome man. A handsome man with strange hair."

We fell silent as he stripped my shirt over my head and unfastened my trousers. As he slid them to my ankles, his chin rested on my pulsing cock. Then his mouth was on me, licking my ball sack and kissing my thighs, making me needful. He rode my cock back to the tip and took me into his mouth.

I explored his muscles while he struggled out of his britches. He lay atop me, throbbing flesh to throbbing flesh. He squirmed so that all parts of him rubbed against me. Then he moved down and took me to the root, sending wonderful sensations throughout me. As my time neared, I fucked his mouth.

"A … Andre, I'm coming." My voice gave truth to the words. I pitched over the edge and tumbled in space while something marvelous happened to my nether regions. I shot gouts of seed into his throat. He choked and came up for a moment, almost drawing a protest before he took me again to accept all I could deliver.

After it was over, he lay against me, his lips against my cheek, his throbbing cock pressing my hip. He started moving against me.

Tentative at first, and then more urgently, finding a rhythm. In the grip of something momentous, I rolled over on top of him. In the weak light, I looked into his lust-filled eyes, and kissed each of them.

Then, as he had done, I worked my way down his hard, rangy body. I paused at his navel, but after washing it with my tongue, I resolutely moved down. My chin made playful circles around his hard cock, rubbed his belly and thigh joints and balls. I licked his column. The taste was not unpleasant.

I came up and pumped him for a few moments, mentally measuring the feel of him against when I did this to myself. Then holding him in my hand, I swabbed his bulb with my tongue, opened my throat, and took as much of him as possible. I gagged, came up, and tried it again. Better that time. Then I worked on him until he made little sing-song cries. It took a moment to realize he was whispering Otter's name. For that brief instant, I was happy to be Otter for him. Soon he gasped and erupted. Every part of him throbbed with the force of his ejaculation. I struggled to take it all. Eventually, he grew quiet and still.

I lay beside him with my hand on his smooth chest. He was breathing as if he had climbed the hollow hill. His hair was damp, his upper lip moist. Neither of us spoke, and I soon drifted into sleep — only to dream of a tall, handsome Teton warrior named Shambling Bear.

# # # # #

I woke lying beside a passed-out, naked man. Tarnation, I was bare-assed, too. Not even my sleeping shift Bits and pieces of the night slowly returned. More whiskey than was good for me. Andre sucking on my pipe. Me returning the favor. My stomach rolled.

I watched the sleeping figure while pulling on my clothes. Every part of him was exposed to my sight. Andre Tiller was handsome … fair of feature and well-formed. That such a man would covet me was a novel idea.

I sat on a hay bale and took pleasure in looking at him. He was a man. No question about it. He'd fathered children and held down a marriage — until murder put an end to it. Yet he had lain with Otter. Of course, Andre had feelings for Otter. That was clear because he'd whispered my friend's name in the throes of orgasm.

A longing struck me so hard I gripped myself in my arms. I had determined on waiting to take Matthew's seed for my virgin mouth. Now it was no longer virgin. Even with these thoughts racing through my mind, I reached for Andre. Though he was groggy, his manhood

Mark Wildyr

rose at my touch, and I tongued him awake. He stretched lazily and murmured a soft good morning before shuddering through ejaculation. Then he tumbled me over and sucked the seed from me. This time we weren't drunk. Hung over, but not drunk.

With both of us naked, I made a deal with Andre to tend the 240 acres James and Otter had planted. He would take sixty percent of the harvest, and forty percent would go to me. As the morning matured, we didn't discuss what we'd done together.

Feeling the need for purification, I tarried long enough for a sweat bath. Which of my deeds would the Christians in town consider more horrendous — murder or sodomy? I rinsed off in the crick, dressed, and cross-cut the prairie straight for home. The late start meant I star-slept that night, but I didn't mind. Maybe Berglund's twisted shade couldn't abide God's fresh air or the scrutiny of His stars. Whatever the reason, he kept to the fringes of my sleep under the glowing heavens that night.

#####

The family, anxious for news of Otter and James, crowded around when I dismounted in front of the stable the next day. Pa told everyone to leave me alone until after I took care of Arrow. But he remained behind to help me.

As we worked, I told how I'd caught the preacher raping a girl and put up such a fuss he'd been run out of town. I told him of burning Billy's journal, about James and Otter leaving me the farm, and detailed my arrangement with Andre Tiller. The important details — the hanging of one man and the bedding of another — never came up.

Pa'd already heard most of it from Dusty when the Yanube City stage came through yesterday. The townsfolk had discovered the reverend dangling from a tree limb off the wagon track near the river's north bank. Yanube City might have bought the idea the bastard had faced up to his deeds and hanged himself, but my pa didn't believe it. Not for a minute. He paused an awfully long time before speaking.

"I killed my first man when I was seventeen. Otter and I caught the cashiered Army captain who slaughtered my father and most of our band. The snake deserved his fate, but I've never got free of the thing. It weighs on my mind to this day. The worst part is that it's a burden you can never share."

With that, he touched me on the shoulder — an intimacy he seldom indulged — and walked to the house with me in his trail.

56

Ma put a warm plate in front of me at the table, and everyone arranged themselves to listen to my news, told between bites. The story came out the same way I'd given it to Pa.

Ma and the girls wanted to bring Otter to the Mead and lay him away with Billy and Cut Hand and the others.

"He's been subjected to enough indignity." My tone was a little more heated than intended. "He'd be mortified at us seeing him like that. He's with friends. Leave him alone."

Pa supported me, and the matter was closed.

Alex followed everything and looked bothered. I could tell he was concentrating on those 240 acres. Didn't make sense. He'd never leave the Mead, and he sure couldn't farm them from here, just as I couldn't. Maybe it was just the idea the land came to me. He licked his lips.

"You gonna deed the acreage over to the family?"

My face burned from disappointment — not anger. "Why would I do that? James and Otter would have deeded it to the family if that's what they wanted."

"It doesn't seem right. Otter was my spiritual grandfather, too."

Pa intervened. "Alexander, was Otter a willful man? Was James?"

"N ... no. He was logical. They both were."

"Then they had a logical reason for doing what they did."

"Still doesn't seem right. It's like we're cut out of an inheritance."

"I'll give you the coins and currency they left me," I offered.

"No," Pa said. "You'll need that to support the property."

"Then I'll give up my claim to the Mead." The words almost stuck in my throat. I couldn't see myself estranged from my birthplace.

"That's for your mother and me to decide." Pa's tone put an end to the subject.

Might as well get the other matter off my mind so long as we were talking turkey. I asked permission to move into Otter's old cabin. From the look Alex gave me, my brother had been considering that possibility for himself.

"Don't know why not if Alex doesn't have any objection. Do you?"

"No. Go on."

We could both see he didn't mean it, but Pa was one to take a man at his word, so he gave me his indulgence.

Since reading Billy's journal, I'd wondered about Alex and his lack of interest in hunting up a presentable girl. That was a harder chore than it sounded. Yanube City, the only town nearby, was a hard day's travel. Most of the farm families scattered along the river wouldn't cotton to the idea of an Indian courting their daughters, not even an Indian everyone thought was three-quarters white.

I gave Alex the once-over. He looked enough like Pa to be handsome, but he carried more of Ma's features than the rest of us. Women would go for him, all right, but my guess was he loved the land more than he'd ever love a woman. He had more acres under cultivation than anyone else in the 150 miles between Fort Ramson and Yanube City.

He had more acres? I blinked. My brother had more or less taken over management of the farm while I wasn't paying attention. Well, he was welcome to it. One day, he'd wake up and realize he'd be working the farm alone. Then he'd find a woman fast enough and start producing little Alexanders to give him a hand around the place.

I moved into Otter's old cabin near the Appleton's abode just west of the stone house the very next day. My new place was one big room with a separate bathing room. It didn't have water piped in, but Otter had rigged up a shower of sorts if a man was willing to pump the water and lift it into the big overhead tank.

# # # # #

The summer scooted by on greased wheels. I traveled to Yanube City to file the Major's will, so the land could be switched over to my name. That got me on the county's taxpayer roll. Well, my share of the harvest oughta take care of that.

After my town business was concluded, I went to the Morrow farm — guess it was the Strobaw farm now — to stow some things in the loft to keep from packing them back and forth between the two places. There was a small fireplace downstairs Otter had used to burn peat for the animals' comfort during the long winter months. He'd built the outhouse — that was what he called the barn — like he'd built his cabin, double-walled with a tabby of mud and hay between, so it was reasonably warm.

I looked up Andre and told him the fields looked pretty good. Depending on crop prices this fall, we ought to do pretty good. Did he ever think about what we'd done for one another? I got my answer at twilight. I heard someone out front of the barn and opened the loft doors to look down on Andre.

Once at the top of the ladder, he shuffled from one foot to the other looking so damned handsome I went over and took him off the tinder hook, pulling him into my arms and giving him a kiss that curled my toes. He was fresh out of his bath, making me wonder how he regarded

58

me since I hadn't had one. It didn't put him off any because he stripped me out of my clothes and knelt before me. Was he pretending it was Otter he was sucking — like I was imagining Matthew doing it for me? He wasn't greedy about it. He took time to play with my balls and stroke my crack while he tongued my rod.

After a minute, we moved to my bedroll. When I was on my back, he started in again. I closed my eyes and surrendered to the wonderful pressure building up inside me. I shuddered through a climax. He did all right by Otter — if that was who he was dreaming about. Then we reversed positions, and I did the best job I could for him.

Like before, we didn't talk about what we'd done. He just got dressed and went home to his daughter. Wasn't shame — at least on my part — but I didn't quite know how to talk about it. That entry in Billy's journal came to me. I liked Andre Tiller. Was getting fond of him. But I can't say I was in love with him. I went back to the Mead the next morning without looking him up again.

# # # # #

Taking care of the forge and the livestock kept me busy. That helped keep my mind off the ghost that haunted me. I'd be working at the forge and see Berglund's pinched face in the flames. Or he'd wake me out of a sound sleep. The more whipped I was, the less he intruded in my life.

A little of my inheritance went to buy four head of beef cattle — one for the family and the other three to sell when the time came. Maybe I'd buy a few more head next year. There was plenty of grazing land and Alex might give up some of the corn crop to put good, tasty weight on the animals since one of the steers would end up in Ma's stew pots.

Pa had finally allowed me to split Otter's coins and currency among my brother, two sisters, and me. The girls would have a dowry, and I would still have enough to support my own household when that came along. After that, things got a little looser between Alex and me, but as harvest time approached, he tensed up again.

We brought in a good crop that autumn. The countryside was still in the throes of depression, so prices weren't so good. That meant we traded instead of sold.

I took another run out to Turtle Crick Farm — that was the name I'd settled on — to see how Andre and I had made out. He'd brought in a good harvest on both places. Since there wasn't much in the way of currency being exchanged — except when some sharpie wanted to steal a man's crop — I told him to barter for things I'd need to establish a home, even if it was in the loft of a barn. We didn't get together again, probably because we went to Yanube City to do some trading before I rode for the Mead. Or maybe it was because I missed Matthew so much right after my orgasms with Andre.

Autumn was short that year. Indian summer hardly got started before winter roared down on us with a vengeance. I was sorta glad to be snowbound. The law wasn't going to show up to haul me off to jail for killing that murdering preacher in this weather. And the more time went by, the less likely that was to happen.

Another recollection haunted me, as well. I'd been the "youth" seen cavorting around naked with an erection — the excuse the preacher from Hell had used to prosecute his hatred of Otter and James. What had they done to incur his enmity? There was nothing about the demeanor of those two to raise suspicion. And then it came to me. A white man living with an Indian. That was all it took to sow the seed of suspicion and hatred.

I tried to put Berglund's shade aside and deal with the festering problem with my brother. Even more troublesome was wondering where Matthew was. The shambling bear I'd seen in my Spirit Dream should have made it home by now. Unless those coyotes on his trail had caught up with him.

In the middle of December, Ma had us put up a *tannenbaum*. She and the girls decorated the tree with bits of colored cloth and pieces of agate and striated river stones in metal frames I'd fashioned so they could be hung from branches.

I'd sacrificed some of my silver to fashion simple crosses for the girls and Jane Appleton and a precious gold coin to make Ma's. None of the women were much for jewelry, but they would wear crosses. I made spurs for all the men. Not the fancy Spanish jingling kind, but good solid working spurs.

The day was a happy one, although there was something missing. Matthew was absent yet another Christmas.

CHAPTER 7

A cabin all to myself wasn't that great when it was blowing and snowing outside. Necessary chores were hard enough, and tromping back and forth between the stone house and my place was just added effort.

However, I wasn't often alone. Reverend Berglund kept regular company. Once, I sat down on the side of my bed for a conversation with the dead bastard. I told him in a very logical fashion he'd taken the lives of two good men, so it was only proper he paid with his own.

He didn't see it that way, of course. He blamed me for flaunting my nakedness and my obscene, jutting penis before the good folk of his flock. *I* killed my friends with my libertine actions, not him.

That brought sweat to my brow, so I explained I was preparing for my holy *hemblecha*. There was nothing sensual about it.

Holy? It was a heathen ritual filled with devil worship and unnatural sex and who knows what other affronts to any Christian congregation. According to Berglund, I'd robbed him of something more precious than gold and silver — the rest of his life.

Otter showed up from time to time to ease my mind on the matter. His specter assured me the guilt was not mine. I longed to accept that notion, but in the light of day, it was elusive.

Was I infected with ghost sickness? Wasn't sure what that was, but I'd heard about it all my life. If this wasn't the real thing, it was a good imitation.

I wasn't totally isolated in a physical sense, of course. Nine others lived at the Mead — counting the Appletons' two small fry — and we had daily contact except during brutal periods of weather. Still, residence in a separate cabin during the winter months altered my pattern of life enough, so I was pleased when spring showed up and things returned to normal.

With the turning of the weather, regular stagecoach runs started again. The drivers speculated the Long Depression ought to end sometime in 1879, so maybe I'd be able to sell rather than barter my share of Turtle Crick's fall crop. Stop dreaming, Strobaw. Planting time hadn't even arrived yet.

Taking advantage of this fact, I invited Alex to go hunting. To my surprise, he accepted. Was he looking for a showdown, too? We headed up Strobaw's Crick and followed the thin forest east past the

Jacobsen place. We'd bagged three red squirrels before the time seemed ripe for talking.

"Alex, we've never been close like a lot of brothers, but it's been worse than usual lately."

"You and Matthew were more like brothers than you and me. You always ran off and left me to do the work." He sounded halfway huffy.

I hadn't intended to let my blood rise, but it started simmering. "Tarnation, you never wanted to put up with us. We did our share."

"Just seemed like you cut me out, that's all."

"Matthew and me have said that about you more'n once. But what's got between us now? Everything changed when James and Otter left me that Turtle Crick acreage. Does it mean that much to you?"

He turned on me, and for a minute, I was desperate to remember if he'd reloaded after shooting the last squirrel. Then the moment passed — if it had ever been there. "It's not the acres, it's ..."

"What, Alex? What?"

"Didn't I mean anything to Otter? I called him grandfather, too."

We sat on a rock, and I thought for a long time before saying anything.

"I think I understand, but I don't know if I can explain it. They shoulda left the land to Matthew, but Matthew's pure blood, and that would've caused problems. He used to go see Otter all the time because Otter would let him feel his red blood. And I went because I think I felt closer to Otter than you did."

"You went because he let you play at being Bear and Eagle."

My breath caught in my throat. "It wasn't play. Matthew was living it. Sometimes he needed to be Bear to heal from seeing his mother and brother lying dead after being shot down by the militia." I took a breath. "You were born a farmer. From the time you were a little kid, you'd rather work in the fields with Pa than play."

"That's what I mean! I'm the farmer. Who better to leave the farm to?"

"You have a farm. It doesn't matter that Rachel Ann and Hannah and I will have a share of the Mead, you're the one who'll run it. You'll make the decisions. And you'll do a better job than any of us would."

I rubbed an itchy eye. "Otter knew me better than anyone else. He knew I'd probably leave the Mead someday ... just as he knew you never would. He wanted me to have a place to go. At least, I'm farmer enough to take care of his place. Am I making any sense?"

"Some. But it still hurt. Otter didn't leave me anything."

"What do you need?"

He turned his coal black eyes on me. "Something. Anything to let me know I counted."

I sighed. I'd have to do it. I'd have to tell him, or he'd never understand. "I didn't talk straight a minute ago. The real reason Otter and James left me the farm was they knew I'd *have* to leave Teacher's Mead one day and would need a place to go."

"Why would you have to leave?"

"Because I'm like they were. I have the same nature they did."

The silence got so deep I could hear Strobaw's Crick running a hundred yards to the west.

"You mean ..."

I nodded. "Yes. That's what I mean. You'll never have to worry about me having fry to inherit my share of the Mead."

"I don't believe you. You can't be like them."

"Why not?"

"You don't act it," he said.

"Did Otter and James?"

"Guess not. Hell, I don't know. You just can't be; that's all."

"Because Ma says it's wrong?"

"Because the Bible says so."

I faced him. "So I'm less of a man to you now?"

"I didn't say that." His face turned red. He wouldn't meet my eyes. "I have to think on this some."

"I expect." I rose and started back to the house. After a moment, he caught up. About halfway home, Alex put his hand on my shoulder and left it there for a long moment. The charley horse building in my right thigh eased and went away.

I'd worried my confession to Alex would make things worse between us, but his hand on my shoulder on the way home seemed to be a true measure of his feelings.

# # # # #

By now, I could not only make the anvil ring in full bell tones, but my biceps bulged as well. Not as much as Timo's or Crow's, but they were getting there. I liked smithing. It was hard work, but I could see the fruits of my labor. I didn't have to wait for the seasons to change like Pa and Alex to know what my product would be. It was right there in front of me at the end of the day.

Rachel Ann sometimes worked the bellows for me, and she was good company — for a sister. Today, she had on a pair of buckskin britches cut down to size. Ma frowned on her girls in trousers, but she didn't put up much fuss when Rachel came out to the forge. The place was tough on housedresses.

"Are you going to see that Killpenny girl anymore?" Rachel asked out of the blue.

I paused, breaking the rhythm of my anvil song. "What makes you think I've been seeing her?"

"You were kissing her out back of the house."

I snorted. "That was last July."

"She's still sweet on you. Why do you think she comes around with Esau?"

"Seems to me she likes Alex better'n me"

"You don't know anything. She'd like to bill and coo with you out back of the barn. Like she did with Matthew."

"Is that so?"

"Yes, that's so. I seen how ..."

"You what?"

"I saw how Minnie looked at you when the Killpennys came to visit last week." She pulled a pretty frown. "Minnie is one Killpenny, and when you put her brother beside her that makes two Killpennys. Do you spell it N-Y-S, or is it like copper pennies, with an I-E-S?"

"With a 'Y.' She likes to be called Min, you know."

"And a skunk would like to be called a mink, but her Christian name's Minnie. Do you have a yen for her?"

"A yen? What do you know about yens?"

"I'm nineteen now. I know all about yens. I've read Mr. Hawthorne's *Scarlet Letter*, you know."

"Does Ma know you read it?"

"Yes. No. I don't know, but I did."

"So who stirs your blood?"

"Any number of presentable young men."

"Hah! You don't know any presentable young men, except your brothers."

"If you and Alex are presentable, I'll pass that litter right by and go for the other kind, thank you."

"Like Matthew Brandt, for example?"

"He's come back, you know," Rachel said.

My heart stopped. My hammer hit a false note. "Back? Where?"

"Alex told me he pitched camp up Strobaw's Crick. I wonder where he went this time."

"Not much telling. He's a gadabout." I couldn't admit thinking it would be nice to pull up stakes and haul off somewhere without a care in the world. It didn't look like the Strobaws were cut out of that cloth.

"I'm surprised he hasn't come over for a visit," she said. "He'll be pining for some of Ma's cooking. I think that's what keeps him coming back."

"Could be." I hit the red hot horseshoe too hard, almost ruining it." So Shambling Bear had returned. I knew why he hadn't come around. Because of what I'd yelled at him that day in the Yanube. Had he gone off and found somebody else? When that thought rippled through me, I did ruin the shoe.

"Shit!"

"John Jacobsen Strobaw! You better be glad Ma didn't hear you."

"Why don't you get out of here? Your jabbering made me ruin half a day's work."

"If that old shoe's a half a day's work, you're a mighty poor smith. And you always said my jabbering was a welcome relief."

"Well, not today. Go on. Scoot."

The sound of hooves pulled us both to the door. As soon as Matthew dismounted, I went back to try and salvage the malformed shoe. Rachel edged out of the building like she didn't want to be seen, but there was no way for her to get out of there and change into a dress without Matthew catching sight of her. I heard him call a greeting. A moment later, he entered the smithy and walked up beside me.

"*Hah-ue, Day-gee-lah.*" He wore faded denim pants and a flannel shirt in deference to Ma's ban on breechclouts.

"Don't call me lover. There's nobody around this place to love." My face went red. I risked a quick look at him and saw he was about to challenge me on that, so I spoke up in a panic. "What are you doing here? I told you not to come around anymore."

He straightened. His eyebrows shot up. "You mean that day out on the Yanube? That was just fooling around. You didn't mean anything by that. Did you?"

I brought down the hammer and collapsed the mangled horseshoe into a solid lump of glowing iron. "Guess not."

"I'd like to see the horse that's going to wear that."

"Starting over. It was ruined already."

His voice went low. "You didn't mean it, did you?"

Now that I knew he was all right, I went waspy. "You're talking backwards again. Like an Indian."

"I *am* Indian. Why shouldn't I talk like one? Answer the question."

"I usually mean what I say."

"You don't want me around anymore?"

I shrugged like I didn't care. It was all I could do to keep from clasping him to me.

"*Ohan*," I heard him speak from a cave. "It's time to clear out."

He was swinging a long leg over his pony before I mustered the strength to move. He took off in a gallop. I ran ten yards after him, yelling for him to stop. He didn't pay me any heed.

I stood for a minute before tearing off my leather apron and making for the corral. Grabbing a handful of mane, I jumped aboard Arrow without stopping for saddle or halter. He caught my urgency and bounded forward, responding to pressure from my knees.

Matthew's trail led west toward the old Pipe Stem hunting grounds. Half a mile from the Mead, I followed him down into a buffalo walk over the Yanube. He'd stopped in the scraggly woods on the south bank for some reason.

To change clothes. Boot prints disappeared, replaced by blurred scuffmarks of moccasins. Without dismounting, I followed his pony's trail to the west. He wasn't galloping or trotting now. Arrow eased through a dense thicket and came to a halt.

Matthew Brandt stood hip-sprung in the small clearing. Except he was Shambling Bear, a Teton warrior, now. Legs spread apart aggressively, his lean, muscled body was naked except for a small breechcloth and ankle-high moccasins. A three-inch scar I'd never seen before ran down his left thigh. A necklace of blue heishi beads brought up from the Spanish territory held a huge bear claw around his neck.

I slid from Arrow's back and walked up to him. Everything I'd planned to say, everything I *needed* to say died. I stood tongue-tied. Neither of us spoke for what seemed like a lifetime.

"Your eyes show who you are," he said. "They're black like mine. The eyes of a raptor. But they have these little pieces of color in them."

"What does that mean?"

"Just that they are different, like Pa's. But your *hin* ..." He reached out a muscled arm to fan my short black hair. "The gold flecks in it are like frozen sparks from your forge. They tell me your blood's different." He fell silent again. His eyes bored into mine. "You'd better leave, John. Go on, get out of here."

"Why?"

"Because if you don't, I'm going to take you."

66

Then I was in his arms. His tongue forced my lips apart and probed my mouth. My breath exploded against his smooth cheek. I sucked his tongue as he ground his hips against me. The ready flesh of his rod pressed against my belly.

He pulled away. "Take off that shirt, or I'll rip it off."

I slipped suspenders over my shoulders. Fumble-fingered, I had trouble with the buttons. Just before he lost patience, the last one gave way. He pulled the garment from me and swept me with his eyes. His fingertips played rough with my nipples. They hardened.

"I want you more'n I ever wanted anybody," he mumbled.

"More than Minnie Killpenny?"

"Shut up." He rummaged around in a buffalo hide parfleche bag and spread a trade blanket of black and red with white zigzag designs on the ground. He loosed the drawstring to his apron, and it fell away. He stood naked and rampant. He placed fists to his hips and waited.

I shuddered. He was allowing me to make a decision. If I walked away now, he would go and never come back. I stumbled toward him. He caught my shoulders and steadied me. He tugged my britches down around my knees and pushed me down on the blanket to fight my boots off. I lay on my back stark naked and watched in awe as he stood over me. Gigantic. Bigger than life. Bigger than my boyhood playmate, my grown hunting companion.

He fell to his knees and leaned forward on his hands. "If you do not leave now ..." He stumbled over his words. "I'll take you like I take my women. You will feel me inside you and know my power."

When I failed to move, he whispered. "So be it."

He thrust his hips forward and placed the tip of his yard on my lips. As he inserted himself, the mass of his cock closed down my breathing passages. I about strangled.

"Easy, Eagle. Wash me with your tongue. Gently, gently."

He withdrew, and I complied. He pressed into me, and I grew agitated again, but when he withdrew, my tongue followed him. He came back again, harder, driving more of himself down my throat. I accepted him more easily now. He fell into a rhythm, giving me moans of encouragement, and I expected to take his seed.

But he pulled away to push my legs apart with his knees. He lifted my ankles so that my butt rose to meet his throbbing cock. I almost rebelled, but in that instant, the tip of his moist rod found my sphincter. I cried aloud as he entered me in one long thrust. He withdrew and slid into me again.

His yard, his cock, his manhood changed my world. Now I knew my nature, my destiny. I sobbed because gentle Otter was no longer here to share my discovery. Matthew misunderstood.

"Soon it won't hurt."

I circled my arms around his slender waist and pulled him into me. "It doesn't hurt. Be a man for me, Bear."

And he was, sparking jealousy because he'd learned this with someone else, some woman or some man. Women. Men. I hated them all and I loved them all. They returned him to me as a warrior capable of beating me into servitude with his penis. At last, I knew what love was. It was Matthew Brandt. Shambling Bear. It was a cock. Strong arms. Hungry kisses. It was being one with this sentient, thinking, human being in the most intimate way possible.

I lunged up to meet his thrusts. Moaning, crying aloud, glorying in the act. It was an urgent, questing movement. It was noise and smells and dancing nerve endings. As he froze in the throes of ejaculation, I filled my lungs and roared, "I love you Matthew Brandt. Shambling Bear."

Be careful what you promise, War Eagle."

It was a warning, but after a rest, he went to work over me again, rendering it meaningless.

# # # # #

We lay side by side with pieces of clothing spread over us against the spring air. At length, I spoke of my *hemblecha* and told of seeing him — as a shambling bear — on his way home. I confessed my disappointment when he didn't show up last year. I related the rest of my Spirit Dream and how Otter and I had puzzled over the meaning of it. The mention of Otter robbed him of his ease.

"I stopped by the Morrow Farm and saw the burned out cabin. Andre Tiller told me what happened. He also told me what you did. I was proud of you."

"Then you should know the rest."

After he heard me out, he pulled me hard against him. "A warrior hides beneath those white man's clothes. No one suspects?"

"No one has come around asking questions. But Pa suspects. No, he knows even without me telling that part."

"Dog Fox knows because that is what he would have done. He has enough red blood to see things a white man wouldn't."

"He is *all* red blood." I told him of Billy's journal and what I'd learned from it.

Bear laughed low in his throat. "Then that makes you one of those dirty half-breeds the whites are so afraid of." He thought for a moment. "Otter was a great man. Maybe it was his death you foresaw."

"I don't think so. Where was all the joy and dancing? Otter thought it might have something to do with a Northern Paiute named Wodziwob who started a ghost dance movement that was supposed to bring back dead Indians and let us get along with the white man."

"What happened?"

"Nothing. The dead Indians are still dead and the whites are still white. Besides, I saw the dancing just before the great man died."

"How did he die?"

"Don't know. Just that he died. Murdered."

"It's a puzzle. But you will know it when you're supposed to."

"Have you been on your Vision Quest?"

"Years ago. Right after I left That's why I went to find Crazy Horse." His mood turned black. "I knew he was going to be a great war chief. They killed him. Murdered him."

When I repeated to Matthew what Major Irons had told us, he said the whites lied. "Crazy Horse spoke up in council after they pushed him to join the army against Chief Joseph and said he would fight until all the Nez Perce were killed. The interpreter didn't say his words right."

"Why?"

"To cause trouble. Or maybe he didn't know any better. When the Star Chief heard what the interpreter said, he ordered his men to get Crazy Horse. They found him at the Spotted Tail Agency where he'd taken his sick wife and talked him into coming back to Red Cloud. After they got there, the soldiers threw him in the guardhouse. When he resisted, one of his guards bayonetted him in the back. Twice. He was murdered."

How do you know this is true?"

His body went tense. "I was standing outside the council and heard what he said to the soldiers through a window. And I was there when he was stabbed. I saw him carried to the adjutant's office where they let him die. They were jealous of him."

"Who was?"

"All of them. Red Cloud, Spotted Tail. Little Big Man even lied about his murder. He said what the whites wanted him to say."

His eyes went soft "He knew me, Eagle. Knew my name. Who I was. I fought beside him. There won't ever be another like him."

We nursed our own thoughts. It was a comfortable silence.

"What's that scar on your thigh?"

He threw his left leg over my groin. The scar was there for me to see. I ran a finger down it. "Does it hurt?"

"Like fire until it healed. After Crazy Horse died, I decided to come home, but the soldiers said we were reservation Indians now. Four of us left in the dead of night. We couldn't get our horses, so we walked. They sent soldiers after us, and there was a fight. Two of us died, but two blue coats got killed, too. They shot and wounded the man still with me. I was trying to help him up when a bullet hit a rock beside me, and a piece of it ripped my leg. It wasn't deep, but it made it hard to walk. I had to leave my companion for the soldiers."

"How did you get away?"

"I tied my apron around the leg wound to stop the bleeding and climbed a tree to wait out the three blue coats tracking me."

"The bear!" Could he hear the awe in my voice? "The shambling bear. There were three coyotes on his trail. I knew they were three men hunting you. I tried to wait and see what was happening, but my Spirit Dream carried me away."

"To the joy and dancing."

I nodded. "Lots of dancing. What happened after you came down out of the tree?"

"I headed east along the White River, but I was weak from loss of blood and didn't get far. I collapsed while getting a drink from a spring and woke to find myself in a cave."

"A cave. How?"

"A healer found me. He managed to get me to his cave in the side of a bluff. When I woke, he was sitting beside me. He took care of my leg and fed me. I stayed with him through the winter and into the spring. He healed me and made me strong again."

This was where he had learned to make man-love. A nameless creature in my belly wormed down into my scrotum. "Who was he?"

"A hermit called Blood-Mark-Boy. He took his name from a birthmark on his neck."

"Did you love him?"

"I made love to him out of gratitude. That was all he asked for saving my life."

"Did you love him?" I insisted.

"Nay, but he made me see that I loved you. I knew I had to come home … to you."

The beast that crawled inside me wiggled a little but was less painful. "So you told him about us?"

His black eyes turned hard. "There wasn't anything to tell. You'd rejected me?" His tone softened. "But I told him about my brother."

"What about now? Are there feelings between us?"

"How can you ask after what we did? We are good together."

"True. But animals have sex and feel good about it," I said.

"I am no animal. I am a man. And I have feelings for you."

"What happens now?"

"Simple. You are mine. I am yours. I came home just to find you."

"Not so simple. Some won't understand."

"I forget you live in a white world. Your ma's world."

"She's your ma, too."

"Yes, but she doesn't tell me how to think. How to act."

"Around the Mead, she does. She protects us from the whites by making us white."

"You'll never pass for a white. You've got too much of Pa in you. Leave the Mead and come with me. We can go wherever we want."

My blood sang at the thought. "Where there are no whites?"

His leg lying across my belly flinched. "There is no such place. I found spots where no one walked, and soon they were there, claiming it all. But we can search for such a place."

"Why, if none exists?"

"Just to be looking. For the adventure."

"I own the Morrow farm now. We could rebuild the cabin."

"And die the same way Otter and James did?"

"I killed the biggest evil. Maybe the others will leave us alone."

"Leave us alone on a 240-acre prison?"

"No, alone on a 240-acre haven. Where we can love one another."

"You speak of a farmer's life to a man who is a warrior?"

His words drew the air from around me, leaving me in a vacuum. My answer squeezed past a constricted voice box. "I will be the farmer. You be the warrior. I'll tend our land, and you can hunt, as warriors have always done."

He sat up beside me and examined my naked body. Then he looked me in the eye. "Get dressed and go home, John."

CHAPTER 8

I was exhilarated; depressed. I was joyful; afraid. In all my parts, all at once. My eyes sparkled one moment and brimmed the next. Bear had left me standing in the small glen without any indication of my future. Our future. Addressing me as John was not a good omen. It didn't take a Spirit Dream to see life as a farmer didn't fit his plans. Now, he would go off alone, consider things, and make up his mind. I would have little say in it.

So I went back to the Mead, retrieved my leather apron from the dirt, and resumed work in the forge, trying to act as if my world weren't crumbling. Rachel Ann came out and peppered me with questions. Where had I gone? Where was Matthew? Was he coming for supper? She got little satisfaction from me, although she likely discerned my unhappy state.

At the dinner table, I deflected questions about Matthew with "don't knows" and shrugs. When Alex said Matthew's camp was no longer on Strobaw Crick, I wasn't surprised, but my heart sank to somewhere in my gut, nonetheless.

"I'll swear, that boy's getting to be downright rude," Ma said.

"He's not a boy!" My outburst drew looks from everyone.

"You're right. He's a man now. Twenty-one this coming August. All of you are becoming men." She teared up. "And young ladies."

I excused myself and headed for my cabin where I grabbed a book from the table and flopped on my bed. Discovering no appetite for reading, I tossed the book aside. All I could think of was Bear. How he'd felt in my arms. Loving me. Leaving me. All in the same hour.

There was a knock on the door. I stood up … hopeful. It was my father wanting to know what was going on. He took a seat at the little eating table near the cooking fireplace. I sat opposite him.

"How come you can read me so well?"

"Anyone could read you tonight. Your chin's been about knee high ever since you came back from chasing after Matthew this afternoon."

"We had an argument, and he ran off again."

"What kind of argument?"

My tongue got thick. How could I tell my pa I'd let a man put his thing up me? My color rose. My throat threatened to close up. It wasn't fair. Back when Pa was young, lying with a man wasn't any worse than a fella doing it to some girl. Now … now it was something else. Why was I ashamed? As much as I wanted to tell him, I couldn't bring myself to admit loving another man.

"He wanted me to go with him. I told him about my farm, and said we … he could go there if he didn't want to live at the Mead anymore. But he said he was a warrior now, and wanted me to be one, too."

"Are you tempted?"

"I am. But I'm a farmer and a blacksmith. I've got responsibilities."

My father sighed. "They made pretty good white men out of us, didn't they?"

I shot him a look. "Seems to me like Ma did that."

"Don't put that on her back. She was just preparing us for it. We made the decision."

"How can a little kid make a decision like that for himself?"

"He can't. But he grows up, and if he's a thinking man, he can decide his future. He may be bent by his childhood, but he's not captive to it."

"Like Matthew? Sounds like you think I oughta try it."

"That's for you to figure out. But whatever you make up your mind to do, you have my blessing."

"And Ma's?"

"She'll fight with everything she's got to keep you off the Warrior Road. But that's because she loves you and would fear for your safety every day of her life. So would I, but I understand how you might feel. Matthew frets our minds like that now."

"I ought to be able to do what's right for me."

"That's the way I figure it, too. Alexander will never leave the Mead because that's what's in his heart. Rachel Ann and Hannah? Too soon to tell, but they'll probably marry some day and go with their husbands. I'm not sure what's in your heart."

I stared at my hands and rubbed a blistered spot. "I'm not either."

"You will. Tell me, have you discovered your nature?"

I studied the top button on his shirt. "Yes."

He nodded but didn't press me further. He didn't need to. My cheeks had flushed when I answered him.

"Then you'll figure out the rest of it, too."

# # # # #

As I left the stable to go to breakfast in the stone house the next morning, I caught movement on the hollow hill. The dawn was just breaking, and the light wasn't good, but sure as shooting, that was Matthew up there. I altered my steps and made my way up the hill.

He was sitting cross-legged on the ground dressed in a white man's plaid shirt and a breechclout fitted with a pair of leggings against the early morning chill. His hair had grown long while he was with the Oglala. This morning, he wore it in braids on either side of his head. The sun edged over the horizon and painted his features a rich copper. He was as handsome as I'd ever seen him.

I sat in the dirt opposite him. "Ma's upset because you haven't paid your respects."

He grunted and then fell silent for a whole minute. "I have decided to go to my father's people in the Laramie country. I want you to come with me. I want the council to marry us in the old way."

"They won't do it. Not anymore."

"We will see. Will you come with me and be my win-tay?"

"I will be your win-tay. I will give you my heart ... every part of me. I will forego everyone else — man or woman — and be yours alone. But I will do it at my farm. I will put no strictures on you except to hold true to me, as I will to you. You can go away and be a warrior so long as you come back to me. It will tear my heart out each time you leave, but I'll put up with it so long as you love me."

"Would I be here if I didn't?"

"If that's true, we can make what I propose work."

He shook his head. "You haven't walked the Warrior Road. A man needs his other self near at hand. When war comes, he needs his mate fighting at his side, watching his back."

"So you're going to walk away and leave me knowing that I have given my heart to you."

"If you deny me your company, I have no other choice."

"We could at least give my way a try. If it doesn't work, then you can leave," I said.

"The other side of that coin is true, as well. You can try it my way and be free to come home whenever you wish."

My inner self seemed empty, yet the dull ache in my gut proclaimed that false. "Will you at least come to breakfast and say goodbye."

"You go on. I will change into clothes that will suit Ma. Eagle, will you lie with me once more before I go?"

Pain ripped through me. "After dinner this evening. In my cabin."

# # # # #

My output at the forge was pitiful that day. My resolve to be strong almost broke when Matthew rode in about mid-day. Everyone was gathered around, eager to hear his latest adventures as I went out to greet him. I wasn't the only one who loved him ... just the one who did so in that special way. He shook my hand and grinned at me, almost undoing me. He was so damned fetching.

I ate pieces of bacon between two biscuits at the forge rather than risk going up to the house and sitting at the table. Before long Matthew and Rachel Ann — wearing her prettiest dress — came out to keep me company.

"Can't you talk him out of leaving again, John? He listens to you."

"Be the first time. He knows he belongs here, but if he's bound on running off somewhere, I can't stop him."

"I'll be back," Matthew said. "I just have to do a little more traveling, that's all. There's a big world out there you ought to see."

Rachel Ann clasped her hands together. "Oh, I'd love to see all those exotic places I've heard about. St. Louis and Dodge City and Lincoln. And New York City! Have you been to New York City?"

"Haven't wandered that far. But I've been to Kansas City."

"Really? Tell me about it."

"Just a smelly, crowded place full of people and horses and cows."

"And theaters and museums, too, I'll bet," she said.

"I guess. But they weren't what I was looking for."

"What was that?"

His answer told me he'd discerned the same list I had seen in my sister. "The usual. Excitement. Women. Found some, too."

Rachel Ann took on a wounded look. "Oh."

Matthew turned to me. "What would you like to see?"

"I'd like to see the end of this day." My face got hot, and I brought down my hammer too hard. No question where Matthew's mind would go with that comment. My sphincter started to itch.

"It's almost over. Ma's fixing a special supper for me. Gonna have a pudding of some kind, I think." He turned innocent eyes on me. "You gonna make room for me in your cabin tonight?"

"If you don't mind throwing your blankets down on the floor."

"Slept in lots worse places than a warm, dry floor."

I quit work early to take a shower in the bathing room before the big supper Ma and the girls had prepared. Matthew kept everyone at the table laughing with stories about his travels. Ma was muted, and worry lines carved her features. The pain of losing him again was clearly as bad as losing Alex or me.

When we were all stuffed to the gullet with food and peach cobbler — instead of pudding — Pa walked Matthew and me to my cabin and came inside to take a seat. Matthew claimed the other chair. I sat on my bed.

"I heard the talk you served the women. What's the rest of it?"

Matthew told him about being with Crazy Horse at Red Cloud's Agency when he'd been stabbed. He described his escape and the fight with the pursuing soldiers. Pa heard him out without speaking.

"Are they looking for you?"

"No, sir. Don't think so. Crazy Horse gave me the fighting name of Red Star and said I was from the Laramie country. Nobody knew me as Matthew Brandt or Little Bear from Teacher's Mead."

Pa grunted. "The warrior's time is ending, Matthew. Most of our people have been pushed onto agencies and had their rifles taken away. They live on whatever the treaties give them. This is your home with people who care for you. There'll be no starvation at the Mead. You can come and go as you please."

"Thank you. I'll come back, but I have to visit my father's people first. Maybe after that."

Pa stood and opened the door before shifting his gaze to me. "Make sure you know your own mind before you make a decision."

"What did he mean by that?" Matthew asked after he left

"I had to explain why I was gone so long yesterday, so I told him you were trying to talk me into going with you."

"What did he say?"

"What he did just now. To know my own mind."

"You didn't tell him about the other, did you?"

I shook my head. "No, but he might have figured it out."

"You were ashamed."

I got huffy until the truth hiding in that statement hit me. "Maybe I was. Things are different now."

"No, we're different. Well, I'm not ashamed. If he'd asked me, I'd have told him I care for you. And that we'd got together."

"That's what you claim. But you don't care enough to stay here."

He stared into my eyes, allowing me to read what he was thinking. He was the man. It was my place to go where he wanted.

He had enough sense not to speak his thoughts. He walked into me, placed a hand behind my head and pulled my lips to his. I had to reach up to kiss that broad mouth.

He stripped off his shirt and shucked out of his trousers. I was slower to undress because I was in boots, not moccasins. When I had shed the last article of clothing, he pushed me over on the bed and straddled my hips. His hot glance made my nipples tingle.

"The smith's hammer has given you muscles. The fingers of his right hand traced those muscles. "Good shoulders. Deep chest." I hardened, pressing against his buttocks. He raised up and allowed my cock to slap my belly. "My wife is hung like a horse."

I grasped his manhood. "And my husband is built like a bull."

The smile slid from his lips as he commenced his mating ritual. He kissed me so deeply I almost thought his tongue was a cock. He rose to smear a bit of fat he'd brought in a tin from the kitchen on his glans before lifting my legs and entering me. His eyes never left mine. The smile came back, making him even more beautiful than before.

I fingered his sloe eyes, stroked his silken lids. He was getting into it now, driving me wild. I ran my hands down his pecs and toyed with his big brown *aze*. Then he leaned forward, raising my butt to pound me harder. The sharp slap of his flesh against mine confirmed this was my man ... my Matthew ... my Bear giving me everything he had.

When his breath began coming in short gasps, he grasped my erection and ran the foreskin over my glans half a dozen times. I erupted, almost dying from the shock of orgasm.

Then he came. Hardly recovered from my own, I watched the excitement on his face as he ejaculated. My heart sang! It was good for him. It was great for him. He felt the way I did. He was giving me his precious body, not just as taking mine.

Matthew collapsed atop me, his heart pounding against my own. Truly, we must be one now. United by some powerful bond I was at a loss to describe. At length, he staggered to the water basin and brought wet towels to clean us both. We spoke little. That would come later. He got back in bed, covered us, and spooned against me. I drifted off to sleep with his soft breath on my cheek.

I woke once during the dark hours with him inside me. He made gentle love this time, and when he was finished, he left his long, semi-erect cock inside me. I sighed and went back to sleep.

He was gone when I woke in the morning.

CHAPTER 9

Early the following day, I decided on a hasty trip to my farm in the hope Matthew had gone there to mull things over before moving on to find his father's people. His pa had been a Burnt Wood or Brulé, one of the Teton Sioux bands. Turtle Crick Farm was a logical place for Matthew to rest overnight before heading for the Laramie country.

Despite pushing Arrow Wind hard, I was too late. Matthew had come and gone. I found sign he'd slept in the loft of the outhouse and taken a sweat bath in the medicine lodge. I rushed to the Tiller farm to see if he was there. Andre had talked to him for a few minutes, but Matthew pushed on this morning.

I spent a miserable night in the loft, listening for my brown-haired neighbor on the ladder, both hoping for and dreading the prospect. But he stayed home, relieving me of the need to decide whether to embrace him or hold myself for Matthew's return. That was foolishness. There was no way to know if Matthew would ever come back. He'd probably abandoned me.

Jeremiah Berglund's shade chose that night to return. The black crow was as hateful in death as he had been in life.

# # # # #

I returned home to resume working in the forge and tending the stagecoach company's horses at the Mead. I also nursed a smoldering anger at my abandonment. My tongue grew sharper and my temper shorter. More than once, I came within a needle's eye of striking out to hunt Matthew down. Damn, him! He'd turned my life upside down and then run off. I almost convinced myself I hated him.

Oh, how I missed Otter. He would have understood my anguish and given me wise words on the matter. But I was robbed of even his comfort. Images of that length of rope dangling from a cottonwood limb at Turtle Crick — now burnt to cinders in the fire pit outside the medicine lodge — fretted my mind both awake and asleep.

A month later, my world lurched again. The good-looking lieutenant I'd met last year rode into the Mead at the head of a squad of troopers. I came out of the forge in time to see him dismount and greet Pa. As I stepped up to them, he turned and called me by name.

"I see you found an excuse to visit the Mead, Lt. Haleworthy," I said.

"Yes, but I'm not sure how I'll be received. I'm looking for Matthew Brandt. I am given to understand he's a member of your household."

Pa nodded, his face giving no clue to his thinking. "Matthew was raised on the Mead."

"I need to speak to him." The Lieutenant paused to instruct his sergeant to dismount the squad.

"My son is not here. He left a few weeks back."

Haleworthy gave him a look. "Your son?"

"As I said, he was raised here. Both my wife and I consider him family."

"What was his destination when he left?"

"Matthew is the family gadabout. He didn't tell me where he was headed." Pa looked at me. "John?"

"No, sir. On my last visit to Turtle Crick Farm, I found he'd stopped over there, but he'd moved on by the time I arrived."

"Turtle Crick Farm?"

"The old Morrow Farm. It's mine now. I inherited it after Major Morrow and Otter were murdered."

A flush rose from Haleworthy's collar. "Yes, that was unfortunate." Was he embarrassed over the deviant life of a military officer or because no one had been held accountable for the murders?

"Why are you looking for Matthew?" my father asked.

"He is believed to be the man called Red Star who rode with Crazy Horse. He and three others fled the Red Cloud Agency after their chieftain was killed. They ambushed the soldiers who went after them, killing two of them."

Pa permitted a frown to show on his face. "He is believed to be this man? That is a strange way of putting it. Is he Red Star or not?"

"I only know what I am told, Mr. Strobaw. Can you tell me if he is that renegade?"

"The Matthew Brandt I have known since he was six years old is no brigand, Lieutenant. He came to us because the militia murdered all the family he had left — his mother and brother."

"I see. Would you tell me if he was this Red Star?"

"In the twenty-nine years since one of yours, a captain named Smith, murdered most of our people, I have led a peaceful life here. I have told you Matthew Brandt is no brigand, and that is my honest belief."

Pa was angry. He'd never strung so many words together when talking to outsiders.

"Pardon. I did not intend to give offense. I am just carrying out my orders." He turned to me. "Can you shed any light on the matter?"

"Only to confirm what my father said about Matthew. And his Indian name is Shambling Bear, not Red Star."

Pa anticipated Haleworthy's next demand and invited him and his men to search as much as they wanted.

The Lieutenant took a hard look at Alexander when they were introduced, but one glance at Ma, and his suspicions faded. There was enough of her in Alex to settle the matter, although he likely confirmed my brother's identification with Curtis Appleton later.

Ma wasn't able to have visitors without offering to feed them. Along about high noon, Lt. Haleworthy was seated at our table inside while his men lounged around the yard eating fried chicken and mashed potatoes. It was soon clear Rachel Ann was smitten again.

Later, the Lieutenant visited the forge where he encouraged me to address him as Gideon. Did his girlfriends called him "Giddy" during moments of passion?

"I regret having caused offense. I was just doing my job."

His plea eased my distaste somewhat. "What would you have done had Matthew been here?"

He looked pained. "My orders were to bring him back to the fort."

"Under arrest?"

"If that was the only way he would come." Gideon managed a boyish smile. "I find Teacher's Mead the most pleasant and thriving farm I've visited thus far. How did it come by that name?"

I'll say this for him. He knew how to get past my personal pique. "My grandfather, Billy Strobaw, was the first white man in this area. He'd graduated from a college back east, so when he started teaching the tribe's children, he became Teacher. Thus ... Teacher's Meadow or Mead. Most folks just call it the Mead."

"Logical. He had another descriptive name, didn't he?"

I banged the hammer a couple of times and then thrust the glowing iron back into the fire ... perhaps a little more forcefully than usual. "Yes. They called him the Red Win-tay."

"Win-tay?" He wrinkled his nose and raised his eyebrows.

"It's a Siouan word meaning 'not woman.'"

"That's a strange appellation." He furrowed his nose again. His flustered look was something to behold. "Oh, I see."

"Things were different back then, Lieutenant ... uh, Gideon. Such a life was accepted among many of the tribes."

He waved a hand toward the stone house. "It's hard to imagine a win-tay building all of this. Damnation, I'm sorry. That sounded ..."

"Like a white man." My voice was flat. "My grandpa was as much a man as anyone in the territory, you and me included."

"Sorry. I've embarrassed you."

I looked him straight in the eyes. They were light blue. "No, you've embarrassed yourself."

"True enough. I say, I like the way you meet things head-on."

"Only way I know how to do it. And if this is a long-winded way of getting around to asking if I know where Matthew went, I don't."

"When you get to know me, you'll find I'm not so devious as all that. I was merely taking pleasure in your company and learning something of this rather strange land I find myself in."

"We met over a year ago. You've been here some time now."

"Yes, but most of what I've learned are things like who the troublemakers are. Where's the next good waterhole if my patrol takes me away from the river. Things like that."

"You oughta be able to learn whatever you need to know at the Rainbow House in town."

"The Rainbow House is a decent place for dining and imbibing. But I don't take to drink well, so I'm something of a stick-in-the-mud."

I laughed in spite of my mood. "You must have some redeeming qualities."

"Oh, yes. I'm keen on racing. My gelding, Brownie, has beaten every other horse on the post."

"Arrow Wind's pretty fast, too."

"I'll take that as a challenge and as an excuse to come back. But now, I must move on. Thank you for your hospitality."

I stood at the door and watched him mount his troop and cross to the south bank of the Yanube. Maybe he wasn't such a bad sort after all — despite trying to arrest Matthew.

Pa showed up at the forge as soon as they were out of sight. "I hope you didn't lie to him."

"Only when I said I didn't know where Matthew was going, and that wasn't much of one. I know what direction he headed, but I don't know any more than that. I think I ought to go find him. He doesn't know they're on his trail. He thinks they haven't been able to identify him."

"If they catch you with him, they'll paint you with the same brush."

"They have to catch me first."

82

"If this is something you need to do, don't leave without saying goodbye to your mother."

# # # # #

After finishing a horseshoe, I decided a ride to Turtle Crick held more interest than starting another. After announcing I was heading out to check on my property, Pa suggested making it a practical jaunt by packing some of our stored vegetables to the man who customarily bought from us. That meant taking the buckboard, a slower trip. That might have been his aim.

I couldn't refuse him, so when I left by the wagon trace on the north shore of the river, I drove a wagon and trailed Arrow along behind.

Bouncing over the rough road put me in a strange mood. I loved this country and knew most of the ground around the Mead. But I didn't know it the same way Cut Hand or Otter or Billy had. Otter could point out the exact spot where the Yanube and the Pipe Stem People had gotten into a skirmish or where someone had been found dead or where a hunter had killed the biggest antelope in the territory. He knew the land not only from his life's journey, but also from oral history. Regret at burning Billy's journal stung me. So much history lost.

I overnighted on the ground beneath the wagon while Arrow and the mare that pulled the buckboard grazed on the short grass of the prairie. I lay with my hands behind my head and took in the night. The tangy scent of mint hung in the air. The horses munching and an occasional footfall as they moved were the only sounds except for the distant call of a whippoorwill. Had the wagon over my head not blocked them, the stars would have made the night seem near to early evening. Despite my anxiety, I slept.

# # # # #

Upon my arrival in town, I made straight for Tussler's Food Market on Broad Street. Thurlo Tussler had bought the bulk of the Mead's crops since he'd opened his business five years back. We indulged in some good-natured bargaining before the bluff Missourian took the whole load off my hands. Part in trade and part in greenbacks. The Specie Resumption Act passed by Congress had taken hold this past January, equating paper money with gold, so I had no reservation about accepting it. The offer of money hinted the depression might be loosening its grip. Next, I headed for Brown's Emporium to fill Ma's list of supplies.

Seven miles north of town, I crossed the bridge spanning Turtle Crick. I was anxious to rub down and feed the horses, not to mention my own craw. I hopped from the wagon seat, opened the barn doors … and froze

It took a moment to recognize the flea-bitten gray Matthew had picked up somewhere after he was forced to abandon Wind Rider at Fort Robinson. He'd christened this one with the same name. Matthew was here. I called out to him, but all I heard was a groan. The green beast seized me by the testicles. Was he up there with Andre getting his pipe sucked? Another groan. Pain not pleasure.

Abandoning the horses, I scrambled up the ladder. Matthew lay on the floor. Blood from a wound in his arm seeped into the planking. I rushed to his side and clasped his shoulders. He fought me for a moment before going limp.

"What happened?"

"John? Eagle? Wh … where am I?"

"Turtle Crick. In the barn." My right hand came away sticky. Something, a bullet probably, had torn his flesh. He'd tried to bandage it, but it was a poor job. The rags were down around his elbow now. He'd bled a lot. His forehead was hot. He had the infection.

After fetching a bag from the corner of the loft that held a few of Otter's medicine herbs, I cleaned Matthew's injury with a mixture of Thyme leaf, white oak bark, and St. John's wort to draw out poisons. Then I brewed a tea of yarrow flowers to help him relax and begin to heal on the inside.

He was out of his head part of the time, but as best I could tell a farmer had shot him while he was stealing milk from the man's cow. It had happened a 100 miles west of here, and he'd been trying to make it back to the Mead. Damned lucky he made it this far. He passed out, so I covered him with a blanket and went down to take care of the buckboard and horses.

I spent a sleepless night holding onto Matthew as he shook and sweated with fever. He was better the next morning, but I didn't trust my doctoring skills and told him I was taking him to get treatment in town. "But I have to warn you; the army's hunting for you."

That caught his attention. Damp with sweat, he struggled to a sitting position. "For stealing milk?"

"Wish that was it. An army patrol came looking for Red Star. Said he'd ambushed some soldiers and killed two of them." I rushed ahead of his denial. "They don't know you're Red Star. They're just suspicious. But we can't think about that right now, you need more help than I can give you. If we were back home there would be medicines." I lifted my hands in a gesture of helplessness. "But there's not much here."

"Can't go to … doctor. He won't … treat Indians, anyway. He'll report me."

"I'm taking you to Timo. He doctored most of the animals in town until a veterinarian set up shop. He'll have what you need."

"You … trust him?"

"Have to take our chances, but I think he'll do right by us."

"Not your neck in … noose." He struggled for breath. "His place … too near fort. Too risky."

Rather than argue, I went downstairs, unloaded the buckboard, and harnessed the mare in the traces before half-dragging Matthew down the ladder. He was still griping when I made him lie down in the back of the wagon. I hid him beneath some blankets, but he complained it was too hot and threw them off. I left our two war horses in the barn and propped the door shut.

The rough road drew groans from Matthew, but there was nothing I could do for that. Before we entered town, I made him cover up with blankets and warned him to lie still. I'd no sooner turned onto the north end of Main Avenue than Lt. Haleworthy and a squad of men came toward me down the road. I whispered a warning and pulled to a halt.

CHAPTER 10

Gideon gave me a fingers-to-the-brim salute as he reined Brownie in beside the wagon. He had a clear view of the buckboard's bed. "Headed back home?"

"Need to do a few things in town before setting out for the Mead."

"Still no sign of that Red Star fellow?"

"Don't know any Red Star. If you mean Matthew, he's a fiddle-foot. Comes and goes. He'll show up one day. What makes you think he's Red Star?"

"One of the Indians at the Red Cloud Agency claimed this Red Star was from the Fort Yanube area. We don't know for sure he's Mr. Brandt. We just need to ask him some questions and clear up a few things."

"So there's a bunch of Indians living on the Mead, and you came riding out …"

"Just …"

"I know. Just doing your job. Well, I've got to start doing mine. Excuse me." I started to flick the reins, but he stopped me long enough to say he hoped to ride out for a visit when he had some free days. I assured him he'd be welcome, but my tone didn't put much meaning behind the words.

We were a hundred yards down the street before I took an easy breath. When I reached the blacksmith shop, I threw open the big doors and drove the buckboard right into the building. Timo paused in the act of working the bellows to stare at me.

"Got a problem, Timo, and I need your help. Come on, Matthew, get up."

From the look on the smith's face, I was glad Matthew had exchanged his loincloth for white man's clothing before we left the farm.

"What's going on, John?"

"You remember Matthew Brandt, don't you?"

"Sure do. Been a while since I seen you. Whoa, looks like you're the one who's got the problem." Timo fingered Matthew's bloody sleeve.

I improvised. "We both do. Matthew tried to Indian up on me at Turtle Crick as a damn fool joke. Instead, he just about became somebody's darling." Timo lived in the backyard of a military fort, so I figured he knew a soldier's term for a dead man.

Matthew came to the aid of my lie. "He shoots me, and *he* gets frothy."

"Dadgummit, I didn't know who you were. Anyway, I got off a quick shot and winged him in the arm. Cleaned it up as best I can, but he needs help." I mustered a grin. "We need to keep this quiet. If you can fix him up, we'll stay at the farm for a couple of days and then go home. Nobody'll be the wiser."

Timo good-naturedly agreed, but he stirred up a moment of panic when he took Matthew by the good arm and led him down the street to his house. Once inside, the smith made Matthew strip off his shirt and lie down on a bed while he got out his medicines. Two minutes later, Timo beckoned me out of the room.

"John, I ain't calling you a liar, but that ain't a fresh wound."

"I tried to doctor it with some of Otter's spirit medicines, but he needs more help than I can give him. We shoulda come straight here, but we didn't."

"It oughta been sutured."

"You can do that. I've seen you sew up horses."

"Needed doing days ago. Not sure it'll hold now."

"Can't you try?"

"If I scrape out all the healed flesh it might take. Hurt like blazes, though."

"He can take it. Please try, Timo. I ... I'll make it worth your while."

"I don't want your money."

I looked him straight in the eye. "I wasn't talking about money."

The big man flushed and licked his lips as he nodded.

When we returned to the room, Matthew was lucid and not sweating so badly. After he took a moment to agree to what we were proposing, Timo gave him a chunk of rawhide to put between his teeth. I got on one side of him and held down his good arm. Timo grasped the injured left arm and went to work with what looked like a wood rasp. Matthew never uttered a sound. He grabbed hold of my biceps and squeezed until feeling was gone, but he didn't fight either of us.

An ungodly amount of time went by before the smith was satisfied. The wound was bleeding now, but he applied an astringent to slow it down. Then he sewed the torn flesh closed with neat little stitches.

Sweat was pouring off Matthew by then, and he had trouble unclenching his jaws so I could take the rawhide out of his mouth. Timo disinfected the site again, covered it over with a proper bandage, and bundled up everything — including Matthew's bloody blouse — to burn. He found an old work shirt as a substitute.

"That's all I can do."

I led the smith out of the room, giving the door a shove as we passed through it. When I halted in the middle of the room, Timo looked anxious.

"You sure it ain't too much trouble?" He sounded like an over-aged swain sorry he'd just asked a girl for a kiss.

"Not if you'll promise never to tell anyone about our accident." I slipped braces over my shoulders and opened my shirt.

Timo had a hungry look on his face as he nodded. His eyes never strayed from my bared torso. "I promise, John." He fingered my left nipple timidly. Then my right. They rose at his touch. "You're so much like him." He put his mouth to my chest.

I stopped him. "Timo, did you ever do this with Cut Hand?"

His eyes bugged. "No! I was just a kid when we stayed over at the Mead that winter. But ... but I've thought about it a lot. I woulda done anything for him. Even back then."

I slipped my trousers down around my ankles. He knelt before me. His big arms went around my waist, steadying me. Rough hands cupped my buttocks. Timo knew only one way to get what he wanted, and that was to go all out. He made audible sucking noises as he rode my pole. To speed things along, I grabbed Timo's head and began to fuck his mouth.

He took it all, drawing breath when he could and enduring my assault. My system discharged, sending hot sparks throughout me. My cum flooded Timo's mouth and throat as I tried to climb up into his warm, moist maw. Even after I went still, Timo moved up and down, drawing the last of my juices from me. Then he curled his tongue around my glans as he pulled away.

Embarrassed, I tugged up my pants and rushed back into the bedroom while still buttoning my shirt. Matthew was lying on his side, turned away from me. When I asked how he felt, he grunted he'd be "*kay*," a Creek or Choctaw word he'd picked up meaning "fine." I rushed to the shop for the buckboard, and this time, he didn't put up a fuss when I told him to lie down in the bed.

I smiled at the smith from the driver's seat. "Much obliged, Timo. Appreciate your help. Remember your promise."

"I will. You keep a watch on his arm." He looked away. "And thank you, John."

"You're welcome." I flicked the reins and sent the buckboard down the road.

After we were well away from town, Matthew had me stop, so he could climb up on the seat beside me.

"What if we run into that army patrol returning?" I asked.

"I don't care." The words were clipped.

I glanced at him. He stared straight ahead with a sullen look on his face. The bouncing had to be hurting his arm, but he wasn't letting on. "What's the matter?"

"The next time you want somebody to suck your pole, close the damned door."

"Wha ... what?" Something ran down my back, likely my soul stealing away.

"You didn't close the door all the way, and you made so much noise, I came to see what was happening. I saw it all. I saw Timo with your *che* in his mouth."

"Aw, don't make anything out of it. I just did that to get his promise not to say anything about you."

"So that was just for me? Looked to me like were getting something out of it, too. You've done it with him before, haven't you?"

The hair on my neck rose. The air was suddenly too thin to fill my lungs. "That's right. It was just for you. Sure wouldn't have done it otherwise." He gave me such a look that I relented and told him about my first time.

He was quiet for a long time after that. "I take care of myself. I don't need you or anybody else making sacrifices for me."

"Sure took care of yourself this time, didn't you?"

I might as well have slugged him. His jaw went tight. "Turn the wagon around."

"What?"

"I said turn around. Take me to the fort."

"You don't have to surrender just 'cause you're mad at me."

He slumped back in the seat. "Naw. I know you did it for me, but it hurt just the same. You're mine, Eagle. Have been ever since you gave yourself to me in that glen on the south side of the Yanube."

I swallowed hard, but this needed to be faced squarely. "Didn't seem like it to me. You fucked me in the cabin and then snuck off in the night. Left me wondering what was going on. I didn't know if you'd be back or not. And you might as well know I got with someone else once, too. Before ... us. But even then I was thinking of you."

He wiped his face with a hand and looked tired. "I didn't have the salt to face you the next morning. Mostly because I didn't know my own mind. But I do now. When that farmer shot me, all I could think of was to get home, so I could see you once more."

It was a simple statement said so deep down that it reached out and grabbed me. Matthew seldom spoke of his feelings, so that was a silver-tongued declaration of love for him.

I clutched his hand. "Matthew. I love you so much it hurts. And when I saw Andre again, we didn't do it because I'd been with you by then and ..."

"Andre, huh?"

"I didn't mean to say that."

"Don't worry, I won't let on. Even if I would like to beat his face in. Stop the buckboard."

I pulled to a halt, and he turned sideways in the seat to face me. "I heard what that army man said. So I gotta go to the fort and face him down. If I don't, I'll have to hide out for the rest of my life. The only way I can be with you is to clear thing up. Turn around."

"I won't let you take that risk for me."

"Then I'll walk back, and I'm not too steady on my feet right now. Take me to the farm, so I can change into a decent shirt. Timo's hangs on me like a blanket. I'll ride back and turn myself in."

I took off my hat and ran my hand through my hair. "No, I'll ride back with you. I couldn't stand not knowing what happened. But not right now. You're sweating, and that will make you look guilty. And you couldn't even explain why you're sweating. They see that gunshot wound, and you're as good as convicted."

"*Kay*. I'm feeling kinda outa kilter right now. I'll be better tomorrow. Take me to the barn and let me get some rest."

Once we got back to the farm, he wanted a sweat bath, so I heated stones for us, despite my fear it would loosen his sutures. But after we came out of the bath and jumped in the crick, he quit sweating and the arm looked less swollen. I made him eat some jerky along with a mug of sweet milk from Andre's place, and then we went to bed. I held him in my arms all night, waking often to check his respiration and temperature. They seemed near to normal.

# # # # #

The next morning, dressed in white man's clothes, Matthew reached over and took my hand before we mounted Arrow and Wind Rider. His grip was stronger. "Whatever happens, you know how I feel."

"I love you, Shambling Bear."

"Not sure I like the name you slapped on me."

"Can't help it. That's what I saw in my Spirit Dream, so that's who you are."

"So be it."

We saw no one on the road, and nobody paid us any attention as we entered town. At the sentry gate, I gave the guard our names and asked for Lt. Haleworthy. Within five minutes, Gideon came running toward us, trailing two troopers with rifles behind him. When he stood before us, I motioned with my chin toward Matthew.

"Look who I found at the farm when I got back from town yesterday afternoon. I told you he'd show up one day. Lt. Haleworthy, this is my brother, Matthew Brandt. I told him you were looking for him, so we came to see what it's all about."

"You're turning yourself in, Mr. Brandt?"

"Like John said, I want to know why you're hunting me. He tells me you showed up at the Mead and searched the place like some outlaw's hideout."

"Not like that, I hope. But yes, I was looking for you. Will you tell me your Indian name?"

Matthew hesitated only a moment. "It's not something I share with strangers, but I was Little Bear until John here changed it to Shambling Bear. You'll have to ask him why."

"You've never gone by the name of Red Star?"

"I've never called myself that name. Why?"

Had Gideon noticed the equivocation?

"The commandant would like a word with you. Are you willing to do that?"

"That's why we're here," Matthew said.

"Good. If you'll follow me."

He led us to the headquarters building where Matthew and I waited downstairs with the armed troopers while Gideon conferred with his superior. When Matthew was escorted upstairs, I tagged along. Gideon introduced us to Major Irons.

The commandant of Fort Yanube reminded me of Major Morrow even though Irons wasn't an attractive man like James. He had prematurely gray hair cut high on the side of his head and was shorter and stockier. It was the military bearing that linked the two. He opened the conversation once he got the two of us seated across from his desk. Gideon stood at his shoulder.

"You've led us a merry chase, Red Star."

My brother shook his head. "I guess you're still chasing him, sir. He's not in this room unless John went renegade on us."

The Major started in on Matthew, referring to some papers in front of him and asking a whole list of questions about where Matthew had been on this date or that.

"I don't carry a calendar around on me, so I don't know if I can recollect all of those dates, but I've been wandering back and forth between the Mead and the Laramie country looking for some of my father's people. He died fighting for the Union against Stand Watie's Confederates when I was just a boy. After the war, some of the bands broke up, and I had trouble finding my family. Only managed to locate one or two."

"You're a blood Indian, aren't you?"

"Yes, sir. My mother was Yanube. We were both survivors of the Smith Massacre."

When the Major asked for more details, I could tell denying riding with the Oglala was tearing Matthew up inside. He got his licks in by admitting he'd liked to have been with Crazy Horse because the chief had been a great man.

When the Major stood, we got to our feet. "I'm going to check on a couple of things, but in the meantime you may go. Don't leave the area. Where will you be staying?"

I spoke up. "We'll be at Turtle Crick Farm for a few days. That's the old Morrow place. I inherited it when the mob shot and burned the Major and hanged Otter." If Matthew could get in the man's face, so could I.

"I see. You're one of the Teacher's Mead Strobaws, aren't you?"

"I'm Cuthan's second son. As I was about to say, after we take care of some chores on the farm, we'll head back to the Mead. You can find us at one place or the other."

"Very well." Irons turned his back, dismissing us.

Gideon walked us downstairs and waved away the two troopers with rifles. "I hope that wasn't too unpleasant."

"Better to take care of it right up front than let it fester," Matthew said.

"True. If you'll excuse me, I'd better get to my duties. I'd still like to visit the Mead when I have some free time, John."

"Welcome any time."

When we went outside, Matthew had to try twice before he mounted Wind Rider. As soon as we were clear of the fort, he expelled air between his lips.

"I was sweating just trying to keep from sweating. Truth be told, I'm all tuckered out."

"Lost a lot of blood. Surprised you did as well as you did."

"What do you think?"

"Irons will send telegraphs and check on what he can. I hope a couple of people you told him about will vouch for you."

"I saw them, but the dates won't match. That doesn't worry me much. They don't live by a calendar any more than I do. Shit, this is going to be a long seven miles. I need to lie down."

As soon as we arrived at the farm, I sent him on up the ladder while I wiped down the horses. When I went up to the loft, I found him sound asleep.

Then the barn door opened and Andre's rich voice floated up. I scampered down the ladder to face my handsome neighbor. From the shine in his eyes, he was anticipating another rendezvous.

Andre's gaze shifted from me to the three horses behind me, so I explained Matthew had come back and was sleeping in the loft. A tic in his jaw signaled disappointment, but he made the best of it.

"Pleased to hear he's back. Is he doing all right?"

Might as well further the lie we'd spun at the army post. "Not so good. I shot him the other day."

"You what?"

I repeated the fabrication that I'd been surprised and thanked the Lord I'd only taken a chunk out of his arm. Andre Tiller is an open and honest man, but I didn't want to take any chances.

"Besides, we had to go to the fort. A patrol stopped at the Mead a few weeks back looking for Matthew, and we had to go see what that was all about."

My neighbor nodded. "They came looking around here, too. Glad you got that cleared up. They were bent on finding that Red Star fellow. What made them think he was Matthew?"

I shrugged. "They weren't too clear on that. Hearsay, I guess. In case anyone asks, Matthew's Indian name is Shambling Bear."

"Nothing shambling about him. He's more like a mountain cat."

"It's a dream name. The fields look good. Are you gonna need help with the harvest?"

"Can always use help, but if the weather doesn't play tricks on us, Libby and me ought to get it done. She's a lot of help for a girl her size."

I grinned at him. "When are you going to find her another mother?"

He flushed. "Don't know. We never get into town much. Not for social things, anyway."

"You're a good-looking man with a successful farm. Shouldn't be too hard to find a woman."

Anytime Andre overstayed his welcome, I now knew how to chase him off. He was out of the barn and headed back home before a dropped penny would've hit the ground.

CHAPTER 11

When we returned to the Mead the following Monday, a surprise awaited us. Lt. Haleworthy — or Gideon as he kept pressing me to call him — had arrived earlier that day for a week's stay. By way of making himself welcome, he'd brought the lavish gift of a bolt of linen for the ladies. His presence, of course, robbed me of the pleasure of surprising the family with news of Matthew's return.

As soon as we exchanged greetings and saw to the buckboard full of supplies and our horses, Gideon once again expressed his delight in the Mead. "This is the most picturesque farm on the Yanube. I'm aching to climb that high hill behind the place. Perhaps you'll accompany me up if you're not too tired from your journey."

"Be glad to, but first I have to deliver a message to Pa from Mr. Brown in town." I had no such message, but I needed Pa to call on Matthew for some chore. He had recovered some strength, but such a climb might tax him.

Just before we started up the hill, Pa snagged Matthew to help prepare for tomorrow's stage arrival. Gideon paced me on the climb. Army life kept him in good shape, although once we stood at the top, he was breathing harder than I was. I forgot all of that pettiness when he showed a genuine interest in the view. He pressed me to explain everything from the stone house to the river flowing in the distance to the Little Island Mountains, a series of hills on the southern horizon. His curiosity about the history of this foreign land where he found himself marooned made him a likeable companion.

After lunch, he remained at the house to regale the womenfolk with tales of Boston. Pa, Matthew, Alex, and I walked the fields for a private talk. Matthew relayed the events of the past few days.

"That explains Gideon's presence. He's here to see what he can find out about you," Pa said.

Alex shook his head. "I thought he was here to see Rachel Ann."

"That, too. But I think it's more to see if he can tie Red Star to Matthew."

"Maybe we ought to let him know Alex's natural name is Red Sun and see if that throws him off." My jest might have set back our reconciliation a tad. I'd already noticed him eyeing Matthew and me. Given my confession while hunting, he could have figured things out.

Pa gave the discussion a serious vein. "Don't say anything to link the Mead to anyone they're searching for. Matthew, when you were here last, I saw a scar on your leg. Did you get that riding with Crazy Horse?"

"No, sir. I got that when I escaped from Red Cloud's Agency after they killed him."

"So it might be known to them if they have an informant among the Oglala."

"I don't see how, but it's possible."

"Then keep it hidden from sight while he's here."

"I'll keep my arm covered, too."

"No. He might have heard about that from Timo. Say something about it at supper this evening."

# # # # #

Some of my animosity toward Gideon rose again around the table late that afternoon. Rachel Ann flanked him on his right, and Hannah sat at his left He paid attention to each of the girls and was courtly to Ma and Jane.

Gideon accorded my pa due deference as we ate, but reserved his real attention for Matthew. What did Laramie look like? Was that Brulé home territory, or had they been driven west like many of the tribes? The questions went on and on.

Rachel Ann, even with stars in her eyes, caught on. Was the flush that crossed her pretty features embarrassment or anger? For his part, my brother-who-was-not-a-brother handled himself well. He described things he knew, and answered with a simple "don't know" if the point of the question was beyond his ken. He managed to slip in a description of our "misadventure" during one of the infrequent pauses in Gideon's conversation.

"Gunshots can be nasty things. Infection, you know," Gideon said.

I waved a hand in the air. "Don't worry. I put enough honey on it to attract bees."

"Honey? Yes, we've been known to do that in Massachusetts, as well. But surely you have more modern means of preventing contamination."

"Why?" Matthew asked. "That one works fine."

"May I examine the wound? Perhaps it requires the attention of our medical officer. I can arrange that for you. No trouble at all."

"It's all sewn up and doing just fine," Matthew said.

"Who did the suturing? The doctor in Yanube City?"

Ma cleared her throat. "I understand you've been at Fort Yanube better than a year, Lt. Haleworthy, so perhaps you know a medical man in town who'll treat Indians. Pray enlighten us."

Gideon's cheeks turned remarkably red.

Matthew spoke into the awkward silence. "John took me to Timo Bowers."

Gideon ran his hand over a stray lock of hair at his widow's peak. It promptly fell back over his forehead, and Rachel Ann was smitten again. "Bowers? You mean the blacksmith with a forge near the fort?"

Pa spoke up. "Timo took care of the animals in this territory for years until a horse doctor came to town. No reason why he couldn't sew up a man's arm. He doesn't charge as much as a medical man."

"I see. Perfectly logical, I suppose." Gideon turned to me. "May I ask what he charged?"

My voice threatened to play out on me, but I kept it steady by force of will. "It's a barter system. When he needs something, he'll expect treatment in k ... kind." Damn, why did I stutter? I shot a look at Matthew and saw his lips compressed like he was holding something inside.

"I gather that system has worked out here in the territories for a long time." Gideon went on to sprinkle a few comments and compliments among the females at the table.

It didn't work on Ma. "More turnips, Lt. Haleworthy?" There wasn't an ounce of guile on her face, but that was a tactic she used on children she deemed being naughty.

"No thank you, ma'am. I am pleasantly filled at the moment. The rumors are true. You set a fine table here at the Mead."

After supper, Matthew and I went out to tend the horses when Rachel Ann snared the lieutenant for herself. We were barely out of earshot before Matthew let out a howl.

"You should have seen your face when Haleworthy asked what you paid for my treatment. Your ears caught fire. It was all I could do to keep from busting out laughing."

"That wasn't for treatment. It was for silence. After you decided to pay a call on the fort, it turned out I gave Timo my joy juice for nothing."

"Nothing? You looked like you were about to blow a head of steam there for a minute. Guess you blew something else."

The moment lost its humor, so we worked in silence until returning to the house to learn they'd decided Gideon would sleep in my cabin.

Matthew and I were expected to share Hannah's room. The two girls would take to Rachel Ann's bed.

Gideon protested turning me out of my home and offered to share the cabin, but I declined. No doubt he would have pestered me all night with questions about Red Star.

We had no sooner gone to bed than Matthew spooned against my back. His groin felt as hot as a coal from my forge. Hushed by the proximity of the family sleeping in rooms around us, I muffled my cries as his hard member — made slick by butter from Ma's table — penetrated me. Soon, I took pleasure not only in his cock stroking my insides, but also in the feel of his muscled belly against my buns, the tender words he whispered in my ear. When he came, he bit my shoulder to stifle his moans. Then I spilled seed across the bedding in great gobs. When we both lay still, I became aware of the squeaking of the bedstead — by its absence.

# # # # #

Gideon Haleworthy had — to use my mother's term — ripped his britches. His continual prodding about Red Star was almost embarrassing. Matthew confided he was tempted to confess just to get the Lieutenant off everyone's back.

The day before he was to take his leave, Gideon renewed the challenge for a race. His Brownie against my Arrow Wind. Matthew promptly invited himself and his gray gelding — more of a light horse than an Indian pony — into the race.

We agreed on a course across the bridge spanning the Yanube about a mile from the starting point, and then west to a large cottonwood some half-mile beyond that and back to the Mead. The route agreed, we haggled over the bet. Everything on Gideon's person was army issue, so all he was free to offer was his West Point ring. Matthew risked two fine beaver pelts he'd picked up somewhere in his travels, and I wagered bits of silver, part of my inheritance from Otter.

Rachel Ann, who by now favored Gideon over her brothers, started the race by dropping one of Alex's bandanas. Brownie, a cavalry horse, got the jump on us. Matthew and Wind Rider tore out next. Arrow was last off the mark. Gideon had a good seat and was in total control of his big mount. Matthew was one with his horse. There was no daylight between them.

I'm a good rider, too, and I knew what my little buckskin was capable of doing. He was fast, but more importantly, he had stamina. He didn't like bringing up the rear in what he recognized as a contest, but I reined him in. I wasn't interested in running him down or killing him on such a hot July day.

By the time we reached the bridge, Brownie had Wind by half a length, and Arrow was pushing them both. Gideon went wide on the turn west. Matthew cut inside, gaining a head. I turned tight. My pony raced alongside Brownie's croup. In the straightaway to the cottonwood, Gideon applied spurs. Matthew kept his head and let the horse pass him. Arrow strained against the reins, but I held him back.

We had elected to travel the stage road to avoid unexpected holes in the terrain, but the going was still rough. Arrow stumbled, recovered, and pulled even harder against my restraint. I gave him a little head. He inched up on Wind. Gideon's big horse couldn't handle the turn as well as the smaller horses, and he lost all advantage as he wheeled. Matthew took the lead with me a head behind him.

Then Matthew eased up. Apparently, he wasn't intent on killing his horse just to win a bet, either. I hadn't realized Gideon had fallen so far behind until we were a quarter of the way across the long bridge before Brownie's hooves hit the planking. Just shy of the farmyard, both Matthew and I turned our mounts loose. Arrow shot past the bigger gray, but by the time we reached the finish line scratched in the sand in front of the forge, we were neck and neck. Alex thought Matthew took it, but Rachel insisted I had. We were more interested in cooling our mounts down than in who won.

In the end, Matthew took the purse by virtue of a toss of one of my silver coins. Gideon was a good sport about handing over his ring. He'd made it a closer race by nipping at our tails at the end, but he lost fair and square.

By the time Gideon returned to the fort, he'd developed what seemed to be a genuine interest in Rachel Ann and asked Pa if he could call on her. Despite Ma's disapproving look, he said yes. My sister went flying off to the stars until she came down to earth later when she realized he'd be fifty miles away three and seven-eighths quarts out of a gallon … if time were liquid.

# # # # #

With Gideon's visit a week behind us, Matthew and I decided to rebuild the burnt-out cabin on Turtle Crick Farm. The fact the place was a mere seven miles from Fort Yanube didn't sit well, but it would give us some privacy we didn't have here. He'd moved his things into my little cabin, but nobody thought anything of barging in whenever they wanted, so we had to be careful.

That thought raised acid in my gut. Why should anybody care if Matthew and I took to one another? Why was it anyone's business? My blood chilled. Otter and James hadn't been anyone's business, either. But the snaky, black-frocked preacher had made it his.

Another thing. If I loved Matthew, why wasn't I willing to share that fact with those closest to me? Because of Ma. That left a bad taste in my mouth, too. Not at her, but at me because I didn't have the grit to stand up to her prejudices.

It took another fortnight to catch up on all the work that needed done in the smithy and elsewhere around the place. I'll admit to some guilt about planning to leave Pa without help with the coach teams, but Alex and Curtis could lend a hand.

We decided to take our leave after the stage from Yanube City arrived in order to change the span of horses one final time. That would make us late in leaving, but we didn't mind star-camping overnight. I checked the calendar hanging on the wall in the clapboard building used for the comfort of the passengers and circled Tuesday, August 12, 1879, with my graphite pencil. The date Matthew and I would begin our new lives.

A year back, the stagecoach company had established another way station about halfway between the Mead and Yanube City. They could push their teams harder if the run was twenty-five miles instead of fifty. The coach usually arrived at the Mead around one o'clock or so. After waiting an hour past the time the stage was due, Matthew and I mounted up and headed out to see why it hadn't arrived. Dusty Skediver was a stickler about his schedule and was never this late. Barnaby Bates, his shotgun rider, didn't even own a watch, but Dusty held the whip-hand on that team.

We weren't more than ten miles from the Mead — at the little rill that once marked the boundary between the Yanube and Pipe Stem territories — before we heard the sound of gunshots. If that was a hunter, he was a mighty poor shot. He was tossing a whale of a lot of lead. Then we heard a deep boom.

"Scattergun," Matthew said. "The coach is in trouble."

We unsheathed rifles and kicked our horses into a canter. I wished for my handgun, but I hadn't brought it along. Matthew's rode on his hip almost everywhere he went. By the time we raised the stagecoach in the distance, it sounded like Greasy Grass all over again … or what I imagined the battle had been. The coach was stationary; the lead horse, down. Four men on horses stood off to the south, firing at the stage.

Barnaby hunkered down behind the coach tossing off useless blasts with his shotgun.

They seemed to be at a standoff until Dusty began working his way to the downed horse. The robbers saw him and circled around to expose his position. Matthew and I reined in and started throwing lead in the direction of the road agents. Neither of us was bothering to aim; we just wanted to stop them from putting Dusty in a bad way.

They didn't even notice us until one man tumbled over like he'd been punched out of his saddle. Everyone stood stock still for a moment before they whirled and spotted us. Thank goodness they were toting handguns, not rifles. We kept up our fire until one turned and bolted for the mountain. The other two collected their fallen companion before racing after him.

I'd just turned to grin at Matthew when an angry hornet whizzed past us. He was faster to catch on than I was. He threw himself out of the saddle and jerked me from Arrow's back.

"Buffalo gun!" he yelled.

We spent an anxious minute twisting our ponies' necks until they went over on the ground. Another bullet whistled by.

"Damnation, I can't see anything down here eating weeds. What's happening?" I came up on my elbows. Matthew pulled me back down.

"Shooter could be sitting off at the edge of the Little Islands. Those Sharps have a long reach."

I handed him Arrow's reins and crab-walked up the road before removing my hat to pop up for a quick look. The robbers were almost at the foothills of the Little Islands. Dusty, Barnaby, and a couple of passengers were standing in the open watching them run.

"They're gone." I stood and clamped my hat back on my head.

Matthew and the two horses got up out of the dirt. We mounted and headed for the stage.

"Thank the good Lord you two come up," Dusty said. He didn't look any worse for the wear, but Barnaby had a blood-covered sleeve. He'd been hit in the left shoulder.

"Came to see why you were late. Anybody else hurt?" Matthew asked.

"Nope. Our passengers and me are all fine. Mad as a pit full of rattlers, but not hurt none."

I took a look at the trace horses while Dusty tended to Barnaby. The animals were agitated, but all seemed unhurt except for the one that was down. "What happened?"

"We were going along like we always done when all of a sudden, Big Black stumbled and went over. Seconds later, we heard a gun boom."

"The man with the Sharps," Matthew said, earning a questioning look from the driver. "He sent us ducking for cover when we started shooting."

Dusty nodded. "After that, four men come riding up on us. Me'n Barnaby got the passengers down on the ground. Them robbers just stood off and kept feeding us lead. They wasn't in no hurry. Waiting till we run outa bullets, I guess. But when I started working my way around to cut the harness from Big Black, they made their move. Then you showed up. Damn, that black was one good lead horse."

We settled rope nooses over the dead animal and dragged him out of the road. Matthew and I were all for heading to the fort to report the robbery attempt, but Dusty insisted on making for the Mead. He had a schedule to keep, and he was already late. The two passengers, one with the look of a gambler, and the other a hard case Texican, backed him up. Barnaby needed patching up, but he could still ride and volunteered to take Wind Rider back to Yanube City if Matthew would ride shotgun. I looped a noose over the wagon's tongue and helped the three surviving horses pull the Concord into the Mead's way station.

Pa tamped down the excitement by sending the womenfolk to warm up the food and show the two passengers where they could go see a man about a horse and wash up afterwards. Matthew and I changed the cut harness on the carriage and hooked up a fresh team. The stage used a four-in-hand set-up so one driver could control all four horses. Before somebody thought that up, it took two drivers to control what were essentially two separate teams.

By the time we sat down, Dusty was finishing up with details about the attempted robbery.

"Been any other attacks?" Pa asked.

Dusty shook his head while his fork tried to find his mouth. "Nope. Not a one. Last time was back during the troubles ten … fifteen years ago. Before my time." He chomped down on a mouthful of Ma's creamed potatoes.

"The Little Islands make a good hiding place," Matthew said. "They're not big, but they're deep."

Pa passed the driver a pan of warm biscuits. "In my day, foreign bands and outlaw gangs launched raids from there."

"Barnaby'll report the robbery attempt, and I expect Major Irons will send somebody to flush them out. Or the sheriff. Don't need no nest of outlaws hanging around and shooting up honest folk." Dusty settled back in his chair. "Matthew, I need a shotgun rider till I get to Fort Ramson. You or John game? Stage company'll pay you a day wage."

Matthew looked at me, but when I told him I needed to repair the harness we'd cut, he nodded. "I'm *kay* with that."

"Deal." Shorty finished off the last of Ma's sour milk biscuits and said he was ready to roll.

"Wouldn't it be better to overnight here and start early in the morning?" Pa asked.

Dusty cocked an eye toward the sun even though it was invisible behind the roof of the eating room. "Lotsa daylight left yet. With a fresh team I can raise the next station in three and a half hours. Depending upon things, we'll overnight there or push on another twenty-five miles to the next station at Beaver Crick. That'll make a easy enough day of it going on into Ramson."

I did a quick calculation. "You can make seven miles an hour?"

"Never figured it that a way. Just know what I can do between the way stations. Seventy-five miles a day's comfortable. Do another forty or so if needs be."

"What're you carrying that they want?" Matthew asked.

"Just these two gents here. I ain't got a spare dollar, but maybe them two has. Course, I got a mail pouch."

The Texican, who looked like he might have some Mexican blood, claimed he just had a little traveling money. The blackleg, tall with the red hair I associated with Irishmen, echoed that, but his signet ring looked like a diamond and his pinkie, a ruby.

Two minutes after Dusty cautioned everybody to visit the "Gent's" a final time, the stage clattered out of the yard and crossed the bridge.

I hadn't realized how much Matthew had worked under my skin, and I got an insight into my future as the concord rolled out of sight. Would the commandant at Fort Ramson have more information on the fugitive Red Star than Major Irons did? Not likely. They shared information over the grapevine.

Matthew was a nomad, but he came by it honestly. Our forebears had always moved on before they wore out the land. Another way the white man had changed us. So he'd go off like this whenever an opportunity presented itself. And if there wasn't an excuse, he'd create one. If I couldn't handle that, now was the time to find out. Something crawled up my spine.

Only when I was lying in bed later did I realize it had been shame. If I was mortified by my love, how could I live it? How could this work? And if Matthew was going to roam the countryside leaving me behind, why even try? The answer came when I woke in the middle of the night dreaming about him. My tool throbbed against the thin bed covers, so I took myself in hand. Afterward, I lay soaking in my own cum, imagining it was his precious seed.

I fell asleep and woke the next morning with my cock hair stiff, and my belly and chest crusted with dried sperm.

CHAPTER 12

Hannah's warning of approaching riders drew me out of the forge Thursday morning in time to see Lt. Haleworthy and a full platoon of troopers cross the bridge. Once on this side of the river, a scout went out on either flank. Crow Johnson, the Absaroka who'd handled the Mead's forge before me, was back. As they drew up in front of the family gathered in the yard, I gave him a broad smile but didn't break protocol by speaking to him.

Gideon's detail had been hunting the highwaymen who'd tried to take the outgoing coach last week. The gang's tracks had led south across the Little Islands until they reached the river beyond the mountains. The road agents had cleared out.

An owl-eyed Rachel Ann stared at Gideon with a silly grin on her face. She hung onto the sound of his voice, but she likely had no idea of what he was saying. I blinked. Hannah was giving the same stupid look to a scout on a pinto beside Crow.

When I cast an eye on him, my mouth went dry. About my own twenty years, he wasn't Sioux or Piegan. Certainly not Crow like Johnson. Cheyenne? Good looking, but different. Matthew was handsome with regular features bearing the stamp of a man. This scout was off-handsome. His features were irregular. Yet taken together they made him as comely as any man I'd ever seen. It prompted me to study the rest of him. What did he look like beneath his flap and leggings? His light skin tone had a slight reddish hue. Long black hair worn in braids. Slender but muscled. He wore no shirt. A bone breastplate covered his chest.

My attention jerked back to the Lieutenant when he asked about Matthew, and was informed he wasn't back from riding shotgun for Dusty to Fort Ramson. Gideon asked permission to dismount his men alongside Strobaw's Crick. While he took care of his troopers, Crow greeted the family, shaking hands all around like a white man.

"You shoulda come back here," Pa said. "John and Matthew are about to set off to rebuild Otter's cabin. James left the place to John."

Crow's features hardened. Otter had been his friend. "Maybe, but I'm signed up for a year of scouting. They'd come haul me back if I stayed." He threw a thumb over his shoulder. "This here's Raven Strongbow. He's a new scout at the fort."

"Didn't know the Crow and Cheyenne rode together," Pa said.

The young man spoke up. "They do nowadays. Can't find no other bloods to ride with around here."

Hannah looked to be swooning at the sound of his baritone. Ma noticed. Her eyes tightened.

Crow ducked his head. "He ain't too bad for a Northern Eater." That was what some called the Northern Cheyenne. The Southern Cheyenne were known as the Roped People. The ten related bands called themselves Like-Hearted People.

Raven shook hands all around just as Crow had. Hannah looked like she wanted to hold hands, too, but only the menfolk got that treatment.

When I started for the forge, Crow tagged after me and pulled Raven along in our tow. The Cheyenne leaned against one wall while my friend and I caught up. After his father had died, Crow married a widow whose dead husband had no available brothers to care for her and brought his new family back to familiar territory. His father had been an army scout, so Crow decided to give the life a try. After a little chinning, Crow worked around to what he wanted to talk about.

"I heard about what happened to our friends. Bad business." He was old-fashioned enough to do the name avoidance thing. "Heard what you done, too. He woulda been proud of you."

Uncertain how much he'd figured out, I nodded my thanks.

"Riding with the army lets you see things sometimes. I seen a familiar-looking paint on a farm near the Little Islands."

"White Patch?" My voice almost caught in my throat.

"Hitched up to a big steel plow."

"Otter's pony and plow?"

Crow's eyes flickered at the mention of Otter's name. "Can't swear to it, but I mentioned it to Raven at the time, didn't I?"

The disturbing scout grunted.

Crow gave me the name of the farmer — Jepsen — and the location of his farm south of Yanube City. He was polite enough not to ask what I intended to do.

A yell from one of the troopers drew us outside. The stage from Fort Ramson was just crossing the bridge. My pulse picked up when I saw Matthew cradling a shotgun in his arms beside the driver. Despite my excitement, I couldn't resist glancing at Raven Strongbow. He was staring at me with bright black eyes. The air seemed heated between us. A shadow of a smile touched his lips. I swallowed hard.

In order to tear loose from some mystical connection to the unsettling man, I stepped forward to meet the stage. He moved up behind me. The heat of his body seemed to warm my backside, sending an itch up my butt. My cock stirred.

Then Matthew's handsome smile claimed me. As he tossed the shotgun to me, I heard the Cheyenne grunt and move away. Matthew hopped down and clasped my hand. Then he punched Crow on a brawny arm and started feeding him trouble about running off and leaving us. When Crow introduced him to Raven, neither of them said anything, but something set my gut to churning. The moment passed after they shook hands American style.

Gideon and his sergeant came over to question Dusty about the attempted robbery last Tuesday. Ma and Jane and the girls showed a woman and her little girl to the eating room. A fat man headed straight to the men's necessary. I got to work unhitching the horse team. Matthew caught up with me as I led the horses through the corral gate. He claimed two big beasts and started removing harness.

"I'll have to go on to Yanube City to collect my pay and get Wind."

"I'll come with you. I'm all packed, so we can go straight to Turtle Crick."

"No, stay here. I've got something I want to try before we leave. Come on, I'll show you."

I followed him outside to the stagecoach. He climbed up and handed down two cages with small birds inside.

"Pigeons?" I said.

"Not just pigeons. Homing pigeons. I'm gonna train them so we can send messages back to the Mead. But I have to bond them to this place, so when we take them with us they'll come back here."

"We'll be able to send messages to the Mead, but how do we get messages from here?"

"We'll get some more birds and bond them to Turtle Crick. Pretty smart, huh?"

"It is if you know what you're doing. You ever trained pigeons before?"

"No, but the man who sold me these explained how to do it. Right now, I've gotta go tell Hannah how to take care of them until I get back. She likes little critters."

Still shaking my head over the matter, I left him to go hitch up the fresh team. As I finished, I noticed Matthew and the Cheyenne scout talking over near the corner of the barn. While Dusty was getting his passengers loaded, I corralled Matthew.

"What was that all about?"

"You mean Raven? We know some of the same people. There were lots of Cheyenne at Greasy Grass."

I felt uneasy and off-kilter as Dusty drove the stage down the road, taking Matthew with him. While I was standing there, Hannah picked up the two pigeon cages and went to set up a cote in the hayloft.

The stage was hardly out of sight before Lt. Haleworthy mounted his troops and got them moving. I went outside to wave goodbye to Crow and get a final glimpse of the scout called Raven. He caught me looking and turned in the saddle to give me a long stare as the column took leave of the Mead.

# # # # #

Matthew rode in four days later — from the northwest. That meant he'd been to Turtle Crick Farm. He gave me a brief greeting before he and Hannah went to check the pigeons. I could hear them talking as I fed and watered Wind Rider for him.

After an hour or so he joined me in the pasture I'd rigged up to hold my cattle, now numbering half a dozen. I'd forged a branding iron, and he smiled when he noticed the way I'd marked the animals — a stylized thunderbird over a standing bruin. An eagle and a bear. What he was thinking brightened his face.

"I told them you'd put in some silver to buy the animals."

He stiffened. "This is not good. If you choose not to tell anyone about us, that is one thing. But lying to hide what we have between us is wrong." He turned and rode back to the house.

I sat astride Arrow while my soul leaked through my boots and puddled on the ground. I finished tending the cattle and returned in time to wash up for supper.

After we took our seats at the table and joined hands over Ma's Grace offering, I determined to tell the family I had found my soul mate. The girls chattered like magpies, but there were plenty of opportunities for me to say my piece. But every time I opened my mouth, I closed it again. I finally spoke, but the words came out different.

"Did Matthew tell you about his homing pigeons?"

He gave me a sad look before explaining his plan. He already had four birds set up in the loft at Turtle Crick. Libby Tiller was tending them until we got there. That way we could send messages back and forth and keep everyone apprised of affairs.

# # # # #

Matthew did not avoid me the rest of the evening; neither did he seek out my company. With my chin somewhere down around my navel, I climbed the hollow hill and sat on a rock, thinking about how important this place had been to our family over the years. The crystal spring bubbling from within the cavern provided pure, sweet water for drinking and washing. The steady, chilled temperature of the cave made it the best preserving room in the territory.

It had also provided a secret hiding place for both body and valuables during the troubles. Most of the family's gold and silver, including that passed on to me by Otter, rested inside.

All of a sudden Pa was standing at my shoulder, startling me out of my thoughts. He'd come on silent moccasins. Or else I was so lost in my thoughts I hadn't heard him.

"Good place to watch a sunset." He sat down beside me. "If I remember, there's a hill for it at Turtle Crick."

I laughed. "That's like comparing standing in a treetop with standing on a stump."

"What's bothering you? You looked like a snapping turtle at the table." When I didn't answer, he took the reins in his own hand. "Did you make the wrong decision? Is the life you selected chafing you?"

"How come you can read me like a book? None of the rest of them can do it."

"More than you think. I'll bet they know most of what's going on in that yellow-flecked head of yours."

"Don't see how. *I* don't know what's going on there most of the time. Pa ... Matthew ... Oh blazes, we got together. I love him." I looked at my father and understood I'd told him nothing new.

"Then why is it troubling you so?"

"He wants to tell the world. At least, our world."

"And you?"

I unsheathed my knife and started digging in the dirt like a little kid. "I can't do it. Every time I open my mouth, my tongue gets tangled up in cobwebs and cotton bolls. What's the matter with me?"

"You're a young man finding his way in a world that's neither red nor white. That's not an easy thing to do."

"You did it. And you're a full blood."

111

"I'm not so sure I could have made it without Billy Strobaw's help. And Otter's. And it wasn't always easy. Many times I wanted to run away and hide out in some *tiospaye*. But Billy saw our future and did everything he could to make sure we were ready to face it."

"I'm not as strong as you are."

"Stop feeling sorry for yourself." His words were as harsh as any he had ever spoken to me. "You come from good blood. Your grandfather and great-grandfather were peace chiefs at a time when everyone called for war. Billy fought his own kind to obtain justice for his adopted people. You were strong enough to go your own way even though you had to wrestle with yourself. So don't talk nonsense."

He drew a breath. "Alexander might be steadier, but he's not stronger. The girls look to you for guidance and friendship, not him. Matthew is a gadfly. He seeks to be a warrior when the way of the warrior is finished. Oh, there'll be more fighting, but it's done. You feel the urge for that life, but you fight it. Matthew might tempt you into a warrior society someday, but you'll be back."

"If I'm so strong, why can't I face Ma and tell her about Matthew?"

"Look deep inside yourself, John. When you know the answer to that, you'll find out how strong you've been."

With that, he started back down the hill, leaving me to puzzle over his words. I sat until twilight was turning to darkness before making for my cabin. I was lying on the bed reading Herman Melville's seemingly endless poem, "Clarel," when Matthew came in. My heart leapt at the sight of him, even though he brought a wounded air with him. I'd figured he would nurse his hurt in the hayloft tonight.

"Where have you been?" I laid the book aside.

"I saw you on the hill talking with Pa, so I spent some time with the pigeons. Hannah's taking good care of them." He paused. "I'll throw my blankets on the floor."

"Please don't. I need you. I've thought about what you said this afternoon. And I understand it's not right to lie to my family. I won't undo the one about the cattle, but I won't tell any more untruths."

"But you won't share everything, either. That's a lie, too?"

"Do Ma and Pa speak of their coupling? No, I won't tell them what we share. That's personal. Ours."

Matthew flinched. "You're ashamed."

"No. I'd like the whole world to know how I feel about Matthew Brandt. That I love Shambling Bear. Pa already knows, but not because I told him. He reads me ... us ... better than the rest."

"It's Ma. You won't tell them because of her."

"That's right. Not because I'm embarrassed to tell her. Well, there's some of that, but it's mostly because I don't want to hurt her. Twice. You're her son, too. And given her beliefs, it *will* hurt her."

"Don't you think she'll figure it out for herself?"

"I hope she does. But I won't slap her in the face by saying the words. Can you live with that, Matthew? Can we build a life together on such soft sand?"

Matthew unpacked the saddlebags he'd carried with him on his trip without responding. Was that my answer? Then he straightened and stared at the wall.

"I accused you of lying, and now I've been false with you."

"How?" My heart wobbled in my chest.

"Raven Strongbow. I knew him at Greasy Grass."

"How did you know him?" I asked through a dry throat.

"His family was at the village Custer attacked. We fought together."

I began to breathe again. "Is that all there is to it?"

Matthew fixed his gaze over my right shoulder. He'd gone Indian on me. "He knows I was at Greasy Grass, and he works for the army."

I remembered the grunt I'd heard from Raven when Matthew tossed his shotgun to me from the stage's seat. "And you know he was there. But why lie about that to me?"

"When you saw us talking, I was making arrangements to meet him in Yanube City. I needed to know if he was going to cause trouble before I said anything."

"Did you talk?"

"He said he owed the army nothing but scouting. And it's like you said. I know he fought at Greasy Grass against Custer, too."

"Matthew, you should have shared your worries with me. I have given myself to you. You accepted my love, and that gives me the right to share your worries. That's more than just lying to me."

I got up to start getting ready for bed. He walked up behind me and pulled me to him. I tried to shrug him off, but he hung on.

"Sharing is new to me." His breath was soft in my ear.

"Horse apples! We've shared things since we were kids." Despite the heat of my words, I settled back against him.

"I've been gone for a long time. I got out of the habit."

"More soft sand."

"Then I'll provide something hard."

His engorged cock pressed against my buns. It didn't burn away my pique, but it melted my resolve. I lifted my arms, so he could draw my shirt over my head. I tingled where he touched me. Went breathless as he pushed my trousers down. Moments later, that hot iron rode up the crease of my buns. His ragged breath fanned my cheek.

"You're mine. I'll marry you if we can find a council to declare it before. I'd go to the stone house and tell the whole family, if you'd let me. So I'll say it aloud to the Great Spirit. You are mine. I am yours."

He entered me while we stood beside the bed. He filled me, not just with the firm flesh of his manhood, but also with his love. His arms around my chest warmed me. His forehead against the back of my head thrilled me. Flesh to flesh. Back to chest. Fundament to manhood.

"Now I am going to fuck my new win-tay until there will be no doubt about how I feel."

He pushed me over the three-drawer storage chest I'd made to hold my gear and massaged my spine and cupped my buns, all while humping me. He worried my nipples until they were sore, always thrusting … harder, deeper. Then he hugged my back to his smooth, muscled chest, giving himself more purchase. He spread his legs and drove into me, his flesh slapping against mine, drawing moans and grunts from both of us.

He exploded. Hot semen flushed my insides. Still he pumped, delivering more of his seed. He mumbled words of love in Lakota. In Dakota. In Yanube. Then he lay across my back so that I shared the thudding of his heart, the singing of his blood.

He fell back across the bed, taking me with him. As we landed on the mattress, he pierced me deeper than ever. He was still rampant. His right hand moved like a teasing feather across my chest, down my belly. He gave my testicles a gentle squeeze. Then he grasped my hungry cock, hooked his heels around my legs, and began to stroke me.

"This is our wedding night," he whispered, raspy from emotion. "Remember me inside you. Remember me stroking your pole. Remember my breath on your neck. My legs on your thighs."

His beat was firm yet gentle. My cock was his, but now other parts of me responded to his steady stroking. My face turned hot. My nipples tingled. My belly danced beneath his palm. My sac drew up. Nerve endings sparked and stuttered. Then orgasm struck. I arched against him while my cum poured out of me. I shuddered through the longest ejaculation I'd ever experienced.

When I grasped his wrist to stop his movement, he flipped us over and began fucking me again. His cock was just as hard, his efforts equally strong, but it took him longer than the first time. That was all right. Giving him pleasure gave me pleasure. Before long, he lit my fire again, and I rose to meet each downward thrust. His cock, the bedclothes ... they were more than I could stand. We came together.

"We're going to have to figure a way to wash our own bed clothes, or everybody on the farm will know our relationship," he said between pants.

"Already do. Washed my own since I moved to the cabin."

I reached up and pulled his naked form to me. He covered us with a damp, sticky sheet, and settled in my arms. Just before I dropped off again, he said he loved me ... in English.

# # # # #

I was sure my happiness — our happiness — betrayed us to everyone at the Mead, but no one seemed to notice except Pa ... until Alex started giving us looks. He'd put five pennies together and come up with a nickel.

Matthew took care of the livestock while I went to work in the forge. I came down off my high horse as I thought about Raven. Could the Cheyenne be trusted? Another thought almost struck me dumb. When they met in Yanube City, had Matthew bought him with his body? Had they gone to the farm and fucked in our hayloft?

Why did I think Raven Strongbow would be interested? Not all men had our particular hunger. My heart slowed again. Because he was interested in me. Just because he perceived something in me — whatever that was — why would he find the same thing in Matthew? My insides shriveled, and I put a name to the feeling. *Jealousy.*

Matthew came through the door at that moment, his lips split in a smile. "The animals look good."

My doubts went into hiding when he dropped a hand on my shoulder and squeezed. He was enjoying the strength of my muscles as I swung the hammer against the barrel rim I was fashioning. "I'm going to start training the pigeons today," he said. "Wish me luck."

"How are you going to do it?"

"They should know this is home now, so I'll take two of them across the river and release them one at a time. If they come back to the loft, I'll repeat that from four different directions, sometimes in the open and sometimes in the forest. When I'm confident they are bonded to the Mead, I'll go farther and do it again."

"Sounds like it'll take some time. I'd hoped to start for Turtle Crick. If we're going to build a house before winter, we have to get started."

"We'll live in the hayloft the first winter. It ought to be all right. Our friends built a sturdy building for their animals."

"Otter insulated his buildings, but there's no proper stove in the place. We'll freeze."

He grinned. "I'll keep you warm."

"Tell me that when we have icicles hanging from our elbows. All right, we'll either live in the outhouse or wait until next spring to move. But there's one thing we've got to do right away." I repeated what Crow had told me about White Patch.

"Get Arrow, and let's go." His lips were grim; his face, flushed.

"Let's talk to Pa first."

Pa was in the field with Alex. Curtis worked just out of earshot, so I repeated Crows words and finished by saying we were going to bring the pony and the plow home.

"You think the law will listen to you?" Alex asked.

"I'm not going to the law."

Pa squinted against the sun. "Not sure that's smart. It won't take much to raise resentment again. There are still people around who tried to take Teacher's Mead away from us."

"I don't want to stir up trouble for you, Pa. But I'm going to go get the pony. White Patch doesn't deserve to end his days pulling a plow."

He was silent for a moment. "Otter branded his horses with a triangle. The white man might turn a blind eye to murdering an Indian and a deviant, but they won't stand for horse theft"

"I'll come with you," Alex said.

Matthew shook his head. "You're needed here. John and I are about to go live at Turtle Crick. We won't be missed if things go wrong."

Pa glanced up at that remark. "Don't do anything foolish. Stealing horses is a thing of the past. At least around here. And we don't need talk of Indian uprisings."

"We're not gonna kill anybody," Matthew said. "But we're going to get that pony."

"And the plow."

"We don't need any more plows," Alex said.

"Speak for yourself. We don't have one at Turtle Crick."

# # # # #

I wanted to get to the Jepsen farm at a decent time on Monday morning, so Matthew and I camped halfway to Yanube City Sunday

116

night. We bedded down in the buckboard I'd driven to haul the plow and looked up at the firmament. It was a clear night, and the span of stars overhead looked like a smear of spilt milk. I pointed out the big dipper.

"Billy and Otter must have looked at those same stars."

Matthew put his hand under my head and pulled me closer. "And Cut Hand and Lone Eagle and all the ones before them. Those stars have been there forever."

"Smell that? Jacob's ladder."

"All I smell are horses and grass. And hay, maybe. Musta hauled hay in this buckboard." He turned into me and pressed his hand against my groin. "Do for me what Timo did for you. Thinking about that still gets my dander up, you know."

"Let me see if I can get rid of some of that dander and get something else up."

I rose to my elbow and opened his clothing. He was already hard. I teased him with my fingers until he grabbed my ears and drew me down on him. The taste of his bulb seemed natural. The feel of his hard shaft in my mouth excited me. He sighed in pleasure as I worked on him, but otherwise he was silent until he suddenly came. I took his seed, all the while nearing my own time.

I threw myself off him and clawed at my trousers, barely freeing my pulsing prick before I shot. He leaned into me and kissed me as he finished me with his hand. Then he lay with his nose against my cheek while I recovered.

"How can anyone say that is wrong?" I whispered.

"It is against nature. Nature provides a cow for a bull. A stallion for a mare."

His answer brought a frown to my brow, but his chin tickling my neck allowed me to disregard his meaning. "Those are mindless beasts who fuck to reproduce. We're more than that. We can choose who we love." I pulled him half atop me. "What am I saying? I didn't choose to love you. It was ordained. You were given to me, Matthew. You were my gift a long time ago when the militia killed your mother and brother. That terrible act put you in my arms."

He tensed. "There is a lot we don't understand."

I nodded. "Somewhere, right now there might be things taking place that will affect us some way in the future."

He turned on his back with a sigh. "More than likely what we are contemplating at the Jepsen farm tomorrow will do that. Do you believe it will be that simple?"

CHAPTER 13

Matthew dropped off to sleep, but his remark kept me awake. How many times had he ridden into danger? Did repeated exposure to peril make it easier to face?

I didn't have to think back too many years before constant danger was the norm, not the exception. The troubles had killed Cut Hand and most the rest of my people. Had taken Dew Drop and Standing Rock. Violence had claimed Otter and James, too, but it was a different prejudice that slaughtered them.

A darkness that had nothing to do with night swept me. I had been the "big kid" flaunting his nakedness in front of the two deviants. No matter I lived to Methuselah's age, I would never be able to shake that guilt. Innocence of what those foul minds conjured up from the muck and mire of their own sinful pasts had not altered the outcome.

A childhood image of Otter powwow dancing with Matthew in the yard of the farm while I tooted on a flute popped into my head. I'd never played one before, and all that came out were discordant noises. But as I lay in the buckboard, I could almost hear echoes of that flute.

# # # # #

Jepsen Farm was a run-down affair lying close onto the Little Islands. A part sod, part clapboard house and a barn little more than a shed was it. Except for a small, poorly made corral where White Patch — all ribs and bones — stood. Jepsen was starving the animal. A lanky man with a long gun in his arms stepped out onto the porch of the shabby house and motioned us away.

"Think he's worried?" Matthew was aboard Wind Rider. Arrow was hitched to the buckboard and none too pleased about it.

"Just about the right amount, I'd say." I flicked the reins.

Jepsen switched from one foot to the other, literally walking without going anyplace as we closed on him. Thin, spiky hair. No shirt. Faded flannel underwear stained with sweat and dirt. Probably a Sesech who'd been through the mud and ended up out here after the Confederacy got whipped. No sign of a woman to take care of him.

"Git outa here!" he yelled as we came near. "Don't want no Injuns on my place. Go on, hear?" He fingered his rifle as we entered his yard, gambling he didn't have the guts to bite the bullet.

"I hear you, but I'm taking my property with me when I leave."

119

"Whut the hell you talking about? Git on outa here 'fore I pop a cap." He shook his rifle for emphasis. The man's mottled complexion and skittering eyes did nothing to improve his appearance.

I pulled up beside the porch. "That's my grandpa's horse over there in the corral. And that's his Deere steel plow lying yonder in the dirt. They were both stolen the night he was lynched."

Jepsen looked to be near swooning. "I paid a pretty penny for that there pinto and plow. Don't know nothing about no lynching."

"Then you've got a piece of paper saying who you bought them from," Matthew said.

"Ya'll ain't got no right to come in here."

"If you don't have a paper, that means you stole them. That ever bother you, Jepsen? Thinking about one man burning up in a cabin while the other one's jerking away his life on a cottonwood limb." My throat almost closed up on me.

Matthew glanced around. "Don't see a cottonwood, but that cabin looks like dry tinder."

"We're going for the horse and plow now. And you're gonna help load the Deere in the buckboard. It's a heavy piece of work."

Jepsen seemed incapable of moving beyond his weird dance from one foot to the other.

"Now!" Matthew said in a low voice. "And put down the rifle."

The weapon hit the porch with a thunk. Jepsen lurched into the yard, making for the corral. No one said a word as we hoisted the heavy plow into the wagon. The stench the man gave off staggered me. A spreading wet spot at his crotch told me he'd pissed himself, and from the smell, done the other, as well — just as if we'd hanged him.

I called White Patch by name as I opened the corral gate. His head came up, and he accepted my noose around his neck. While I tied him to the back of the wagon, Jepsen worked up some courage.

"You boys in trouble now. Real trouble. Ya'll know what they do to horse thieves around here?"

"Don't worry, we won't ask the law to hang you. And that's where we're headed, straight to the Sheriff's Office. You see that triangle on the pinto's rump? That's Joseph Otter's brand, and there's plenty in Yanube City who'll swear to that."

Jepsen stood rooted to the ground as we headed for town. Matthew kept an eye out until we were beyond rifle range.

"That true about going to the sheriff?" he asked.

"Yes, but I'm heading to the fort first. I want to test the military's attitude about the murder of an army officer. Then we'll tackle the sheriff. I met him once, and he's apt to be a problem."

We took Main Avenue through town to the fort. The sentry box was unmanned, so I drove the wagon right up to the headquarters building. A sergeant came out to challenge us.

"I need to see Major Irons."

"He's busy."

"Then I'll talk to Lt. Haleworthy."

The orderly disappeared inside. A few moments later Gideon came out and listened as I related everything that had happened.

He rolled his eyes. "Might've been smarter to pick up the sheriff before going to see Jepsen."

Matthew gave a dry laugh. "You figure the sheriff would take a ride on the word of two Indians?"

Gideon colored. "Let me see if I can get a word with Major Irons."

We waited a quarter of an hour before Irons appeared on the veranda of the headquarters building with his lieutenant in tow.

He eyed Patch and glanced into the wagon as he acknowledged us, so Gideon had already told him our story. I gave him an abbreviated version, anyway.

"That's a civil matter. You should be talking to the sheriff."

"That's where I'm headed next. But there was an army officer murdered June a year ago, so I came to you first."

"Retired. A retired army officer. No, this is sheriff's business."

I took up the reins. "That's where we're headed now. Thank you for your time, sir."

"Lt. Haleworthy, why don't you escort these gentlemen down to the sheriff's office? You might stick around and see if anything comes up that might be of interest to us."

The Major disappeared back inside as Gideon went to claim his mount. In minutes, we were making our way back down Main to the Sheriff's Office. The big raw-boned man came out to meet us. He still had a moustache big enough to make eating messy.

"Sheriff, I'm John Strobaw."

"I know who you are, Strobaw. You, too, Brandt. I keep tabs on what goes on in my county."

Did he know I was the man who had yelled rape and drove the snaky preacher out of town ahead of a mob? "Then you should be interested in what we have to say."

I told him exactly what had happened, going into great detail in the presence of the Sheriff, one of his deputies, and Gideon — plus a couple of passers-by who'd stopped.

"You oughta come seen me before you went tearing off and trespassing on a man's private property."

"Would you have gone with them?" Gideon asked.

Landreth gave him the fish eye. "What's your business here?"

"Major Morrow was a retired army officer. His murder is a matter of interest to Major Irons. And it looks like these two men have uncovered something useful."

The Sheriff turned back to me. "Looks to me more like I oughta take you in for horse thieving and robbery."

"I have a piece of paper that says I own this paint. Jepsen doesn't."

"What piece of paper?"

"I inherited everything Joseph Otter owned. I've already filed his will with the proper authorities. If you check, you'll see it lists three horses by description and by brand, a triangle." I nodded toward Patch, "And it lists this one by name."

"How come it don't list all three by name?"

"Because Otter didn't name any of his animals except his war horse," Matthew said.

"His what?"

"His riding horse," I said. "By all logic, either Mr. Jepsen was with the mob who murdered Major Morrow and Otter or he has a bill of sale from someone who was. Why don't we go ask him which it is?"

"Now hold on. I'll do my own investigating. You two get on outa here. I need you, I know where to find you." The Sheriff stomped back into his office.

Matthew grimaced. "That will be the end of that. He'll not do another thing."

"No, he'll hope it all blows over," I said.

"Why is that?"

"Hell, Gideon, everyone in town knows who killed Otter and James. But they were just a couple of *berdaches*, so who cares?"

"*Berdaches?*"

"Deviants," I said. "And to make matters worse, one of them was a dirty Indian. Hard to work up much sympathy — much less justice — for a couple like that."

Gideon mounted his horse. "What will you do now?"

"We're headed for Turtle Crick Farm. We're going to rebuild and settle there."

"Then we'll practically be neighbors."

"Yes, neighbors," Matthew said.

# # # # #

White Patch was glad to be home. Maybe it was my imagination, but he seemed to be looking for the man who had cared for him most of his life. Past his prime now, Patch would never have to pull a plow again. He'd still be a decent riding horse so we figured on giving him to Libby Tiller after we built him back up. She would value him to the point where his care would be assured.

We knew our intent was right when Andre showed up with his daughter soon after we arrived. Libby was delighted to see the paint and scolded us for not feeding him right. Sadness replaced joy when we explained the situation.

She and Matthew went to check the pigeons, leaving Andre and me to inspect the fields while I told him of today's events. Andre was handsome in a different way from the other men surrounding me. His features remained stubbornly fair. His hair was sandy brown, and he had a spray of freckles across his nose. Libby mirrored him except for her mother's chestnut tint to her locks.

Since I had decided my own nature, I was more perceptive about others, and what I saw in his face was hunger ... for me. A momentary flush of pride brought a mild unease. Was I becoming a man to flaunt himself in front of others? No, the core of my angst was that we were going to be neighbors. And if my guess was right, Matthew would turn into Shambling Bear and disappear for long periods of time. It was time to face this man-to-man.

"Have you found a prospective mother for Libby yet? She needs a mother, you know."

He removed his battered hat "There are one or two likely candidates down at the church. But I haven't mustered enough interest to make the effort."

By the church, he meant the Main Street Methodist Church in Yanube City. I was never able to figure out the name of that place. It sat on Main Avenue. Yanube City didn't have a Main Street.

"When are you coming back to the farm?" he asked.

"Matthew wants to train the pigeons at the Mead. He's asked my sister, Hannah, to help." I glanced at the outhouse loft. "He's proposing the same thing to Libby right now."

123

He stared at the hayloft doors as if he could see through them. "She'll jump at the chance. She's already pestering me to get a pair."

"Andre …" I paused when he turned eager eyes on me. "Matthew's coming to live with me on the farm. That means … well, it means we can't do what we did together anymore. I thought you should know, just in case that was holding you back from looking for a woman." I blushed at my pretentious words.

"I think about what we did. A lot." He glanced at the hayloft again and cleared his throat. "But I understand. Matthew seems to have recovered from his gunshot wound."

"Andre, do you know Timo Bowers in town?"

"The smith? Yes. He made my cooking stove."

I paused. "He doesn't have a wife, either."

CHAPTER 14

We stayed an extra day at Turtle Crick in order for Matthew to show Libby how to take the pigeons out for short flights. As she had undertaken the care and feeding of Patch, we made good our aim of gifting her with the pony. She was ecstatic. Given the recent flare-up over the pinto, I wrote a piece of paper conveying ownership to Liberty Belle Tiller.

On Wednesday, we left the spare buckboard at Turtle Crick for our later use and took to the saddle for our return trip to the Mead. Arrow seemed to appreciate being restored to the status of a war horse.

"Cross country or by the river road?" Matthew asked as we clattered over the bridge.

"Road. I want to stop by the smithy on the way back."

Halfway to town, we met a patrol led by Lt. Haleworthy and paused to exchange pleasantries. As we started for town again, Raven reined in beside us.

"Not much to do when I ain't on duty. Maybe I can I spend some time at your farm?"

"You can sleep in the loft if you overnight. Just don't eat the pigeons."

Matthew, who looked none too pleased at my invitation, spoke up. "But first go to the farm west of the place and meet Andre Tiller. He tends John's farm while we're away. His little girl will need reassuring. Her ma and brothers were killed by renegades."

Raven grunted and rejoined the column.

As we dismounted at the forge; Matthew asked why we were here.

"We're gonna need a cook stove. Besides, I want to try and take care of a problem. Come on. You'll see."

Timo was working the hammer when we came through the doors. He gave us a big smile. "Do something for you?"

"We decided to rebuild Otter's cabin, so we're gonna need a stove."

"You can forge anything I can."

"Except a stove. That might be more'n I can handle. And a water pump. The murderers stole that, too."

We agreed on a price before I undertook what I'd come to do. "Also wanted to say thanks for your help when we needed it a while back. And to say we can't do what we did that day anymore."

The burly man blushed like a doe-eyed swain as his gaze slid to Matthew. "Oh. That's all right. Appreciated when ... well, uh."

"But I was thinking. You know Andre Tiller, don't you?"

"Don't see him too much, but he's a pleasant fella."

"Handsome, too. It strikes me he's in his prime and has needs. But he doesn't have a woman, either."

I waved goodbye and walked outside before the smith died of mortification. Matthew caught up with me wearing a big grin.

"You know what the Cheyenne call deviants? Matchmakers."

I swung a leg over Arrow. "Shut up, Matthew."

We rode down Main on our way to Maartens Lumberyard at the south end of town. Maartens's sons had once helped Otter rebuild the outhouse when it burned, so they had a good idea of the size and layout of the cabin. I intended to buy lumber for the cabin to avoid cutting down trees. They were too scarce in this part of the country for that.

Mr. Maartens was a little stiff when two Indians entered his office but loosened up when he learned I was Otter's "grandson." He probably didn't suspect we addressed our elders by that term out of respect. The idea was helped along by the fact I'd inherited the farm.

I explained I wanted to expand the size of the cabin by adding a decent-sized sleeping room. James's and Otter's house had been a single big room with a separate bathing enclosure added onto the west end. After Mr. Maartens did some calculations, he gave me an estimate that about knocked me out of my boots. He calculated it would take $350 dollars for the materials, including thrown glass windows, and another hundred for his sons to do the work. Steep, but I didn't hesitate taking him up on the deal so we could have our house before hard winter set in.

Abner, the older son was a plain, outgoing man something shy of forty. His brother Jonah was handsome and pretty much lived inside himself, at least around strangers. Younger than Abner. More like thirty.

The sons were familiar with the tabby of grass and clay Otter used for insulating his buildings. Before we left for the Mead, I almost beggared myself by agreeing to fork over the entire amount in a combination of greenback and hard chink. We arranged to meet Abner and Jonah at Turtle Crick in a week to make sure they knew what I wanted and to hand over payment.

It was late when we left the lumberyard, so we returned to the farm to start out fresh tomorrow. We might as well have gone on down the road because Matthew spent half the night imitating a stallion.

# # # # #

For most of the following week, I divided my time at the Mead's forge between fabricating things needed here and household items Matthew and I would require upon moving to Turtle Crick. When the time came to go meet Abner and Jonah, Matthew stayed behind, claiming it was only right to contribute as much as he could before we left for good. He prevailed upon me to take his four white pigeons with me. Anxious to see if they would make the fifty-mile flight back to the Mead, he asked me to release two of them.

I started early, since I had no intention of overnighting on the road. It was after dark by the time I arrived at the farm, and when I lit a lantern in the barn, I was startled to find a long-maned pinto such as the one Raven rode. When I called out, he answered from the loft.

"My first day off. You said I could sleep here." Dressed in a breechclout, he joined me as I rubbed Arrow down.

"I remember. Uh, did you go see ..."

"I done what you told me. Tiller showed me to his daughter. But I seen I made her skittish and told her I'd feed the pigeons tonight."

I put the birds in the cote with the others and discovered how clever Matthew had been. The pigeons from the Mead were white. The Turtle Crick birds were gray so could tell where each called home.

Tired, I washed up in cold water and made ready for bed. Raven had thrown his blankets near the ones I'd left behind. Once in our respective bedrolls, we lay in the dark and talked a few minutes. I learned he was the sole surviving member of his family. The rest had fallen when General Mackenzie attacked Dull Knife's sleeping Cheyenne village on Powder River. He'd had seventeen summers at that time. He'd been on his own ever since.

"Matthew tells me you were at Greasy Grass."

"I fought there. It was good." His voice deepened. "Maybe it wasn't so good. Things went wrong after that. Greasy Grass was why my family died at Powder River."

"We forget that actions echo down through time. How is it that you now serve the army that killed your people?"

"I want to know as much about them as I can. I want to know how they fight. I want to see it from their side."

"Dangerous words."

"You gonna betray me?"

"I hold no love for the army. Although when the whites fought the big war among themselves, the militia held power here, and they were worse."

Raven would understand. It was Col. Chivington's Colorado Militia that slaughtered his people at Sand Creek. That was back in '65, but it was burned into the memory of most blood people, regardless of age or tribal affiliation.

I didn't keep the conversation going for long. I turned on my side and took in the aroma of the barn. The musk of the big animals below carried up into the loft, softened by the odor of bales of hay. The world was silent except for the occasional flutter of a wing from the cote. I drifted off to sleep thinking I would take a sweat bath tomorrow.

I came half-awake as Matthew spooned against me. I sighed in anticipation when he pulled my shift down. I arched my back as he parted my buns and probed my sphincter. He entered me strongly. His hands circled my chest and pulled me to him.

"Matthew," I mumbled as his hard male member thrummed me.

Minutes later, I came fully awake and tore out of the blankets, almost tripping on my under shift. Matthew was at the Mead!

"What are you doing?" I stared into the darkness, balled fists held in front of me.

"Being a man for you."

His deep voice struck a chord. It would have been easy to lie back and take what he was offering. But that would be unfair to Matthew.

"I seen the way you looked at me at Teacher's Mead. I got hard when you looked at me down there."

My outrage faded a bit. My interest probably had shown to one who was looking for it. "You got the wrong idea, Raven."

A Lucifer rasped on the rough floor, and a moment later he lit the lantern. Yellow light danced across his tight muscles. His pectorals were flat and hard, centered with dark aureoles on a hairless torso. He sat on his heels, stretching the skin over his smooth thighs. An upward curving prick strained out of a black bush and throbbed in the uncertain light, engorged to the point of bursting.

He grasped himself. "I … I'm close! I have to finish."

"Raven, go outside …"

My words died as he leaned back on one arm and stroked his member. Pearl drops — the clear moisture that comes with excitement — glistened at the end of his large slit. I couldn't take my eyes off him.

Muscles played in his chest and stomach as he increased his rhythm. He spread his knees, revealing a heavy sac. I caught myself licking my lips and froze lest he find encouragement in the act.

He closed his eyes, rose to his knees, and thrust his groin toward me. Seed erupted from his cock and splashed on the floor. He flogged himself until the gushing became an oozing.

"I knew you wanted me," he rasped.

"You're wrong." Aware my cock was making a liar out of me, I wadded my blanket in my lap. "I ... I have a mate. It wouldn't be right."

He smiled, which gave his dark features a sardonic look. "A mate? Matthew? You called out his name while I fucked you."

My skin crawled. Had I given him an advantage he could exploit? "Matthew would keel haul both of us if he heard you say that."

"Keel haul?"

"It's a riverboat term. And it's not something you'd want done."

I returned to my blankets as he rose to wash himself. I was doing my best to ignore the ghostly feel of his big cock inside me when he snuffed the lantern and spoke into the sudden darkness.

"You and Red Star, huh?"

CHAPTER 15

The next morning Raven demonstrated no awkwardness over the night before, but I kept my distance. Mindful of the chore Matthew had given me, I took out one of the white pigeons, affixed a message saying I'd arrived safely and released it. The little creature rose, seemed to pause for a moment, and then streaked off in an easterly direction.

"Pretty smart," Raven said. "If some hawk don't get him."

"That's why we send two." I removed a second white bird from the cote and repeated the procedure.

We had just finished a spare breakfast of pemmican when a heavy wagon rumbled over the Turtle Crick bridge. The Maartens boys had arrived. After I made the agreed payment, we unloaded the wagon and stacked the lumber and other items.

The foundations of the burnt-out cabin appeared sound enough to use again. Before the morning was out, the brothers had demonstrated they knew their business. They would require little help.

The weather was warm even though we had passed into September four days ago. When both brothers shed their shirts to work, Raven eyed the younger brother, Jonah, and shook his head. He mouthed a Cheyenne word I took to mean "too pale."

All four of us went to work leveling the ground for the new sleeping room. We finished that heavy chore in late afternoon before Raven and I went to the sweat lodge. Once inside, he grew rampant. I told him to go jump in Turtle Crick. The cold water would take care of that for him.

The brothers were ready to head back to town by the time we dried off, so Raven accompanied them on the ride back to Yanube City. I watched them go and wondered if I'd handled the problem of Raven Strongbow adequately.

# # # # #

Early the next morning, I stopped by the Tillers' to say hello and ask Libby to tend the pigeons. Abner and Jonah were already on the job by the time I got back. Given we would be able to use most of the standing insulation walls of the burned out cabin, Abner estimated the job would be finished by the end of October, well before the Canadian winds blew winter down on us.

Shortly thereafter, I crossed the bridge with cages holding four gray pigeons tied across Arrow's croup. A few hours into the trip home, weather overtook me. In this territory, rain might drench a man near to drowning while fifty yards in any direction the sun swamped him in his own sweat. Today, heavy clouds to the east were dumping buckets of water on the Mead.

I'd been cross cutting the country, but if I was in for a soaking, it would be easier on Arrow to take the road. The pony responded to the reins and angled south toward the wagon trace on the north side of the Yanube River. I took out my slicker, fixed my hat hard upon my head, and plowed into a bracing shower. A short distance later, I rode out from under the chilled rain into the welcoming warmth of the sun. The ground was wet, so I held Arrow at an easy walk. At this pace, I might have to overnight in less than ideal circumstances.

In the early afternoon, shortly before picking up the wagon track, I reined in at the sound of gunshots. Rifle fire. I was halfway to the Mead, which put me about twenty-five miles from Yanube City. Wasn't a hunter — too sustained. The stage way station was the only thing in the area, so I kicked arrow into a lope and emerged through the thin line of trees on the north bank of the river.

Gunfire had died away, but smoke rode a breeze half a mile to my east. A few minutes later, I stood on the north side of the river and looked across at the way station. As feeble flames licked at damp timbers, four riders hazed the relief team of horses out of the corral and headed south for the mountains. I jerked my rifle from the scabbard and took a bead on the closest rider. It was an improbable shot, but I lifted the barrel to give him a lead and squeezed the trigger. A long moment later, he pitched from the saddle and rolled in the grass. The others kept riding.

I found the closest walk across and forded the river. As my pony pounded around the corner of the smoldering building, I saw arrows protruding from the walls. Arrows? Marauding Indians stealing horses?

The recent rain had kept the flames from catching hold of the building. Nonetheless, I found a bucket and doused the timbers before going inside. Charlie Bates, the way station man lay face down on the floor, dead. Charlie was Barnaby's brother. The highwaymen had returned to draw more Bates blood. Serious blood this time. I covered him with a canvas from the stable while I figured out this was Thursday. The stage would be coming in from Fort Ramson.

I walked out to check the fallen bandit. He was dead. He must have been a rough-looking man because he sure was a rough-looking cadaver. Not an Indian. A white man. Where was that Sharps rifle that almost got Matthew and me the last time we encountered this gang?

I left him where he lay and talked my way to his horse, grazing a hundred yards away. Once he was in hand, I mounted and rode back to the charred way station. It made more sense to go meet the stage than to ride the twenty five miles to Yanube City, so I switched to Arrow's back and led the outlaw's roan straight down the stage road.

I raised the coach halfway to the Mead. Dusty pulled the team to a halt when I flagged him down. My heart dropped into my stomach. Barnaby rode shotgun.

"Trouble, Dusty. The highwaymen are back. They hit the way station. Barnaby, I'm sure sorry, but Charlie's gone. They shot him dead and set the station on fire. Shot some arrows in the walls to make us think renegade Indians did it."

"How you know it wasn't Indians?" Even in the dusk, Dusty's face was as red as Barnaby's was ashen.

"I shot one of them. A white man."

I offered to ride for Yanube City, but one of the passengers, a hefty young man, volunteered to take the brigand's horse and go for the law. Barnaby wanted to go see to his brother. I checked the pigeons after the coach rumbled down the road. The birds had taken a slapping around when I'd kicked Arrow into a run. One of them was dead. Broken neck. But the others seemed okay.

I headed into the rising darkness with another dead man on my shoulders. Damnation, why did this bother me so? Berglund and the road agent deserved what they got. Let it go! Easy said; harder done.

Night was well established, and the Mead was dark when I unsaddled and saw to Arrow before carrying the three surviving homing pigeons up to the cote in the loft. Only one of the white birds I'd released had made it back.

Matthew issued a challenge from the cabin door before I reached it. He threw it wide and embraced me upon hearing my reply. We were no sooner inside than he lit a lamp and started undressing me.

"Let me clean up. I smell like a horse."

"You smell like sex."

My lover drilled me as if I'd been gone for weeks rather than days. During the height of it, a ghostly image of Raven almost put me off. The thought died under my lover's impassioned assault.

Later, as we lay fighting for breath, I told him of the attack on the way station. His response made me sit up.

"Had a feeling somebody's been watching us. I climbed the hollow hill a couple of times. But all I saw was a flash of light across the river."

"Coulda been a long glass. Did you say anything to Pa?"

He shook his sleek head. "After what you've told me, I'll say something to him tomorrow."

"The Mead would look like rich picking for outlaws. And they'll know the stage pays hard money to act as a way station."

"They'll also see a bunch of rifles here. We won't be as easy as Charlie alone at a way station," Matthew said.

"They didn't get much there other than horses. The Mead might look like it's worth the risk."

"You think we should wake Pa?"

I scratched an itchy place on my left temple. "No. But let's tell him at the breakfast table."

I managed to get some sleep before Matthew recovered enough for another session. Then he spooned against my back for the rest of the night, giving me a warm, safe feeling.

The household rose early each morning for pressing chores, such as milking cows and tending animals, before gathering for breakfast. Matthew scaled the hollow hill a couple of times before we sat down at the kitchen table in the stone house.

"Middle of the night, ma'am," I said when Ma asked when I got back. "Pa, those highwaymen are back. They killed Charlie Bates and tried to burn down the way station west of here."

Pa settled everyone down and heard my story. Then Matthew contributed his disturbing suspicions.

"You climbed the hollow hill more in the last few days than you have since you came back," Pa said. "I think you're right. Someone's been keeping an eye on us. Maybe they've decided there are too many of us to tackle, but we can't count on that."

"They might not feel the same way about the Jacobsens," I said. "We ought to alert them."

"Rachel Ann, ride over to say hello to your uncles. Take the back way. A sheriff's posse or the soldiers from Fort Yanube will be on the highbinders' trail, but your uncles oughta keep a careful eye out."

He turned to me. "You figure they know you killed one of them?"

I wiped my lips with a napkin and pushed my chair back. "Don't see how. I was on the north shore of the river. They'd already started for the Little Islands. It was just a lucky shot."

"They might take it personally if they know who you are."

I shook my head. "Not unless one of them snuck back while I was seeing to Charlie."

"They must be awful desperate to hit a way station," Alex said. "The only thing they could expect was the horses they took."

"And if they're that desperate, they might decide to take us on," Pa thought for a minute. "Jane, you stay near the house. Keep the fry close." The Appleton's son and daughter were the only children on the place.

We broke up and went about our chores. All the men toted rifles or had one close by. Rachel Ann wore a handgun strapped around her waist when she rode for the Jacobsen place.

Matthew and I hazed the cattle into the near pasture, still penned in by the Pennsylvania zigzag fence Billy and Otter had erected all those years ago. Then I went to work in the forge while Matthew stood guard atop the hollow hill. It must have been about high sun when I heard a whistle and stepped outside to see him waving.

I turned to the river. Something like a dozen horsemen rode hard on the other side of the water. Some headed for the bridge, but a few splashed across the ford near the big cottonwood upstream. Pa shouted for everyone into get to the house. I grabbed my rifle and a band of cartridges and made straight for the hollow hill. Matthew and I would guard our backside.

Billy Strobaw and Cut Hand had built their home like a blockhouse. Pa and the others could defend it against any attack, but the forge and other outbuildings were vulnerable to torching. I got to the top of the hill in time to see the five raiders who'd splashed across the Yanube turn and approach the house from the west where they figured we were blind. The other six or so thundered up the road brandishing pistols. Except for one, who rode with a long-barreled rifle. The Sharps buffalo gun. He'd get close and try to punch through the thick, hinged shutters centered with gun slots protecting our windows.

Matthew and I put about ten yards between us and sprawled behind a rock outcrop. So far, the bandits gave no sign they had spotted us on the hill.

"How come you brought three pigeons?" Matthew called.

Pigeons? Now? "One broke his neck when I rode hard for the way station. How come there's only one white one in the loft?"

"Figured you'd messed up and just sent one."

"Nope. Two."

"Hawk got him, I guess. You tackle those bastards coming in from the west. I'll open up on the ones coming up the road."

"You see the sharpshooter?" I asked.

"Got him spotted. That son of a bitch is dead. He just doesn't know it yet. Uh-oh," Matthew said.

The marksman had pulled up at the edge of the forge and was dismounting when Matthew's bullet caught him in the head. Pa and the others let loose from the house as soon as they heard a gunshot. Things got kinda confused. I had my hands full scattering the bunch riding up on the blind side of the house. One jerked sideways out of his saddle, and another grabbed his shoulder and let his horse get away from him before they figured out where I was.

The others started shooting and broke for cover. We didn't have much to worry about so long as they stuck to short guns. As one kicked in the door to my cabin, I shot him in the butt. He fell with a howl and started wiggling around behind the building. The other two took off back toward the river.

I glanced at Matthew and saw he was shooting the big Sharps rifle to pieces so none of the other outlaws could use it.

Five of the raiders milling around in the yard didn't seem to be hit. The narrow gun slots in the shutters made sighting a moving target difficult. Nonetheless, the desperados began taking cover behind the outbuildings and pulling long guns. Not good. I didn't want a siege of the place.

"I'm going to the east hill!" I grabbed my bandolier, ducked down behind the crest, and dropped down on the lower mound. From here the east side of the barn was visible, and I drew a bead on the killer taking refuge there. He moved at the last minute, and that saved his life. But he wouldn't use his right arm for a while. It was spurting blood.

I was about to slither down the side of the hill and try to flank the raiders when fresh gunshots broke out from the thin screen of trees east of the Mead. Jacob and Christian had heard the gunfire and come to our aid. Within minutes, the gang pulled out, beating it back down the road toward the bridge. Half their horses ran without riders.

My two uncles stepped out into the open just as one of the raiders turned and threw a hail of lead at them. Christian pitched backwards into the dirt.

I raced down the hill. Not Christian. He was my happy-go-lucky uncle. By the time I got to him, sober-sided Jacob was helping him to his feet. Christian cradled his left hand in his right armpit.

"You hit bad?" I halted at his side.

"Naw. Bullet hit my rifle, tore it outa my hands and knocked me on my bum." He pulled his hand from his armpit. His little finger jutted out at an awkward angle. "Damn, that hurts."

As Pa and the others joined us, renewed firing came from across the river. The fleeing highwaymen had run right into a troop of cavalry. Within minutes, the remnants of the gang had been rounded up. Half the troopers headed back down the stage road toward the fort with their prisoners. The rest crossed the bridge with Gideon Haleworthy in the lead. Raven rode at the rear of the column.

Gideon gave a fingertip to the cap salute. "Anybody hurt?"

"Just a broken finger." Pa motioned to Christian.

"Naw," Jacob said. "Outa joint. I fix it."

He grabbed his brother's hand and jerked on the finger before anyone had any idea of what he intended. Christian gave a howl, stowed his wounded digit back in his armpit, and did a little dance.

"Lucky timing," Alex said to Gideon.

"Not luck. We've been out ever since word came of the attack on the way station. Tracked them into the Little Islands and found their camp. They'd left two to guard the horses they stole, but they gave up without a fight. Crow and Raven found their trail down out of the mountains. We were in the foothills when we heard shooting."

"Don't see Crow," Pa said.

"He went back with the detail taking prisoners to the fort."

"Might take a look around and see if you find any more of them."

Matthew called from beside my cabin. "There's a wounded man over here,"

The troopers found three injured and two dead men. One had the look of a Mexican, another was a blood. The rest were white.

After we helped the troopers load up the dead outlaws, I glanced up and saw Raven talking to Matthew. They reminded me of cur dogs with ears laid back and legs gone stiff. Crap! Was the Cheyenne telling him what happened in the loft?

As Gideon took his leave, I watched Raven as the troop made its way down the road toward the bridge. When I turned, Matthew was standing ten feet away staring at me. Without uttering a word, he stalked into the barn. I followed close on his heels. Once inside he whirled and planted his feet.

"Why didn't you tell me Raven spent the night at the farm?"

"I haven't had the chance."

"You had all last night."

"We had other things on our minds last night. And besides, we were worried about the raid on the way station. Hell, I didn't even tell you about the pigeons until we were in the middle of a shootout." My attempt at humor failed. "There's nothing to worry about, Matthew."

"Then why did he ask me if I was willing to fight for you?"

The anger in Matthew's voice shook me. What had Raven told him?

He shook his head. "We pledged ourselves, John, so I expected you to be true."

"I have been true."

"Then how did Raven know about us?"

With a chill in my heart, I told of waking and thinking *he* was inside me. I spoke of calling out Matthew's name, and realizing he wasn't in the loft with me, and scrambling up from my blankets.

He slammed his fist into the wall and then grabbed my arm. "He fucked you?"

I wrenched from his grasp. "I put an end to it as soon as I came awake. I did nothing wrong except maybe watching him abuse himself."

"You did what? You didn't throw him down the ladder?"

The idea hadn't occurred to me, but I couldn't tell him that. "I didn't touch him or willingly allow him to touch me. I told him I could never be with him. And then he called you Red Star."

Matthew trembled. His pupils dilated. For a moment, I feared he was going to attack me. Maybe it would be better if he did. I could defend myself with my fists. Violence might release his resentment and put it in its proper place. Instead, he stalked to the ladder and climbed into the loft, warning me not to come up.

I finished an anxious day of work and checked the loft. He wasn't there. As I headed to the stone house for supper, I spotted him sitting atop the hollow hill. I had no appetite, but everyone would know something was wrong if I didn't fill my plate. The meal was likely good, but it was mush to me.

By the time I snuffed out the lantern in the cabin and took to my bed, Matthew still hadn't appeared. I fretted half the night, but he'd have to get over his rage in his own way. In the meantime, I'd go about my business and wait for him.

The next morning Wind Rider was gone from the corral. I climbed the hill behind the house, but there was no sign of a horse and rider. Had he gone to call out Raven Strongbow? Would they fight until one was dead and the other was condemned by the law? Had he decided I wasn't worth fighting for? I felt a little better upon discovering the white pigeon was gone. He'd taken it with him, so he was likely on his way to Turtle Crick.

I scrambled to finish the morning chores and was late for breakfast. When Ma asked about Matthew, I said he'd taken off somewhere.

I didn't do as good a job of feigning an appetite this time, and when I started for work, Pa walked with me to the forge, wanting to know what happened,

"We had a fight." His gaze moved over my face. "Not fisticuffs. An argument."

"Over that Cheyenne?"

Not much got by Cuthan Strobaw. "Raven was at the farm when I got there. He stayed the night"

"Did you give Matthew cause to mistrust you?"

"No. At least not to my way of thinking."

He didn't challenge my equivocation. "Where's he's gone?"

"I dunno. Maybe he's gone for good this time."

Pa looked me in the eye, something he rarely did. "Is your bond so weak?

"We're feeling our way. Neither of us knows how the other one feels. Not exactly, anyway." I kicked dirt with the toe of my left boot.

"What are your feelings?"

The words came hard and caused me to break out in a sweat. "I've always loved Matthew as a brother. I don't know when this deeper thing came alive. But it's there, and I'm afraid for him."

"Afraid he'll go after the Cheyenne scout."

"He's not stupid. He won't just go to the fort and call Raven out. But I'm afraid Matthew won't come back at all. He took the pigeon with him, so maybe he intends to stay in touch."

"What are you going to tell the others?"

"Nothing. This isn't the first time he's run off. Everyone more or less expects it now."

"Not running off in the middle of the night. You have to tell your mother, Son."

I looked away. "I ... I can't. I wouldn't know how."

"Then you need to look inside and see if you've found your true self. How can a man live his life hiding the thing he feels strongest from those he loves?"

My nerve endings jangled. "How did Otter do it, Pa? How did he and James live that life?"

"It was a different time. When Cut Hand brought Billy Strobaw down out of the Little Island Mountains, no one questioned their right to love one another. They created lives of honor and dignity. When Otter claimed Billy's love, things had not yet changed because they lived inside our community. But when the *tiospaye* died, their lives turned. They were isolated here at the Mead, but even so, they were exposed to the white man's world."

I sat on a bench against the wall. He claimed a place beside me before continuing. "Otter and James had a rougher road because they lived closer to that foreign world. In the end, the way they chose to love killed them."

"It's not right!" I stood and paced, trying to loosen my cramping muscles.

He glanced up at me, revealing a web of small wrinkles around the eyes in an otherwise smooth face. "Nay, but it is the way it is. The rightness or the wrongness doesn't matter. Only the reality counts."

I plopped down beside him again. "Why do they condemn one man loving another?"

"My knowledge of the whites was framed by Billy. While many of them believe man-love is condemned by their God, Billy thought their condemnation was caused by fear of those who were different. In truth, hatred of *berdaches* may be no different from hatred of tribesmen. They fear contamination. It is ironic, but while their laws temper their ability to kill men of the blood, their churches allow them to murder deviants."

"Ma's not a hater."

"No, but she's a believer. She takes what her bible says to heart."

"But the bible was written by men."

"According to her, they were men inspired by God."

"Then why should I condemn myself in her eyes by telling her who I am?"

"Because her love for you will overcome everything else."

"It'll conflict her. Why lay that burden on her?"

"She can bear it. And she deserves to know who her son is. Just as you deserve to have her support."

"She won't support me. She might send Matthew away. She might even send me away."

"Do you know her so little? She could never send either of her sons away. She loves the one of you as much as the other. Besides, sooner or later, she will see what is right under her nose."

"But Matthew and I are going to Turtle Crick."

"No matter. In time, she will know. Tell her, Son. And then share it with the others."

My soul shriveled like paper in flames. "I'm all right with how I am until I think of telling her. Then I feel like something's wrong with me. How do I tell her?"

"Through the honesty inside you. I will send her to the forge where you are most comfortable. Tell her here among the things familiar to you."

I swallowed hard. "Why not wait until Matthew comes back, so we can tell her together? He's been after me to tell the family, so he'd be in favor of it."

"If that will be easier for you. But what if your fear comes true and he doesn't come back."

"If he doesn't come back, there won't be a need to tell her."

"Will you not still be who you are ... even then?"

"I don't know, Pa. I don't know."

# # # # #

Pa didn't send Ma to the forge, but she came the next morning on her own. I'd missed breakfast to take care of a cut on one of my steer's legs. She brought me a plate.

"You need to keep up your strength." I'd heard those words from the time I was a little kid refusing to eat my peas.

"Thanks. Sorry I missed breakfast."

"What's wrong, John?"

I shrugged. "Worried about Matthew."

"What's different about him disappearing this time?"

I looked into her blue eyes and thought about the time she'd almost smothered Matthew hugging him to her breast after he'd run off to Otter's when he was a child. What Pa had said was true. She loved Matthew as much as she loved the children she bore.

We walked to the bench against the wall where I sat beside her, took a deep breath, and started talking. She clutched my arm, and I could see she took my words hard. She's a fair woman, and she grew even paler as I revealed more and more. She said nothing until I finished. Then the forge fell silent for so long I grew ashamed.

"Are you sure, Son?" she asked at length.

"Sure of what? How I feel about Matthew. Absolutely. I'd give up my life for him. My soul, too, I guess."

She flinched. "Don't say that. Don't even think it."

"Why not. That's what you believe."

"In my head. But in my heart, I'm not so sure. Billy Strobaw and Otter taught me and my brothers. Educated us. If anyone had a soul when he died, it was Billy. He was strong. He was a believer, yet he managed to reconcile the way he lived with his faith.

"Otter was one of the best men I've ever known. When Billy died, he protected the family and fought our battles for us. Loving men like them have made me question things. And now that my own son is strong enough to tell me he's chosen that life simply adds to my doubts. I'm not pleased by what you're telling me. It's a harder road you've chosen than my other children ... except Matthew, of course. But you're man enough to travel that road if that's what you want."

"It's not what I want, Ma. This life chose me. I didn't choose it. I know things would be easier all around if I'd found some girl ... woman to fall in love with."

She surprised me with a rare vulgarity. "It's this damned country. There aren't enough girls your own age. It's ... it's an unnatural situation."

"That's not it. I tried to get interested in Min Killpenny. It just didn't work."

"Not much wonder. She's a silly thing." She looked stricken. "Shouldn't say things like that. I think Alexander's been sneaking off to see her."

My eyebrows climbed. "Alex?"

"Is Matthew as set on this thing as you are?"

"Yes. He's been after me to tell you all along."

"Why didn't he do it? He has a mouth and knows how to use it."

"Because I asked him not to. But there's something I haven't told you." I put her back on the bench and told her about Raven.

"That man assaulted you!" She stood. "And Matthew's gone to confront him."

"I don't think so. He's just gone off to think things through."

"He's gone to face him down. Go get Cuthan. You have to go find Matthew. Right now!"

# # # # #

Neither Pa nor I felt Matthew would act rashly, but Ma was adamant that we had to go find him. Just before we rode out of the yard, Pa's sharp eyes spied a pigeon heading for the loft. I scrambled up the ladder and recovered a scrap of paper from the leather sheath strapped to one of the bird's legs.

"At farm helping build cabin. Need time. Matthew."

Weak with relief, I scooted down the ladder and headed to my cabin for pencil and paper. On the way I thrust the message into Ma's hand. A few minutes later, I sent one of the gray birds on its way to Turtle Crick Farm. Then I went to talk to my parents.

"I sent a message saying I'm on my way. Don't see a need for you to go, too, Pa."

"Go bring him back, John."

"Tell him I said to come home right now." Ma used her tone for rebuking naughty children.

#####

I started late in the morning — taking the gray Turtle Crick pigeon with me — and should have overnighted, but I traveled the wagon road until arriving at the farm in the wee hours. I lit the lantern hanging on a nail just inside the barn door and removed Arrow's saddle and bridle. When I turned to get the curry brush, Matthew was standing behind me with a knife in hand. He was naked but for a cotton loincloth.

"Thought it might be Raven," he said.

"What if it had been?"

He flipped the blade and tossed it into the nearest wall. "We'd have a frank talk."

"With knives?"

"If that's what it took to get my point across. You made good time. You almost beat your pigeon."

"Apparently your idea works." I indicated the cage on the floor by the saddle. "I brought the gray pigeon with me."

"Good. You can take the white one when you go back tomorrow."

"I'm not going back. Not until this thing is settled. They know about us, Matthew. I told Ma and Pa both."

"How did they take it?"

143

"Pa already figured it out. It was a pole axe to the head for Ma, but she handled it like she handles everything. Said for me to bring you back home. Not sure if she's going to take a switch to you or hug you to death."

A smile touched his lips. "So you were afraid for nothing."

"She's hurt, Matthew. But she told me she'd never known finer men than Billy and Otter, so her belief all deviants are bad was already shaken. But it's hard to accept that two of her sons will live that way."

"Are you sure we can make it work?" He set out oats for Arrow. "Seems like we're on that sand you talked about. I think it shifted beneath our feet."

"For you, maybe, but not for me. I did nothing wrong. I defended myself against Raven after I knew what was happening."

"John, for such a smart man, you can be so damned dumb. You don't even realize what you've done."

I took a step backwards. "What do you mean?"

"When you didn't throw Raven outa the loft after he tried what he did, you let him know he had a chance with you."

"Whoa, now ..."

"Stop and think, man. He fucked your ass. Raped it, if you're telling it straight. And you didn't break his neck. So what does he do? He lets me know he's ready to fight me for another go at you. You've set us on a path that's gonna be hard to get off of."

My throat went so dry I had trouble speaking. "I'll make him see. I'll make it clear. You may be on sand, Matthew, but I've found a mountain to plant my feet on. And I say this knowing if this thing doesn't please you, you'll go marry a woman and have a host of small fry. I can't do that."

"Why not?"

"I don't have the interest or the will. I love Shambling Bear. And I will always love him even if he throws me over and says he wants nothing to do with me."

Matthew licked his lips. "I'll throw you over, all right. But in a way you'll like. If you climb that ladder over there, I'll fuck you until you yell for me to stop."

"I don't want you to fuck me, Matthew. I want you to love me."

He grinned, which made him unbearably handsome and impish at the same time. "We'll do a little of both."

He went on up to settle the pigeon in the cote while I finished tending Arrow. I gave Matthew's pony, Wind, a handful of oats and patted his long nose before going up the ladder. Matthew stood in the middle of the loft. He was naked, yet not rampant. I never tired of watching candlelight play off his coppery skin. Long muscles rolled with every movement. He lifted my shirt over my head.

"Truly," he whispered. "No man has ever had such a handsome mate. It makes me proud that you want me."

My heart threatened to burst when he pushed me down on the bed he'd scrounged from somewhere and tugged off my boots. Then he fumbled with the buttons of my trousers. In moments, I was as naked as he was. My chest swelled as he studied my body, pleasure lighting his black eyes. How had I found favor with such a beautiful man?

He fell upon me and lowered his lips to mine. Teased me with a pretend kiss. Seized my lower lip between his teeth and worried it like a puppy at play. He sucked my tongue into his mouth, sending shivers all through me. My engorged cock pressed against his. I was aware of various parts of me all at once. The mouth he was deep kissing. My chest where his hard torso pressed against my nipples. My belly against his as we drew breath. The soles of my feet where his toes rubbed against them. It was as if we had melded into one.

Then Matthew took me by surprise. He moved down my body to suck my nipples and explore my navel. His chin was in my bush. Then he made the earth move by sliding up the underside of my turgid pole to take my glans in his warm, moist mouth. Surprised and delighted almost beyond endurance, I lost control. I managed to mutter a warning before my eruption. Matthew came off me and finished me with his hand.

"Th ... thank you."

He said nothing, but covered his large member with my semen and raised my legs. His entry was strong and steady and exciting. Our eyes locked as he hovered over me and applied himself earnestly. This was the fucking part. After a Herculean effort, he emptied inside me and dropped on the mattress at my side. It took a long time for him to recover enough to go for the water ewer and clean us both. Then I slept better than I had for weeks.

CHAPTER 16

Early the next morning, I wrote a message saying I had arrived safely and Matthew was all right. After the pigeon was on its away, the two of us went down to see what progress the Maartens had made on the cabin. The interior of the structure was almost restored, although the sleeping room was still just a frame. Our new home would be tight and snug ... and private.

Abner and Jonah showed up soon thereafter and went to work. Matthew picked up a hammer and joined the brothers while I went to see Andre.

I rode through our fields on the way to the Tiller place and found the crops in good shape. We would have a good harvest. Halfway there, a gunshot drew me to a halt. Was Matthew hunting? Or had he happened upon a serpent? Then another sounded, closer this time. When the third report came, I pulled Arrow around and raced for Turtle Crick.

Both of the Maartens were standing near the cabin. As I opened my mouth to ask what had happened, Matthew, rifle in hand, tore out of the barn on Wind and headed across the bridge. I followed hard on his heels.

He made his way south on the wagon track but soon deserted the road. The prairie looked to be flat, open ground, but it was veined with sudden gullies that Otter had called ha-has. As we neared the first one, Matthew disappeared down the hill. When he was in my sight again, he had slowed to a walk and was leaning over to search the ground. I pulled up beside him.

"What happened?"

"Somebody tried to bushwhack me. There! There's his tracks."

"Be careful, he might still be around."

Matthew dismounted. "When I tossed lead back at him, he took off like the skunk he is."

"Did you see who it was?"

"Have you gone dumb again? It had to be Raven."

I slid from Arrow's back. "Shooting at you makes no sense."

His voice turned harsh. "He's had a taste of your buns and wants more. To do that, he has to get me out of the way."

"A man doesn't kill because he wants another man's companion."

"You remember all that history Otter made us read? How many lives did one man's hankering for Helen of Troy take?"

"That wasn't history. That was myth. Anyway, that was different. Paris wanted King Menelaus's wife."

He gave me a withering stare. "What difference? Are you my mate or not?" His scorn was palpable.

"Maybe it is the same. But I never thought of anyone fighting over me."

"I told you what he said at the Mead. Now he's tried kill me."

"Then we better ride for the fort and settle this thing."

"Ride for the fort and tell them what?"

I absorbed Matthew's words as we followed tracks in the grass. He halted to pick up a shell casing.

"Looks like army to me. Does that convince you?"

"If that doesn't, this does. See the scrape mark on the pony's left front shoe?"

"It's been scored by a rock or something metal. That should make the horse easy to identify," he said.

"I noticed that mark when he was at the Mead. The shooter was Raven. We've gotta report him to his superiors. We'll claim there's bad blood between the two of you. He has to keep a close mouth on the thing, or I'll reveal what he did to me. He'll be caught in his own loop."

"Maybe." He sounded doubtful. "I don't trust him. He's bad medicine."

"How are we going to clip his horns if we can't turn him in?"

Matthew's black eyes bored into mine. "I can think of one way."

"Killing him?"

"At least, calling him out. After that, let the better man win."

"What about the Maartens? Do they know you were shot at?"

"They were there when the bullet plowed into the wall right beside my head. But they didn't see who it was any more than I did."

"Let's try to convince them it was a careless hunter or else they'll paint it as something else."

"You go feed the Maartens a story. I'm going after Raven."

"He'll head straight to the fort where you can't touch him." I paused. "Let's go deal with the Maartens and do a little planning."

"It's not you with a target on your back."

"True. But that's the smart thing to do."

He ignored me and followed the tracks in the grass until they rejoined the wagon track and headed south toward the fort. That must have satisfied Matthew he was safe for the moment because turned Wind and headed back to the farm.

"Catch him?" Abner paused in the act of driving a nail.

"Found where he was. Looks like a careless hunter. When I threw some lead back at him, he hightailed it."

"Gettin' so a man can't walk in his own yard," Jonah said.

"Better'n it was when militia was riding." Both Abner and his brother retained traces of a Dutch accent.

"We're riding to town to order a couple of things from the blacksmith," Matthew said. "You need us to bring anything back?"

Abner squinted at the sky. "Got everything we need for today."

Although I hadn't known we needed anything from Timo's shop, I reclaimed Arrow and went along with Matthew. Once out of sight of the brothers, he skirted the farm and headed north toward Trickling Water. Neither of us spoke on the ten-mile trek to the stream. Despite the history lessons Matthew alluded to, I'd never heard of two men fighting for the favors of a third. But why not? Men fought over women. Was this so different?

That thought hit me so hard I reined in. Matthew didn't notice. He must be in deep thought, too. I caught up with him, and soon thereafter, we arrived at the brook.

Matthew dismounted. "Somewhere around here there's a cave where Otter buried some of Dull Lance's people."

"It's on the north side of the crick."

We splashed through the water and walked the far bank. Most of the terrain was too flat to accommodate a cave opening, but after backtracking to the west, we located the adit. Weeds and brush had almost hidden it from view.

"You gonna disturb the ghosts of those people?" I asked.

"No. I was just curious if we could find it."

I plopped down in the dirt and spooned a palm of cold, clear water. It tasted sweet. "You come up with anything yet?"

"The civilized thing is to go talk to Raven."

Was he being sarcastic? "I'll go with you. He's got to hear from me that there's no place in our lives for him, except maybe as a friend."

"No!" Matthew's word was so explosive, I looked up at him. "There's no place for him in our lives at all. Not after raping you and trying to bushwhack me."

"To be fair, he didn't know about us when he tried to do it to me that night. Until I gave it away when I thought it was you, that is."

149

"Why was that, again?"

"Horse apples, Matthew! I was asleep when he ... did that. I woke up thinking of you."

His raptor's eyes softened. "That's good, but that's also bad. He knows how it feels to make love to you, and he's determined to complete the act. There's another way, you know."

"How?"

"We could join a *tiospaye*. There are some still around. Then we could live as husband and wife."

Husband and wife. The terms jarred me. I hadn't thought of it like that. Was I womanly for accepting Matthew's physical love? "Is that still the custom among the bloods?"

He picked up a rock and tossed it into the shallow water. The ripples disappeared downstream in the blink of an eye. "Not so much anymore. The white man's infected us all. A lot of the People have gone to Jesus. Some are just doing and saying what's expected, but some take it to heart. Trouble is you never know which is which. The council might marry us, but a lot of people would mock us."

"According to Otter, that happened in the old days, too. But still, Two-Faces got respect."

Matthew ran a lean hand down his face. "I don't know. Maybe no one would be willing to marry us, but I'd feel safer there."

"There will always be Raven Strongbows ... even there."

"True. And there are too many whites among the tribes nowadays. Some in authority, others looking to see what they can trade or steal."

I watched Arrow crop grass from the prairie floor. Wind Rider drank from the crick. A hawk soared overhead and took a sudden dive toward something in the grass. All the Great Spirit's creatures were predators. Were we no different from the beasts? My heart felt like a lead ingot in my chest.

"So we kill him or we run away, is that it?"

He looked at me with such love that I almost swooned ... like a woman. Maybe there was some female in me. He gave his attention to twirling a long blade of grass between his fingers.

"Do you ever think about that preacher you killed?"

"All the time."

"How about the highwayman you shot?"

"Not so much. That was less personal."

He straightened his shoulders. "I think about the men I've killed. There was a Crow scout for Custer at Greasy Grass. He probably wasn't a bad man. And then there was one of the white soldiers who chased us after we left Fort Robinson. He may not have died, but he was hurt pretty bad."

"But they were trying to kill you."

He rose straight from the ground, effortlessly. "Does it matter?"

I stood beside him. "Yes, I think it does. I don't regret killing either of those men. They were evil." My words were rushed and perhaps not deeply felt, but I sought to ease his mind.

"Evil. Does that make it right? And Raven? Is he evil because he wants someone I find more desirable than anyone else on earth?"

I was on firm ground now. "If he tried to kill you because of his hankering for me, he's evil."

# # # # #

Finding Raven wasn't as easy as it sounded. We rode past the fort several times without spotting him, although we saw Crow off in the distance once. On the second day, I went up to the sentry box and asked for Raven. The private on duty told me the scout rode out with a patrol down south somewhere near the Little Islands.

Thursday morning, we arrived in town in time to see Gideon lead a large patrol out of town and up the stagecoach road toward Fort Ramson. He had both his scouts. Crow went south to cover their right flank. Raven crossed the bridge to cover the left from the north bank of the river. Both he and Crow would race to get ahead of the column, but that suited us fine. We put Arrow and Wind into a fast gallop on a more roundabout route.

Ten miles east of the fort, we turned south to the wagon trace and allowed the horses to blow. Soon we heard a pony. A minute later, Raven rode into view, his rifle propped on his thigh. Matthew's was in his saddle holster, as was mine. But we both had side arms handy.

Raven drew up and regarded us, looking every inch the proud Cheyenne warrior. Despite the coming autumn, he was dressed only in loincloth and moccasins. His long black hair flowed loose, fluttering in a breeze off the river.

His eyes fixed on Matthew and then moved to me. "Red Star. War Eagle."

"My name is Shambling Bear. It has always been Bear."

"What do you want?"

"What do I want? I want to kill you, but Eagle convinced me not to do that. Even though you tried to bushwhack me."

A slight smile played across Raven's lips. "I do not need Eagle's protection."

"Nor do you have it," I said. "You try to kill him again, and we will both be after you. Knife, gun. It doesn't matter, but we won't live under a threat from you."

"You suffer no threat from me." His pinto pawed the ground.

"Any threat to Bear is a threat to me."

"Don't you like two warriors fighting over you?"

"I would sooner have one as my mate and the other as a friend, but it is too late for that. You have destroyed that possibility."

"When Red Star is no longer around, I will take you as my *he man eh*. You will come to accept me."

"Never. My man is here at my side, and that's the way it will always be."

"I gotta get back to scouting. You gonna try to keep me from passing?"

Matthew rode to Raven's side. "You asked me a question once. Yes, I will fight for Eagle. And I'll not hesitate to kill you."

Raven kicked his pinto down the trail without once looking back.

Matthew watched the scout out of sight before splashing into the nearest walk across in the river. "He's up to something. Let's see if we can get a word with Crow. Maybe he knows what's in the Cheyenne's head."

Gideon halted the column as we approached. He waited until we were near before hailing us. Two troopers rode up and flanked him on either side.

"We were just headed to the Mead," he said. "Matthew, I'm sorry, but I have orders to arrest you and return you to the fort under guard. You've been identified as the fugitive, Red Star."

CHAPTER 17

The two troopers flanking Gideon disarmed Matthew. He put up no resistance, but had he done so, I'd have battled right alongside him. But to what end? There were twenty soldiers, at least.

"Who made this claim?" I asked.

"I was merely told to bring him back to the fort."

Crow rode in from the south to join us. He must not have known the patrol's mission, but he'd heard enough to grasp what was going on. "Lieutenant, maybe it ain't my place to speak, but I know this man since he was a fry. He was living right at the Mead all the time I was there."

"Thank you, Scout, but that doesn't alter my mission."

At Gideon's instructions, one trooper shackled Matthew's arms behind him while another grasped Wind's reins. The column wheeled about and reversed direction back toward the fort. I sat for a moment debating what to do. I wanted to ride at Matthew's side every step of the way, but I had to let Ma and Pa know what was happening. I turned Arrow toward home before realizing Turtle Crick was closer. Pigeons could deliver the message, allowing me to join Matthew at the fort.

As I bolted for the farm, my muscles spasmed at the sight of a horseman on the north shore watching like the trickster bird he was named after. As Arrow splashed across the river, Raven rode south along the wagon track. Did he hope to throw me down and take me like a woman? Well, he'd find out I was no woman. As my horse reached the far shore and labored up onto dry ground, the Cheyenne scout bore down on me.

Rather than run, I reined in. As he drew his pinto to a halt by my side, I launched myself from Arrow's back and thrust him from his saddle. We dropped heavily to the wagon road. He was stunned. I sat astride his chest with my knife blade pressed against his right eye.

"I should kill you for the coward you are." Spittle sprayed from my lips.

He struggled for breath. "I ... did it ... for you."

"Liar! You did it for your own selfish reasons. You've denounced the finest man I've ever known."

"Then kill me and be done with it."

"Words! Stupid words. You're a fool as well as a coward. What made you think I'd want you?"

He was recovering now, but he remained frozen. A flick of my blade would take out his eyeball. "You looked at me. And I saw where you looked."

That shook me. Had my careless eyes sentenced Matthew to death?

"When I made love to you," he said, "it was almost more than I could stand. I've been with a win-tay before … but never like that."

My hand shook so much he closed his eyes before I brought myself under control. "I got away from you as soon as I woke. I told you no, Raven."

"And I said I'd fight for you."

"By trying to bushwhack Matthew? By turning him in to the army? You're not a man. You're a yellow dog."

I stood and backed away. He rose to his feet. I felt as if scales had fallen away from my eyes. He was still handsome, yes. Achingly so … but he stood revealed as a jackanapes, a craven, conniving, no-account. "If you are a man, you will go to the fort and tell them you were mistaken."

I mounted Arrow and rode for the farm.

# # # # #

After sending a message to the Mead by two pigeons in case one was struck down, I took time to let Andre know what had happened. Then I headed for town to visit every merchant where the Strobaw family had been doing business for fifty years seeking the support of those who had known us as both man and boy. Only two, aside from Andre, lent any support — Caleb Brown and Timo Bowers.

I received a bitter lesson that day; one I should have learned at my father's knee. I was an Indian. Nothing more; nothing less. It didn't matter that I was educated. Or had European blood. Or that I was a landowner. Those were just adjectives in the white man's language. I was still an Indian. That was the noun. I wasn't even a citizen of this land that had belonged to my ancestors. What was it the Union general named Sheridan had said? "The only good Indians I ever saw were dead." And he'd been in charge of packing us onto reservations.

Nor did it matter that Caleb was the owner of the largest mercantile establishment in the territory or that Timo had done business with everyone in town or that Andre was a successful farmer. When Major Irons admitted us to his presence, he was inflexible. His duty was clear. A credible identification had been made, and he was obligated to act.

154

Despite his rejection of their entreaties, Irons gave Caleb every courtesy and Timo and Andre honest respect. He treated me as an irritant, although he did permit a visit to Matthew in the guardhouse after searching me for hidden weapons. Having just lately discerned my true status, I wasn't as stoic as Matthew about his situation.

He listened while I told him everything that had happened since I'd left his side. Then he asked what came next.

"Major Irons said they're going to transport you to Fort Robinson for trial."

"How?"

"They have a wagon with bars on it they haul prisoners in. Matthew, promise me you won't try to escape."

"At the first opportunity."

"Don't say that! Think what that would mean. You'd be a fugitive for the rest of your life. The army and every lawman in the countryside would be looking for you."

"That's better than hanging. At least I can die fighting."

I gave up trying to talk sense into him and told him I was coming to Nebraska with him. Now it was his turn to argue, but I held my ground. When it was clear I was agitating him rather than lending comfort, I rattled the cell door and called the guard.

"Raven will come for you now. You insulted his pride, so he'll rape you first and then kill you. Go stay with Andre tonight."

"No. I'll be where he can find me if he comes looking."

A corporal appeared, putting an end to talk. As I left the guardhouse, Crow was standing at the corner of the building.

"How is he?" He walked me to my horse.

"He's handling it so far."

"Was it Raven?"

I nodded. "Tried to bushwhack Matthew the other day. When we faced him down, he told the army Matthew was the man they were looking for. Red Star."

"I figured. Where are you staying tonight?"

"At Turtle Crick. Where's Raven?"

"Over in the barracks where the scouts sleep. It ain't nothing but a cabin, but you gotta call things the way the army does, so it's a barracks."

"Is he free to leave tonight?"

"He can get away. You worried about him coming for you?"

"He thinks ... uh, well ..."

"He's thinks he's got a hankering. He don't just think it, John. He's got it bad. Wants you like the rest of us want a woman. We've been known to kill for our doxies. Guess that kind ain't no different."

"Crow, can you get me Matthew's gray? I'm going to Fort Robinson with the detail, and I'll need a spare to spell Arrow."

"Be better if you asked Lt. Haleworthy. Somebody might accuse you of being a horse thief if I snuck him to you."

I looked up Gideon and made my argument for the horse. I told him flat out I was going along with the jail wagon and needed another mount. He argued before ordering a trooper to bring Wind Rider. After that, I set off for the farm.

When I arrived, I bedded down the two horses and went to inspect the progress the Maartens had made on the cabin. It was almost habitable. I went up to the hayloft to retrieve my blankets and found one of the gray pigeons with a message saying Ma and Pa would be in Yanube City tomorrow. They must plan on traveling most of the night.

After eating some jerky and a tin of peaches, I threw down my bedding behind the unglazed front window of the cabin. I slept fitfully with my long gun in my arms until something brought me awake. The sound of a hoof. Whoever was there hadn't come across the bridge, or I would have heard him earlier.

The moon cleared a low-hanging cloud as Raven slipped from his pony and stood with his back to me. As he stared at the barn, I lifted my rifle, sighted close to his head, and squeezed the trigger. He chose that moment to move so that my bullet must have scorched his ear. He dropped to the ground and twisted around.

"Don't shoot, it's me, Raven."

"I know who it is, you miserable coward. That shot was a warning. The next one will punch out your eyeball."

He got to his feet, his hands held out to show they were free of weapons. "Let me talk to you. Tell you of the love in my heart. You know the power of my loins, now let show you the beauty of my love. I have brought a love flute. I will play ..."

I threw a shot into the ground at his feet. Then another. And another. He danced backward, an oddly graceful maneuver. "Take your flute and get out of here, or by God, I'll kill you."

"Put away your anger and look inside yourself. Even after you knew it was me loving you, you didn't do nothing about it. You watched me finish, and we slept side by side the rest of the night. A man who didn't like what I done wouldn't let ..."

156

When I cocked the rifle, he strode to the pinto and regained his saddle. But he didn't give up. "I will be back, Eagle. I'll keep coming back until you're mine. I want to run my hands through that strange lightning hair. It excites me … even now. I want to hold you in my hands. Measure you against me."

My rifle roared again, and his horse drummed across the bridge. I went outside and watched for as long as I could see his indistinct form in the shadowed moonlight.

I couldn't sleep after that. What was the matter with me? Because I hadn't reacted with violence, both Matthew and Raven believed I had a weakness for the scout.

Around about dawn, I dropped off into such a deep sleep I woke with a start as Libby rode into the yard on Patch. I watched her jump down and go inside the barn. A few minutes later she threw open the loft's hay doors.

"Mr. John, you out there?"

I stood and waved. "Here, Libby."

"My dad says to come over and break the fast over some eggs and pork. He figures it's gonna be a long, hard day."

"I expect he's right. You go on, I'll be right behind you. How's White Patch treating you?"

A smile so wide it almost split her lips brightened her face. "He's the greatest horse in the world." As she scrambled out of the barn and took to the pinto's back, I hearkened back to the days when life was that simple for me, too.

Andre packed my belly with food and sent me on my way. I rode into town with a prickly feeling on my back. Timo came out of the forge and waved me down to ask if Matthew was all right. Everyone else I met pretty much turned their backs on me. As rude as my people thought the white man's stare was, I was now disconcerted no one would meet my eyes.

As I dismounted at the sentry box to request admittance, a wagon came down the street. My pa cut a striking figure: handsome, broad-shouldered, flat bellied with thick black hair worn loose. But I realized for the first time what people in town saw. Another Indian.

Ma sat beside him on the wagon seat, bright yellow hair spilling out from under her no-nonsense man's hat. Pretty. Even from this distance. They'd pay no more mind to her than they would Pa. She was nothing but a squaw woman. Why was dust falling from my eyes all of a sudden? Because it was time to grow up.

At least, Gideon showed my family some respect ... deference, even. He came rushing up as the wagon pulled to a halt and held out a hand for my mother. She accepted it as daintily as any Boston matron and stepped down into the dirt. Gideon got us in to see Major Irons in record time.

Irons was courteous enough to the Strobaws of Teacher's Mead, but when Ma demanded to know who'd denounced her son, he permitted a bit of impatience to show. Nonetheless, he sent for Raven Strongbow. His manners showed some strain after half an hour with no sign of the scout. Gideon, dispatched to see what the problem was, returned to whisper in his superior's ear. Irons went mottled as he sent for all the scouts.

Before long, three dusky men filed into the room, Crow at their head. I doubted this room had been so full of Indians since it was built.

"Where's Raven?" the Major asked.

"Ain't seen him this morning, sir." Crow paused before adding. "Pinto's gone."

"When did you see him last?"

"When I took to my bed last night."

Irons questioned the other two scouts, a Miniconjou Lakota about Crow's age from up on the Cheyenne River and another man I didn't recognize ... maybe a Mandan. Each denied knowing anything about the missing man.

"Dammit!" The Major muttered an apology to my mother. "I want him found. Found and standing right here in front of this desk. I won't tolerate desertion. You understand me?"

Since no one knew who he was addressing, everyone in the room shouted, "Yes, sir!" Except the three of us.

# # # # #

The major's orders were never carried out. Raven was gone ... vanished. I believe the commandant would have cried foul play had not the scout's belonging been missing, as well. The sentry was of no value in the matter because there were too many ways on and off the post without passing the guard box.

Had I convinced Raven he had no future with me? Had shooting at him done the trick? Somehow, I doubted it. After the major cleared us out of his headquarters building, I saw Crow and Pa standing beside the wagon talking. Nearby, Ma had Gideon by the sleeve asking what this latest event meant for Matthew. Gideon had no answers.

There was nothing more we could do today other than wrangle permission for a short visit with the prisoner. They allowed us to stand outside the guardhouse window and speak to Matthew through the bars. Ma almost teared up, but she stuck out her chin stubbornly and told him everything would be all right. Talking to Matthew through iron bars depressed all of us, including him.

# # # # #

We were a glum bunch sitting around a cloth on the Turtle Crick cabin floor picking at the meal Ma had put together. I chose that time to tell them what was going on, even confessing to shooting at Raven. I couldn't tell if the red spots on Ma's cheeks were from fear or outrage.

"That snake denounced your brother from personal pique."

She seldom called Matthew my brother. Was she trying to insinuate incest into what he and I held between us?

My father spoke up. "It doesn't matter, his motive. Whether he runs away or not, he's done this thing and set off these events."

"If he doesn't return," Ma said, "perhaps the Major will turn Matthew loose."

I shook my head. "We have to face the devil. The Major has had a credible identification of Red Star, so he'll send Matthew to Fort Robinson, gambling others will remember and identify him."

"Probably true," Pa said. "But maybe none of our kinsmen will inform on him."

"We can't rely on it. Matthew told me some of the Lakota at the Red Cloud Agency were jealous of Crazy Horse."

I elected to sleep in the hayloft and leave the partially finished cabin to my parents. As I left to turn into my blankets, Pa stepped outside. I took the opportunity to caution him to listen for Raven.

"No need. Crow Johnson told me the Cheyenne will not be returning. He sounded certain of his words."

I climbed the ladder to the loft in a daze. If what Crow intimated was true, would the discovery of Raven's body rebound to the favor or the detriment of the Strobaw family and Matthew Brandt?

CHAPTER 18

The next day was Saturday, and by the time we arrived in Yanube City, the town was crawling with farm families trading and buying supplies. We ran into the Killpennys at Brown's Emporium where Ma and Pa stopped to thank Caleb for trying to help Matthew. Our neighbors were shocked to learn of his plight. Min's eyes fixed on me. Was she writing Matthew off as a lost cause? Then she must have remembered the brief intimacies I'd failed to follow up because she asked after Alexander.

We wrangled permission at the guardhouse to see Matthew. His appearance left me with my chin hanging. He was wild-eyed and edgy. If this was his state after only two days in the jailhouse, I feared for him on the upcoming trip. Maybe he was right. He ought to take the first opportunity to escape that came along.

While Pa and I watched through the windows, Ma talked her way into the cell and sat with him on the little cot. Her presence settled him, but that would be transitory. She put her lips near his ear and spoke long and earnestly. Whatever she said, afterward he was calm enough to talk to us through the bars without appearing half mad.

When we were waved away by a guard, Pa and I went to see if we could catch a word with Crow. The scout let us know scuttlebutt had the jail wagon bringing a deserter from Fort Ramson and was due to pick up Matthew later today or tomorrow. Then it would head southwest to Fort Robinson.

Crow figured a stage could make the 200-mile trip in forty-eight hours, but the army prisoner transport wagon wouldn't have way stations to switch to fresh teams, so it was a five-day trip. Five days in an open wagon with iron bars as protection against weather and four nights locked up in the jail wagon or in some army guardhouse wouldn't improve Matthew's attitude.

Gideon told us Irons had telegraphed Fort Robinson and informed them the witness against Red Star had deserted, sparking a bit of hope. While we waited for a reply, the jail wagon arrived. The reinforced Conestoga had a small enclosed section behind the driver's bench. South of that sat an iron-barred cage with benches affixed to the floorboard. The roof was closed against the sun. Canvas gathered along the top could be released to drape over the cage as protection against the elements. A grim way to make a five-day trip. The prisoner locked inside was a hard-looking white man made even whiter by a layer of dust from the hundred-fifty-mile trek from Fort Ramson. According to Crow, he was a deserter.

At length, a grim-faced Gideon came outside to tell us the major had received a reply to his telegram. There were others at Fort Robinson who could identify the fugitive, Red Sky. Matthew was to be sent forward tomorrow morning.

I spent the rest of the day getting myself some paperwork. If the white world was going to look at me like an Indian, I didn't want to be some nameless wandering tribesman. Caleb Brown, Theo Tussler, Eric Maartens, and Timo Bowers joined us down at the local attorney's office to attest to my identification. Richard Bacon created an official looking document identifying me as John Jacobsen Strobaw, a quarter-blood Yanube with the earth name of War Eagle. The paper described my appearance in detail, down to scars on my arms and hand. These white men came up with the same description of my hair as most blood people: "A full head of black hair shot through with blond hairs, appearing as stars in the dark night."

The traveling photographer was still in town, so I have paid a quarter to sit for an image to put with the paper. To protect against the hazards of travel, the lawyer wrapped the document and my image in oilskin.

# # # # #

Ma loaded a pack with jerky and pemmican and tins of food while Pa saw to it I had ammunition and a little gold and silver — the latter hidden throughout my goods and on my person. We stowed Matthew's rifle and six-shooter — both recovered from his jailors — aboard Wind. My own pistol was snugged around my waist, and my Henry, with sixteen .44 caliber cartridges in the loading sleeve, was tucked in Arrow's saddle scabbard. After that was done, we said our prayers and headed for town.

We arrived in time to see Matthew, shackled at both wrists and ankles, loaded aboard the jail wagon. Ma and Pa didn't even have time to say goodbye before the driver popped his whip and the team of four horses started moving. Matthew saw us and raised his hand in farewell. I kicked Arrow into a trot, and leading Wind Rider by the reins, rode to catch up with the detail.

Ten miles out of town, the wagon rumbled to a halt, and a man with sergeant's chevrons on his arm stood on the Conestoga's bench and faced me. He cradled a shotgun in his arms.

"Injun, this here's an official army prisoner conveyance detail. You get on outa here. We don't need no company."

"This is a public road. I'm up to no mischief. One of those men in that cage is my brother, and I want to ride along to make sure he's all right."

"That killer's your kin, huh? Well, this here may be a public road, but the spot we're traveling belongs to the army. I catch you in range of this shotgun I'll consider you a renegade bent on breakin' his brother outa prison. I'm authorized by the military to shoot you dead if I figure I'm under assault. Now go on, get outa here."

"Sergeant, I'm a peaceful man and don't court trouble. But you can rest assured I'll be close by."

"Go on. Get on down the road."

"No, thanks. I'll trail along behind. Here, let me give you a peace offering." I sparked the sergeant's nervousness by reaching into one of my saddlebags and hauling out four small cans. Regretfully, they were the peaches packed in sweet syrup I liked so much. Nonetheless, I tossed them to the driver. "Two are for the prisoners."

The sergeant cursed some more as he sat down and prodded the driver to get started. The NCO watched over his shoulder as I allowed them a head start. Good. Hope he broke his damned neck. A possibility since the wagon wasn't slung on thoroughbraces like a stage. Every bump in the rough roadway rattled the spines of everyone in that conveyance. I remained within easy sight of the wagon for the rest of the day.

The two troopers surprised me by pausing for the night on the road instead of making for a town or an army post. They pulled to the side of the track at twilight and made camp. I unlimbered my long glass only to find the sergeant studying me through a pair of field binoculars. The driver was heating up a meal.

They had elected to halt in the midst of a broad, flat plain devoid of trees or brush of any meaningful size. I found a salt bush to provide some screen before settling down to a meal of pemmican and another precious can of peaches. Aware the sergeant knew my location, I waited until darkness before moving a distance on the other side of the roadway to spread my blankets and get some sleep without benefit of the warmth of a campfire. Such flames would have been welcome. The night had turned frigid.

In the wee hours, I left my hobbled horses and set off down the road by the light weak light of a quarter-moon. Near the wagon, I moved off the road and went into a crouch, covering the last few yards on my belly like a slithering serpent. Snorts and snores came from the area around the campfire. The two troopers. The sound of a rasping saw came from the portable cell. The white deserter.

A soft whippoorwill's cry told me Matthew was on my side of the wagon. He was awake and aware of my presence. As I moved into position, I grasped the hand he held out to me. He pulled me to the bars. His dry, cracked lips closed on mine. He was dehydrated.

Without a word, I removed the cap of my canteen and placed the vessel in his hands. When he'd had his fill of water, he handed it back. We froze as the trooper supposedly guarding against my slitting their throats stopped snoring and changed positions. A moment later, he resumed his night song.

Matthew put his lips to my ear. "Beloved." I thrilled to the word and nodded against his hand cupping my neck. "Get me out."

"No. I have a plan. You'll have to endure it to Fort Robinson." A violent shake of his head. "Have to," I whispered. "Or be a fugitive. Do you trust me?" A pause and then a short nod. "Then be patient."

I gave him a little pemmican to fortify the meal the soldiers had fed him before beginning the laborious process of returning to camp.

Before dawn, I moved my bedroll and horses back to the saltbush so the soldiers wouldn't catch on to my tricks, but it was wasted effort. After the jail wagon moved off down the road, I took a look around the area and saw boot prints. One of the soldiers, probably the sergeant, had sneaked up to my abandoned camp. Had he intended to hamstring my horses or do me in?

I mounted Wind before the wagon was out of sight and set out at an easy pace. A river lay before us a few miles in the distance. Would the wagon cross or remain on this side? Was there a bridge, a ferry, or a ford?

It was a ferry, and the jail wagon was halfway across the broad stretch of the Little Sioux River. My animals could swim it, but the effort would take a lot out of them. I'd wait until the ferryman returned to this side and pay my way across.

The distant figures talked on the south shore for a long minute before the wagon went on its way. To my consternation, the ferry didn't budge. I'd been out-coyoted. The sergeant had warned against aiding me across the river. Painted me as a renegade, I expect.

Before there were ferries, people had crossed the river by means of buffalo crossings, and those were often near the ferry stations because that is where the trails took prospective customers. This one lay half a mile downstream. The horses could walk a good part of the way, but there was one span of about fifty feet that looked deep and swift

As there was no evading it, I sent Wind splashing into the water while Arrow followed along behind. When the water reached the horse's belly, I slipped out of the saddle and hung onto the pommel as the gray swam for the far shore. I released my hold on Arrow's reins as soon as I was convinced he would follow.

Just when I grew concerned the current was taking us too far downstream, Wind got his feet on solid rock, and I eased back into the saddle as he walked up out of the water. Arrow, smaller and less affected by the current, regained the shore to my right.

I stripped and wrung out my clothing while the horses blew and regained strength. Dressed in damp pants and shirt, I checked saddlebags on both animals. Everything was soaked, but I'd dry things out as soon as I had the chance. The important thing was the oilskin had protected my identification paper and photograph.

I switched to Arrow's back and set off to intercept the wagon. Upon regaining the road, there was no sign the vehicle had passed. I'd been flummoxed again. The sergeant was smarter than I gave him credit for. He'd crossed the Little Sioux within my eyesight and arranged to force me to ford the river. Once he knew I was across, he'd returned to the north shore again and taken the road west, leaving me hornswoggled on the wrong side of the water. Tracks in the dirt confirmed the wagon had reversed course and returned to the river.

After hobbling the horses, I walked back to see the ferryman on the far shore sitting beneath a scrap of canvas he'd rigged as protection against the sun. I waited until he lay back on a pallet and pulled a hat over his eyes.

I went back to dig a pair of damp gloves out of one of the saddlebags, remove my gun belt and every other extraneous thing on my person except for my knife before returning to the river. The ferryman was just as I had seen him last. I gripped one of the guide ropes anchored to this side, wrapped my legs around the hemp, and began hauling myself across the river hand-over-hand.

Things went well for the first half of the distance. Upon reaching the middle of the river, the dynamics of the thing changed. I was now pulling myself up a sagging rope with my back to an armed man who'd most likely been warned I was intent on scalping him and stealing everything he owned.

Three quarters of the way across, my biceps were burning. Soon thereafter, my back began to strain. Chest muscles cramped so much I almost dropped into the river and swam the remainder of the way. Then my thighs started to lose strength. A sudden charley-horse almost brought a cry from me. Any minute, there'd be a shout of alarm from the ferryman. Still, I laboriously placed one almost numb hand in front of the other and pulled myself along until I bumped my head into the piling rigged to hold the ropes.

My calf muscles threatened to refuse, but I managed to lower myself to the ground without crying out. Then I had trouble keeping to my feet. It took a minute for my body to agree to obey my will. When I felt strong enough, I stole to the sleeping man's side and snatched the rifle from his arms. He came awake with a start.

The pudgy, balding man with long sideburns came to his feet with a wheeze. "Please, boy. Don't do nothing. Don't ..."

"I'm not going to do anything, you are. You're going to take me across to get my horses, and then you're going to bring me back."

He didn't seem to hear me. "My scalp ain't gonna do you no good. Look at it, no hair."

"No, but those side burns will make good ear muffs."

His button eyes grew to half-dollars. "Please! I got a family."

I poked his belly with the rifle barrel. "Get me across the river. Now!"

His short legs wouldn't carry him as fast as he wanted to go. He almost tripped getting to the ferry. But when we were aboard, and he gripped the tow rope to begin our crossing, his arms bulged with muscles, and his chest was full and hard. He might have appeared to be a frightened little man, but in reality, he was a frightened big man. Potentially a dangerous man.

Nonetheless, he wanted to be done with me, so he made a short trip of it. He waited for me to leave the ferry, but I poked him in the butt with the rifle and drove him ahead of me to the horses. Then I prodded him back to the river and had him shove off.

"How much is the fare?"

"Huh? What?" His pig eyes bounced around as he pulled against the rope. "Ten cents. Five extra for the horses. Just had one fare today, so I ain't got no money."

"I don't want your money. I'm no deadbeat. I pay my way."

He almost jumped into the river when I stuffed some coins down the neck of his shirt. Once the horses and I stepped off the ferry onto the shore, he pulled himself out into the current again. I smiled and lifted the rifle. He almost went to his knees before I pitched the long gun into the shallows where he would be able to retrieve it. He might lose some cartridges to a good soaking, but he'd be able to dry and oil the weapon without loss.

He was scrambling to reverse course when I mounted Arrow and rode east, trailing Wind along behind.

# # # # #

The pattern of the wagon tracks told me the driver was flogging his team hard. There were places where one or two of the wheels had left the road after hitting deep holes or washed out places. I'd not raised the jail wagon by the time a town loomed ahead of me around sundown.

I pulled up well outside of the settlement and considered what the sergeant would do. There was no sign of soldiers, but there might be a sheriff's or marshal's office in town. Would he try to set the local lawdog on me? Sharing a cell with Matthew for the night wouldn't be bad, but they'd keep me locked up until the portable jail was far down the road. If they found the gold and silver on me, they'd claim I was a thief. Where in the world would an Indian come by riches like that? I was no longer tethered to the world I thought I knew.

After a wide detour around town, I took refuge in a ha-ha, which sheltered me from the wind, yet was close enough to keep an eye on things. Exhausted after a hard day, I took time to change clothes before eating. After checking on my animals, I fell asleep.

A distant coyote woke me well before dawn. Gambling no one was keeping watch, I walked straight down the road into the darkened village. The place was a bugtown so small it had probably never even heard of gas lights. A lantern had been left burning in a store window. I found the empty army wagon beside the livery stable. The prisoners would be at the jailhouse.

As I started for the jail, the crunch of a boot sent me ducking into a darkened doorway. A man emerged from an alley onto the street. A badge on his chest glinted in the light of the lantern. Praying the glare of that lamp hid me from his sight, I stood stock still. He paused a minute before sauntering off in the opposite direction. I took a deep breath and headed around behind the jailhouse.

The back of the adobe building opened onto a small alley. The window had no glass, but the bars were hatched, some running up and down, and others running sideways. I sidled closer and made like a cricket serenading its mate. A moment later, Matthew's drawn features appeared. I poked my fingers through the bars and felt a thrill run down my leg when he sucked them into his mouth. Desire whipped through me with such force I almost staggered. "M … Matthew," I whispered low in my throat.

"It's all right." He spoke in a louder whisper. "No one here except the other prisoner, and he's snoring so loud I can't sleep."

"But there's a night watchman, so we need to be careful."

"Get me out of here, John. Use Wind and Arrow to pull out the bars or something. I can't take being penned."

"We're almost halfway there. Two more days and we'll be in Robinson."

"Maybe, but Sgt. Roscoe pushed the horses so hard today he might have to wait overnight for them to recover. Besides, when we get there, they'll just lock me up there until they get around to hanging me. I'd rather get shot on the run."

"Trust me, Matthew. Please."

"I do. But I'm going mad. I've never been locked up in a cage. It gets so bad sometimes I don't think I can take another breath. Get me out!" His voice rose dangerously.

"I know it's hard, but you have to stay where you are. I've …"

I hissed a warning and stepped back into the dark shadows. A moment later, the lawman stepped into the alley and paused to strike a Lucifer. A flame flared. He drew on a long cheroot as he squinted against the light. Then he dropped the match in the dirt and completed his circle of the building, giving the darkened window a quick glance as he went. Although he walked within an arm's length of me, he was blind to my presence. His night vision had been destroyed by the match.

Satisfied he was gone, I sneaked back to the window. "I've got some gold and silver on me, Matthew. When we get to Robinson they might not have any witnesses who know you. If they do, I'll buy some to deny you're Red Star."

His hands clutched my fingers again. "Sounds thin, but I'll hang on somehow."

"I've got to go before people start stirring, but here's some pemmican. My canteen and a can of peaches won't fit through the bars."

Moments later, I started to ease my way out of town. In less than fifty yards, a big dog stood in the street, barring my way. He growled low in his throat. His ears flattened. I slipped my knife from its sheath even though I didn't want to kill the beast. That would alert the sergeant I was here.

As the animal started to advance, I pulled some jerky from my pocket and tossed it on the ground. The dog snatched the meat from the dirt. His ears went up, and in the false dawn, his tail wagged a bit. Moving cautiously, I circled around the beast and tossed a second piece of meat down the street behind me. As he took off in pursuit of the tidbit, I headed the other direction. Before I'd cleared the last building at the edge of town, a voice called out.

"Who's there?"

CHAPTER 19

Heart thudding like my anvil hammer, I whipped around the corner and pulled my handgun. Pressed hard against the side of the building, I waited for the lawman to make his move.

"Oh, it's you, you sorry old hound. Where'd you find a piece of meat? Go eat it and leave me alone."

My organs were going crazy. I stood against wall until my eyes stopped swimming and my stomach settled. Then, staying clear of the roadway, I headed for the horses to pack my blankets and to saddle Wind. A stand of trees in the far distance signaled a rill or spring. I'd hole up there until the jail wagon passed.

After washing sweat from my face in a spring at the base of three stunted trees, I filled my canteens and tried to grab another few minutes of sleep. Waste of time. My insides were still churning. I watched from behind a screen of bushes as the wagon passed later. The sun was well risen, but it was still early when they rumbled down the road. I allowed them to get almost out of sight before mounting up.

The hot September morning passed slowly. I stopped when the wagon halted, taking these opportunities to relieve myself and restore the circulation in my extremities. Each time the wagon moved again, I'd switch horses to ease the burden on each.

A little after high sun, a low bank of dark fog rose ahead and to the left of us. A few minutes later, it became clear the roiling menace wasn't *p'o*. It was *shóta*, smoke. A ground fire. Tribesmen sometimes set them to refresh the earth, and *Wakinyan's* lightning often ignited them. The question was — did it burn on the far side of the river to the south of us or did it lie in our path?

Sgt. Roscoe had halted the wagon and raised his binoculars to figure that out. At a more distant remove, I allowed his conclusion to dictate my actions. The wagon started forward with a lurch, telling me the prairie fire was on the near side of the river. The wind in my face would bring the conflagration right at us.

I abandoned my strategy of remaining at the edge of Roscoe's sight. The sergeant would be too busy to watch his rear, anyway. I touched heels to Arrow's sides and set off at a lope straight down the trace. Before long, smoke swept across the landscape ahead of the fire. How far behind were the flames? My fear at the moment was for Matthew.

That wagon was wooden, except for the bars which would hold its prisoners inside the cage to be roasted alive.

The jail wagon plunged into the heavy bank of smoke and vanished. A minute later, a suffocating mix of smoke and ash raced over us. Although blind, Arrow thundered onward beneath the urging of my heels. Wind, began to pull on the reins, almost jerking me from the saddle. I halted. Coughing and gagging, I dismounted and splashed water from a canteen on pieces of clothing to use as blinds on the two horses. I soaked a bandana and pulled it over my nose before taking a set of reins in each hand and walking down what I judged to the invisible road.

When I perceived orange flames ahead, I mounted Wind, dug at him with my heels and urged the blinded animal straight at the wall of fire. Arrow gave me his trust and followed the pull of his reins.

As the heat became near to unbearable, the roar of flames grew so loud the horses could not hear my reassuring words. Wind fought me and reared, but I kept my seat. Through the billowing gray cloud, I saw a parting of the flames. The road! There was little fuel on the road. Perhaps we could make it through. *If* I could keep the horses from panicking. When Wind balked and refused to go on, I slipped from the saddle and led the animals toward the opening in the flames on foot.

There was little oxygen in the gasses whipping around us. I tried to breathe shallowly. Each breath seemed to sear my lungs. I prayed the ponies would not draw in these noxious fumes. Wind stumbled, but recovered. He tried to shy away, almost dumping me on the hot ground. I stayed on my feet and tugged. He took a step. Another. And he began to move. Arrow remained at my side.

When it got so bad I had to hold my breath, I tried to make a run for the opening in the flames, but my legs wobbled. Fighting panic, I continued apace as the roaring flames got nearer and nearer. Yes, there was an opening. Almost beyond my capacity to hold my breath, I picked up the pace, and then — in an instant — the flames were behind us. The smoke cleared, pushed free of us by the west wind. The hot earth smoldered, but at least, we could draw a breath.

I removed the blinders from the horses, but continued to lead them by the reins for some distance. When our surroundings were cool enough, I halted and used the rest of my water to bathe their eyes and coats to free them of hot ash. Both gentled at the treatment. After dousing my own face and eyes, I gave them a good inspection and judged us lucky. We had come through unscathed except for some minor blistering — unless there was internal damage. That I could not discern until I'd ridden the mounts a distance.

The jail wagon was nowhere on the road in front of me, so it must have survived the fire. Too concerned for their well-being to push the horses, I resisted the urge to canter and set off at a slow walk.

After about five miles, I topped a rise and saw the wagon halted on the road ahead. I turned back down the hill, dismounted, and walked to where I could watch with my long glass without exposing myself to the troopers' view. They were replenishing their water supply from a roadside crick. Sgt. Roscoe handed over a canteen to the white army deserter. He drank and then squandered the rest by pouring it over his head. Roscoe was slow in the doing of it, but he brought Matthew a refilled canteen.

While I had no wish for the army men or the other prisoner to see me, Matthew needed to know I had survived the fire. Judging the three whites otherwise occupied, I mounted the hill and stood in full view for a brief second. My mate spotted me and gave a small sign.

After the jail wagon disappeared over the hill, Wind carried me to the spring. I stripped and bathed in the frigid water while keeping a close eye on the horses as they drank downstream. If their internals were damaged, the cold water might agitate them. Neither showed any discomfort. I drank, changed into less smoke-heavy pants and shirt, and hit the road at a leisurely pace to allow the animals to recover their strength. Even so, I raised the wagon by late afternoon.

Sgt. Roscoe and his detail met up with a company-sized army unit at dusk and sheltered with them that night. I made no effort to contact Matthew, instead locating a coulee where I got a good night's rest. The next morning, I followed the wagon at a distance, and that is how the next two days went. As he got close to his destination, Sgt. Roscoe stopped playing cat-and-mouse and rode hard for the fort. He'd managed to cut one day off his journey.

# # # # #

Fort Robinson sat in a broad, shallow valley surrounded by hills and buttes and more trees than I was accustomed to seeing. Like Fort Yanube, it had no walls surrounding it. The Red Cloud Agency and its thousands of Lakota and Cheyenne and Arapaho Indians had moved from the North Platte River to this country on the White River back in '73. The U.S. Government established a military camp named after a dead Lieutenant Robinson at the agency in the spring of the following year. The fort was to protect the agency, they claimed. Hogsplatter.

Controlling the tribesmen after an Indian agent was killed was the real reason. In a few months, they had moved the camp a mile and a half to the west of the agency. Two years later, they renamed the post *Fort Robinson*. That had a permanent sound.

The army encampment might be but six years old, yet Crazy Horse's assassination wasn't the only stain on its reputation. In September of '78, just about a year ago, Dull Knife and 150 of his Northern Cheyenne fled north after being forced to relocate at the Darlington Agency on the Southern Cheyenne Reservation. After a long, difficult running battle with the army, they gave up on the effort to return to their homeland in Wyoming and Montana and headed for the Red Cloud Agency. Intercepted, they surrendered and were taken to Fort Robinson.

Despite months of negotiations, Dull Knife and his people refused the order to return south, so the military confined the entire band to a barracks with bars on the windows and withheld rations, leaving the Cheyenne without food or wood for heating in the midst of a bitter winter. On the night of January 9, 1879, the tribesmen broke out of confinement and fled. The army pursued the band, and over a period of days killed many of them.

After Crazy Horse's murder in 1877, the Red Cloud Agency was moved up on the Missouri in the Dakota Territory. Instead of thousands of tribesman who once inhabited the area, I saw only a few abandoned building and a half dozen tipis and lodges on the perimeter of the military fort.

While the jail wagon made straight for the flagpole flying the American flag, I headed for the nearest skin lodging.

I am not a particularly social man. Despite my blood and appearance, I have never been around many Indians, save my own family. Nonetheless, I spoke Lakota, so I dismounted and hailed a stout, dark man of about fifty in front of his lodge. His initial wariness vanished the moment I removed my hat and ran a hand through my hair. The sole visible physical inheritance from my Scandinavian mother — her golden hair sprinkled among my father's thick black ones — grabbed his attention. When I was a child, Otter had often run fingers over my scalp and noted that in the old days, my gold speckled head would have been big medicine. Perhaps it held some power now.

We shook hands Indian-style. His eyes remained on my forelock the entire time we exchanged identification and provenance. Buffalo Leg had heard of the Yanube and their massacre by the Americans almost thirty years ago. I thought of confiding my mission but decided to take this man's measure first. As he would take mine. That was why it was courteous to speak of small things before raising big things. He invited me inside the tipi where he introduced me to his wife, Sweetwater, and his son, Crow Hop. The younger man was a few years past my own age.

We had not gotten far into our get-acquainted-talk when someone outside shouted news of a blood captive brought to the fort in the army's jail house wagon. Some of the men, including Buffalo Leg and his son decided to walk over and take a look for themselves.

I held my tongue and went along with them. Both of Sgt. Roscoe's prisoners were already in the guardhouse by the time we arrived, but word was going around that *Wicháhpi Luta* had been captured. Discerning some puzzlement in the crowd, I played ignorant and asked Buffalo Leg who this Red Star was. The old man admitted he didn't know. In fact, no one seemed to know, but he must be a big killer because the army had gone to the trouble of bringing him all the way from the Dakota country where he'd been hiding.

Before long, we heard talk the army was looking for someone who could identify this murderer for them. Money was being offered to anyone who would step forward. That concerned me. Most of these people would not betray a brother for the white man's money, but as in any society, there were always a few who would.

Buffalo Leg and Crow Hop began to throw glances my way and expressed a desire to return home. Although I would have preferred to try and get a glimpse of Matthew, it was best to stay with them. Halfway back, they paused to engage me in conversation.

"They say the army brought this man in their jail from the fort that bears the name of your people," Crow Hop said.

These two men were not greatly infected by the white man's bad manners — as I was — but I didn't have a week to spend edging up to the subject, either. So I chose a path somewhere between. "Yes. I was there when they arrested my brother and put him in jail. He was denounced by a Cheyenne scout who was jealous over ..." I stumbled. "Over the favor of a woman."

"Women sometimes cause men to do bad things," Buffalo Leg acknowledged.

"So I came along to see if I could be of help to him, but the soldiers chased me off every time I came near."

"Afraid you wanted to shoot them and set him free, I expect." Crow Hop's attitude showed he would likely have approved of doing just that.

Buffalo Leg suggested I stay close to my brother and resumed his journey home. Concerned my story might have frightened them, I asked if I could return to their camp at nightfall. The old man assured me they would care for my animals and have blankets and a meal for me when I came back.

Because there were a number of tribesmen in and around the fort, I walked around to get an idea of the design of the place. It was not difficult to find the guardhouse and determine it was unapproachable by stealth. Discarding the idea of asking permission to visit Matthew, I moved around to stand in plain sight on all sides of the building, hoping he would see me through a window and know he was not abandoned.

I returned to Buffalo Leg's camp at sundown, and contributed a chicken I'd bought at the sutler's store on Robber's Row at the edge of the post. I hadn't known such traders dealt with anyone other than soldiers, but my coins were as welcome as anyone's. Now, my presence need not be a burden on Buffalo Leg's larder. Before we retired that night, the old man and his son asked a few more tentative questions. Even so, the time had not yet arrived for blunt talk.

The next morning, I returned to the fort and joined a group of young men sitting around talking and smoking. It was a mystery how these people survived. No one seemed to have any industry. They hung around the fort as if this was all that mattered in their lives. I sat where I had a good view of the front of the guardhouse.

Along about mid-day, the jail wagon pulled up to the squat, ugly building, and Sgt. Roscoe hopped down from the seat and went inside. A few minutes later, he came out again with a prisoner in shackles. I couldn't see who it was, but it was not Matthew. In short order, the wagon made its way out of the fort and headed east.

Starting a conversation among the young men about what would happen to the new prisoner, proved fruitless. They were more interested in gambling with a deck of white man's cards. I gave up and returned to Buffalo Leg's camp.

I wasted three more days talking to everyone about what was happening inside the fort. Several times I came close to entering the headquarters building to plead Matthew's case, but something held me back even though I was frantic over the state of his mental condition.

Early that afternoon my benefactor was ready to talk. "Put on your hat and come with me."

I covered my head and fell in behind him. He led me past a rotting building that must have once served as a storehouse for rations. Beyond that stood what probably had been the Indian agent's house. Our destination was a smaller house that also looked unoccupied. Nonetheless, a man sat in a chair on the front porch.

"This was *Mahpiya Lúta's* house before they moved the agency up on the Missouri. They call it Pine Ridge Agency now." There was a note of disapproval in Buffalo Leg's voice.

He led me up on what had been Red Cloud's porch and greeted the tallest man I'd ever seen. Standing in the presence of these two, I began to understand Matthew's attraction to the warrior's life. I respectfully removed my hat and caught the tall man's reaction. I started to replace it, but he waved for me to remain uncovered.

The stranger nodded to Buffalo Leg. "It is as you said. He has hair like the night sky. That will be my name for you. *Hin Hauipe Skan ...* Night Sky Hair."

"I am honored to accept it," I said.

Buffalo Leg introduced me to *Mihpiya Icántagye*, Touch the Clouds, a Miniconjou chief and a close friend of Crazy Horse. This man had covered the body of his companion with a red blanket as he lay dying on the floor of the adjutant's quarters near the guardhouse. The Miniconjou was aptly named. He must have stood seven feet tall.

"*Nitune he?*" he asked in the abrupt manner of a white man.

"My American name is John Strobaw. My natural name is War Eagle."

"Strobaw. You are kin to *Winkte Lúta?*" Touch the Clouds asked.

"The Red Win-tay? Yes, I was of his fire. My grandfather was Cut Hand, last chief of the Yanube. My father is Dog Fox, named Cuthan Strobaw by the Red Win-tay, his adopted father. I came from the Dakota territory to help my brother who was arrested by the army and brought here in their jail wagon."

"*Wichápe Lúta,*" Touch the Clouds said. "Red Star."

My heart sank. Here was one who could identify Matthew. I forgot my Indian manners and reacted like a white man. "His American name is Matthew Brandt, although his natural name is Shambling Bear."

The tall man nodded. "And his fighting name is Red Star. You told us why you came, but what do you want?"

"I want to take my brother home. They claim he's a murderer, but he's innocent."

"Who knows who is innocent and who is not? He rode with us, so he may have killed."

"To kill in battle is not to murder," I argued. "Besides, there are many who have killed white men in wars, but they are not arrested."

"You are right. Red Star was but a sapling when he rode with us. Nonetheless, he did ride and fight. His crime was to run away from the agency when *Thashunke Witkó* was killed. They sent soldiers after him and his companions, but he escaped."

"He told me Crazy Horse had tried to send him away, so when his chieftain was murdered, he left and made his way home."

The tall man looked thoughtful. "How do we know you are who you say you are?"

I reached into my shirt and pulled out Lawyer Bacon's document. "I have a paper a white man — a legal man — prepared saying who I am."

The Miniconjou studied the writing for a moment. I had no idea if he could read. He took a long look at the photograph and compared it with my own face before asking, "How much will you risk to free your brother?"

I didn't hesitate. "Anything."

"The army has two men who will identify Red Star. They are not of good standing with the People, but the whites do not care."

My heart plunged into my nether regions. "So there will be a trial?"

"Yes, but they are not ready yet. When the sun is midway to its high point tomorrow morning, these two men will identify Red Star in front of the guardhouse for all to see."

"Who are the witnesses?"

"One is a drunk, and the other grubs for money like the white men he serves. Cover your hair, and Buffalo Leg will take you home with him. He will have you at the guardhouse tomorrow. Be prepared to do as he instructs you. Will you do this?"

"Yes, sir." I clamped my hat down on my head. "I know why I'll take whatever risk is necessary, but why are you willing to help?"

"Young Red Star has done nothing that most of our men have not done. It is not right to point him out because he escaped and returned home. This I have argued before the Agent and the Army, but they have not heeded my words. I have something in mind, but it is a thin plan that might not work. Go now, and let me do what I must do."

"If one of the men is a money grubber, let me give you this." I placed a small gold coin in the tall man's hand.

CHAPTER 20

The next morning — a Monday by my calculation — Buffalo Leg suggested I dress in breechclout, moccasins, and hat before leaving for the fort. On the way to the guardhouse, we passed the adjutant's office where Crazy Horse had breathed his last. Buffalo Leg made certain we arrived well ahead of the expected crowd and took care to see we remained at the forefront. Touch the Clouds arrived and stationed himself at my side.

The crowd stirred like a herd of cattle shifting at midnight when a man with silver leaves on his shoulders arrived with an American in civilian clothing; Lt. Colonel Steffington, the fort commandant, and the Pine Ridge Indian Agent, respectively. They were joined by another officer, who Touch the Clouds said was the man assigned to defend Matthew — a Captain Hughes.

Soldiers with long bayonets affixed to rifles arrived with two Indians in tow. One had the loose-jawed appearance of a sot while the other looked like a red man wearing a white face, one twisted with avarice. Touch the Clouds confirmed they were the witnesses.

As a hot September sun rose over us, the guardhouse door opened, and two soldiers emerged with a shackled Matthew between them. My heart stuttered at my lover's appearance. His normally lustrous hair hung lank and matted. Wild eyes burned from his skull. Dark bruises marred his forehead. At his appearance, the crowd grew restless. The guards held them back with the knives on their rifles.

Touch the Clouds pointed to the pair of Indians between two troopers standing opposite Matthew and called out in a loud voice. "These men are not good witnesses. They are not men of standing."

"Are they not Lakota?" The colonel was a blond man with more than a touch of gray in his muttonchops. "Are they shunned? Outcast?"

"Nay, but they are not trusted. Their words do not come from straight tongues."

"As long as they are members of your tribe who were here during the time in question, then the identification will proceed."

Taking me by surprise, Touch the Clouds snatched the hat from my head and pushed me forward so that I was standing at the shoulder of the guard on Matthew's right.

The Colonel pulled the witness with the look of a drunk forward. The man stumbled. He was likely in that condition at the moment. "Tell me if you know this man?"

As the drunkard swayed and tried to focus, Touch the Clouds, now standing behind me grunted. "*Dho!*" The sot's gaze swiveled as he looked for the source of the exclamation.

"Answer me, Thomas Long Lip," Col. Steffington said with more than a trace of impatience. "Do you see the renegade, Red Star?"

The witness gave a loose-necked nod and pointed a shaky finger … at me. "I see 'im. Right there."

My stomach dropped somewhere down around my ankles. A sheen of sweat popped out on my upper lip as I remembered the question Touch the Clouds asked last evening. Did he plan to exchange me for my lover?

"What?" the Colonel exclaimed. "What are you trying to pull?"

"Tha's him. Right there. I 'member them stars in his hair."

"You straighten up and identify the proper man." Steffington's muttonchops bristled.

"Beg pardon, Colonel," Captain Hughes said, "but he made his identification."

"What do you know about this, Captain?" The senior officer's eyes smoldered.

"Just what you do. The witness identified someone other than my client as the renegade, Red Star."

"Take him away." The older officer beckoned the other witness forward. "You now, you tell me if you see Red Star."

The tribesman with the crafty look walked with a shuffle, as if his right leg was injured. Confusion replaced craftiness. His eyes focused over my shoulder a moment before he nodded at me. "That's him. I remember the star hair. That's how he come by his name."

The Colonel looked down his long nose and sputtered. "That's yellow hair, not red, you idiot. The man's name is Red Star, not Yellow Star." Steffington planted himself in front of me, panting so hard his breath fanned my cheeks. He'd had mutton and onions for breakfast. He reached up and rubbed my hair before examining his palm. He plucked a few hairs from my scalp and studied them.

The Captain stepped to his side. "I think under the circumstances, you should release my client. Your two witnesses have failed to identify him."

"As you were!" the older man barked and motioned to the guards. "Return the prisoner to the guardhouse. And lock up this other one until I get to the bottom of this."

Two privates hustled Matthew and me to the adobe guardhouse. A rank, sour odor clogged my nostrils when they shoved me through the door. The troopers took Matthew straight to a cell and removed his irons, but they held me in the anteroom where the jailer had a desk. Dressed in an apron and moccasins, I was practically naked, but that didn't keep them from searching me.

Rough hands probed my *thaghe*, my testes, and lifted my *che*. They stripped moccasins from my feet and searched for some sort of weapon hidden in them. They didn't find one, but they did discover the document prepared by Lawyer Bacon and the photograph in my apron. A short, powerful man wearing sergeant's stripes tore open the oilskin and glanced at the writing. He tossed everything on the desk and moved in front of me with fists planted on his hips. He was a hater. His bristly face displayed his character.

"You're the renegade Injun that followed Sgt. Roscoe all the way from Fort Yanube, ain't you?"

I kept my mouth shut. Moving so fast I didn't even see it coming, he buried his right fist in my gut. I doubled over. A grunt escaped me. I fought for air. The sergeant grabbed my hair and lifted me up to face him. I heard an animal howling. Matthew.

"Shut up, redskin," the sergeant said over his shoulder. He poked my chest. "You ... I ask you a question, you answer. Er you that Injun?"

"I ... followed the ... the jail wagon here."

"Jail wagon," he said with a sneer. "That's a genuine, official U.S. Army prisoner transport vehicle. How come you followed it?"

"Watch ... over my brother."

"That prisoner over there's your brother? Then how come that paper says your name's Strobaw. That ain't the name he give us."

I was able to breathe easier now. "Lived with us since he was six summers. Raised ... uh, like my brother."

"So you know he's Red Star."

"Don't know anything of ..."

I saw it coming this time, but that didn't make it hurt less. The blow left me hanging helplessly in the arms of the two troopers supporting me. My insides felt like something was busted. They dragged me across the room and threw me into the cell adjoining Matthew's.

Nauseous, I collapsed on the floor. It was all I could do to drag myself to a narrow cot covered with rough blankets.

As my eyesight cleared, I saw Matthew peering at me through the bars. From the glow in his dark eyes, he would have killed the sergeant if he could reach him. I tried to smile and let him know I was all right … an uncertain conclusion at the moment.

The burly sergeant studied my identification paper and wadded it up as if to discard it but changed his mind. He left the guardhouse, taking the document, my photograph, and his two companions with him.

The pain in my gut eased as I surveyed my surroundings. Four cells opened to the front room where a sentry could keep an eye on the occupants. Matthew and I were the only prisoners. He remained pressed against the bars closest to me, but I didn't go to him. We'd reveal ourselves for sure. Then they wouldn't need a trial to hang us.

"Are you all right?" Matthew's voice cracked.

"Be all right. Bruise. That's all."

"I'll kill that bigoted son of a bitch!"

"Cut out that talk. He give you that knot on the head?"

"And a couple more. Name's Hanlihan. He doesn't like it I can talk better than he can."

I tried to laugh, but it hurt my belly. "Then don't talk better than he does."

"What were you and Touch the Clouds trying to pull out there?"

"It's called confusing the issue."

"Hanlihan'll beat your head in if he catches you talking fancy like that. Otter shouldn't have educated us so well." He sat down on his bunk. "So what happens now?"

"They don't have any witnesses against you, so maybe they'll let you go."

"Maybe, but they have two who say you're Red Star. They'll hold onto you, and we're no better off. Besides, those two will say whatever Steffington wants as soon as he straightens them out."

"That captain. Does he have a spine?"

"He speaks his mind about the law book he's arguing out of, but he's got no power. The Colonel will run right over him."

Neither of us felt like talking. I longed to touch Matthew, but if I had, I risked losing control. As the light failed, the air grew crisp. A breechclout and moccasins didn't provide much cover. So I used the sour blankets on the cot. Somebody entered and lit a lamp, but he left again. I went to sleep hungry because nobody came to feed us.

# # # # #

The next morning, the guardhouse door opened admitting Hanlihan and two privates. He threw a shirt and pair of pants through the bars. "Git dressed like you was civilized."

I struggled to my feet and loosed the strings to my apron. When I was dressed in the baggy clothes, the sergeant opened my cell. The two privates grabbed me by the arms and pulled me through the door without bothering to shackle me.

Every step provoked a sharp pain in my belly, but I was determined not to let them know. Once inside the headquarters building, Hanlihan respectfully knocked on a door, opened it, and reported. As soon as he pushed me through the door, he was dismissed and instructed to wait outside.

Three men occupied the plain, stark room. The mutton-chopped Colonel sat behind an oak desk. The Pine Ridge Indian Agent and the Captain who handled Matthew's defense had positioned ladder-back chairs on either side of the senior officer so they had a good look at me. My wrinkled identification paper and camera image lay on the desk in front of Steffington.

"Who are you?" he asked without preamble.

"Just who that document says I am. My name is John Jacobsen Strobaw. I'm a blacksmith at Teacher's Mead fifty miles east of Fort Yanube. I'm also a landowner. I inherited a merestead from Major James Morrow. He farmed 240 acres on Turtle Crick seven miles north of the fort until he was murdered in June of '78."

"What are you doing here?"

"My brother was falsely arrested, so I came to keep my family appraised of his situation. As a matter of fact, I'd appreciate sending a telegram to ..."

"Not possible. Military traffic only."

"I informed Fort Yanube of my intent before I left. I also tried to explain to Sgt. Roscoe, who was in charge of the prisoner transfer, but he chased me off with a shotgun. I held back far enough, so he could see I was no threat until we arrived here."

"Your brother, you say? Red Star is your brother?"

"I don't know a Red Star, sir. Matthew Brandt was orphaned when he was six years-old and brought to Teacher's Mead. My parents raised him as one of our family. He's my brother, Colonel, as surely as if my mother had borne him."

"What's his Indian name?"

"Shambling Bear."

And yours?"

"War Eagle. That's what we call ..."

He waved a hand in the air. "Yes, yes, I know. That's what you call a golden eagle. But that's not what Touch the Clouds called you."

"No, sir. When he saw my hair, he named me Night Sky Hair."

The Colonel took me through my activities since I'd been in the Fort Robinson area. He displayed particular interest in how I knew Buffalo Leg and Touch the Clouds.

After I explained, the agent spoke up. "I told you to get rid of the Indians hanging around the fort."

Steffington shot eye-daggers at him. "They serve a useful purpose now and then." He turned back to me. "How did you manage to get my witnesses to identify you as Red Star?"

"I didn't manage anything, sir. I'd never set eyes on those two men before they nearly stopped my heart by saying I was someone I wasn't." I cleared my throat. "But it seems like the important thing is they misidentified me as this Red Star fellow."

The Captain stirred in his chair. "He's hit it right on the head, sir. *Both* witnesses identified a man we know can't be the fugitive. You've confirmed that by wire with Fort Yanube. I believe it's time to release ..."

The Colonel's complexion flamed. "Not so fast, Captain. I'm going to get to the bottom of this. Those two witnesses correctly identified Brandt as Red Star just the day before. I want to know why they changed their testimony."

"I'm not so sure it was proper ..."

"Don't lecture me on proprieties, young man."

The Captain stiffened in his chair. "I wouldn't presume to do so, sir. But I assume you'll allow me to be present any time you question the witnesses."

If anything, the older officer got redder in the face. With any luck he'd burst a blood vessel, and we could go home.

Hanlihan no sooner got me back to the guardhouse than he let me know it wasn't over. The same two privates held my arms while the sergeant planted his feet in front of me and let go with a right. To the belly again. My lungs lost air. I had trouble getting it back again.

Matthew started howling until one of the guards walked over and took a swing at him with the butt of his rifle. Matthew backed up against the back wall and started screeching again. Hanlihan gave me another vicious punch and then held me off the floor by the hair of my head while the two privates opened Matthew's cell and clubbed him unconscious. If I'd been able, I'd have taken up his howling, but I was having trouble getting enough oxygen for breathing.

"All right, boy, you ready to tell me how you got to Thomas Long Lip and Walks-Crooked?"

"Wh ... who?" I wheezed.

He fired a short one right to my heart. "Don't go dumb on me. The witnesses against your friend over there."

I leaned against him and tried to hold onto consciousness. "Never saw ... until yesterday."

He hit me again, but it didn't matter much because I was already blacking out.

I came to sprawled on the floor of my cell. The first thing I saw was Matthew's worried face as he pressed against the bars.

"Are you all right?" he asked.

"Damned if I know. You?"

"Sore head. Move, man. See if everything works."

It was all I could do to turn over and get to my all fours. Standing was beyond me, so I crawled to the bunk and levered myself up. Then I lurched over to Matthew. He steadied me with hands through the bars. Hanlihan and his thugs were gone for the moment, so I leaned my forehead against his and drew strength from his touch.

Matthew heard boots on the porch and shoved me toward my bunk. I managed to collapse on it without sliding to the floor. A trooper, one of Hanlihan's pet privates, brought tins of something that was supposed to be food. He lit the lamp and left.

Whatever was on the plate was nearly inedible. I shoved it aside.

"*Yuta*," Matthew said. "Eat. Keep up your strength."

I forced it down and had a fight with my sore stomach to keep the mush from coming up again. Nobody lit the fireplace in the anteroom that night, either. I managed a little sleep anyway.

#####

The next morning, as I listened to reveille and the formation calls, the iron bars in my cell seemed to be closing in on me. I was about to ask Matthew if a man ever got over that feeling when Hanlihan opened the door and stepped aside. The Colonel and the Captain entered, followed by Touch the Clouds and Buffalo Leg. Then the two false witnesses were shoved into the room by guards and placed in front of the cells. The one called Thomas Long Lip looked drunk. Walks-Crooked just seemed frightened.

The Colonel's voice echoed around the room like icy thunder. "Now, has anyone intimidated you or threatened you to influence your identification?"

Long Lip just stared with his mouth gaping. The other one shook his head. "No, sir."

"Then, for the last time, tell me which one is the man called Red Star? You there, Thomas Long Lip, which one is he?"

The drunken man glanced back and forth between Matthew and me, looking more confused by the second. After a moment, he turned to Sgt. Hanlihan. "Which one was it you wanted me to say was him?"

Hanlihan was a man of heightened color, and his anger rose up out of his collar. The Colonel turned on his NCO, muttonchops standing out straight.

"What does he mean, Sergeant?"

"Don't know, sir."

"Why don't we ask Thomas Long Lip?" the Captain said. "Thomas, did ..."

"Just a minute, sir!" Hanlihan's eyes danced dangerously. "You can't believe nothing this drunk says."

"Exactly what I've been arguing all along," the Captain said. "Nor the other one either." He turned back to the witness. "Did Sgt. Hanlihan tell you which man to identify?"

Long Lip nodded. "But I don't remember which one he said."

"Sergeant, outside!" The Colonel started for the door.

"Just a minute," the junior officer said. "Brandt, what are those bruises on your head?"

Hanlihan was so agitated he almost darted between Matthew and the Captain. "He was putting up a fight, so we had to subdue him."

"What was he doing out of his cell?"

"A call of nature, sir."

"Why? He has a slop bucket. I see it underneath the cot." The captain turned to me. "How about you?"

I met the red-headed sergeant's hate-filled eyes as I lifted my shirt. A grunt issued from the Colonel as he saw the angry bruises. He spun on his heel and marched out the door yelling for the sergeant to follow. Long Lip and Walks-Crooked vanished without a sound.

The Captain went out, leaving Touch the Clouds and Buffalo Leg standing in the anteroom. Both were stern-faced, but I saw a glint of satisfaction before they turned and followed him outside.

"I know Touch the Clouds, but who's the other one?" Matthew asked when we were alone.

"A decent man who helped us when we needed it. His name is Buffalo Leg."

"How you figure they got the witnesses mixed up?"

"My hair. I think they got the one called Long Lip drunk and kept talking about the stars in my hair. The other one got confused and followed Long Lip's lead, or else they bought or threatened him."

Before we could say more, the Captain returned with a Major, a medical man who examined both Matthew and me. He claimed we'd recover and had us locked away again.

When we were alone, Matthew asked if I was sure I wasn't busted up inside?

"You sure your brains aren't broken like an egg yolk?" I came back at him.

We laughed aloud. Not because it was funny, but because there wasn't much else we could do. It set my insides aflame again and probably gave him a headache.

"I love you, John," he said in English.

"I'm *Wanbli* now. And I will be until we get home. And Eagle loves Bear ... *Mathó* ... something fierce. Come over to the bars, and I'll show you just how much."

"Never know when they're going to come in. Besides, I haven't put water to my person since they locked me up. My smell would turn your stomach."

"I'm not much better. Oh, Bear, I'm getting hard for you just thinking about it."

"I'm in the same shape, *Wastelahapi*. But I don't dare come over there. I'd lose control."

Calling me "Beloved" set my groin aflame. "Iron bars might inhibit you some."

"Maybe, but I can think of a couple of ways."

The mental image got to me, and I laughed again, which made me cough. That hurt, but there wasn't any blood. Maybe the doctor was right; nothing was seriously wrong.

Then Matthew brought me back to reality. "How's this thing gonna end?"

CHAPTER 21

We sat in our own stink as the fort come alive the next morning. Thursday, if I calculated right. My unwashed flesh bothered me more than my aching gut. We dreaded Hanlihan's arrival, yet he was our sole contact with the outside world. He didn't appear at his usual time … a mixed blessing. A hullabaloo outside the guardhouse about mid-morning left us feeling helpless. Several shots close at hand increased our anxiety.

No one had come to check on us until a private I'd never seen before arrived with two tins of food around the noon hour. We'd no sooner wolfed down the boiled beef and potatoes than he and another trooper brought containers of warm water and bars of soap. As soon as they left, we stripped and turned the bathing water black with grime. The two men returned to sluice us with buckets of fresh water — cold this time. I felt near to clean again. Our spirits rose with the bath.

"Do they clean a man up to hang him?" Matthew quipped.

# # # # #

Halfway through the afternoon, the guardhouse door opened again to admit a peaked-looking Capt. Hughes with his left arm bandaged and hanging in a sling. The medical man who'd examined us yesterday was with him. No one volunteered information as the sawbones gave us another going over and confirmed we weren't seriously or permanently injured in some way.

I noticed how skinny Matthew was. His breadbasket was almost concave. His system had eaten up all his fat and started devouring muscle. I hadn't been in the army's tender care as long as he had, so I wasn't in such bad shape.

Buffalo Leg and Touch the Clouds entered as the medic departed. I was almost as happy to see the clean clothes they brought as I was to see them. A pair of my pants fit Matthew, but one of my shirts hung on his reduced frame like a tipi skin. Still, he acted like they were New York opera clothes.

After we were dressed, Capt. Hughes told us we were free to go. As the officer started leave, I asked for the return of my identification paper and something saying Matthew was clear of the charges.

He paused on the threshold. "No charges were filed."

"Doesn't matter. The whole territory knows he's been accused. He could spend the rest of his life getting hauled back to the army's guardhouse. We need a paper."

"There isn't a paper." He didn't have muttonchops like the colonel, but if he had, they'd have been standing out straight. Looking ill, he hitched his left shoulder like a man in pain.

"Then create one," I said. "Captain, I'm not trying to be a hornet in your beehive, but this is important. Give us something that says Matthew's free."

Hughes sagged into a chair at the desk and ordered one of the privates to bring him pen, ink, and some official Fort Robinson stationery. "And Mr. Strobaw's identity paper. It's in the Colonel's office," he added.

I chomped down on the urge to ask what had happened to his arm. When the enlisted man returned, Hughes passed Lawyer Bacon's paper to me – together with my photographic likeness – rested his left elbow gingerly on the desk, and started writing. At length, he sat back and reviewed what he had written before signing the paper with a flourish. The he handed over a document bearing witness that while Matthew Brandt, a Teton tribesman who also went under the name of Shambling Bear, had been detained and questioned over being a fugitive follower of Crazy Horse named Red Star, no evidence had been presented to support this claim. After a due and deliberate investigation, Matthew Brandt (Shambling Bear) had been released and was free of suspicion.

After thanking the Captain, I folded the document and stored it with mine inside my shirt. Then we trailed the others out into the bright sunlight. I blinked several times before my eyes adjusted enough to see Buffalo Leg had both Arrow Wind and Wind Rider saddled and waiting. He and Touch the Clouds mounted their animals as Matthew and I climbed uncertainly aboard ours.

Touch the Clouds led the way to what had once been Red Cloud's house and dismounted. We sat on the porch around the Miniconjou's chair and remained silent while he considered what to say.

"There was trouble over at the fort this morning. Sergeant Hanlihan got his stripes cut off for beating you." He gave a dry laugh. "Most likely, for messing up Steffington's plans. Hanlihan's a skunk. A lizard. He went outa his head and threatened the Colonel. When Steffington said he was throwing him in the guardhouse with you two, Hanlihan lost whatever brains he had. He pulled his handgun and started for the guardhouse." The tall man paused. "He was gonna kill you. Hughes stopped him, so Hanlihan shot him. That's why his arm was wrapped up like that."

Matthew and I looked at each other.

"Then Hanlihan stole a horse and run off into the buttes. They sent a patrol after him, but they lost him. He might be mean and crazy in the head, but he's a good at soldiering."

I nodded. "So that's why they let us go. They didn't want to be responsible if he snuck back and shot us through the bars."

"That's the way I figure it," Touch the Clouds said. "The medical man ordered Hughes to bed after he patched him up. But the Captain said he had to do right by his client first. He's a good man."

The Miniconjou's judgment drew murmurs of agreement from us.

"Here, this is yours." He held out a hand holding the gold coin I'd given him.

I closed his long fingers around it. "No, it's yours. I'm sure you can do more good with it than I can when the winter comes and rations grow scarce."

"It will be well used. I swear this to you."

"I found more of the white man's money in your bags while I was looking for clothes for you to wear," Buffalo Leg said. "So I took some to buy stores from the sutler." He held out a bag.

I accepted it and rummaged around inside for a coin comparable to the one the Miniconjou had. "Use it for your family."

Touch the Clouds cleared his throat. "You are both men to make your own decisions, but maybe you oughta rest here till morning. You can take a sweat bath and get rid of all them jailhouse poisons before you leave. I'm gonna throw my blankets down at my old friend Buffalo Leg's lodge tonight. Tomorrow I go back to the Cheyenne River Agency."

On impulse, I spoke up. "Touch the Clouds, are you part of the council at Cheyenne River?"

The tall man nodded. "I sit on the buffalo robe. Why?"

I got up off the floor. After giving me a puzzled look, Matthew stood beside me. "We don't have councils at Yanube for me to acknowledge this man as my husband. You're as close to one as we can get, so we want to declare our marriage before you in the old way."

Touch the Clouds nodded. "Then so be it. Buffalo Leg and me are honored to witness for you. Is this your true will, Shambling Bear?"

I'd expected to feel a modicum of shame at such a personal moment, but my heart swelled so big it cramped my chest as Matthew answered.

"Yes. War Eagle is my other self."

The two Sioux elders stood and joined hands with us. "Let it be as you want. Be good to one another. Eagle, don't get jealous when your husband takes another wife. Be faithful and obey him in all things," Touch the Clouds said.

Somehow I didn't think that was the way it was done in Billy's time, but the simple words made Bear happier than I'd ever seen him, so it was enough. Our two friends told us where to meet them on the White River for the sweat bath early the next morning and withdrew. Bear grinned and led me inside the dusty, drafty house before clasping me to his breast and kissing me on the lips.

"I felt that right down in the *thaghe*," I said. "Was what I said to them all right?"

"It was good. Now there's one place on Turtle Island we're not hiding our true selves."

My belly and sides were sore, and Matthew's head still ached, so it was a crippled up pair that made love in Red Cloud's old cabin that night. Bear reciprocated again and about drove me mad with his mouth and tongue on my hard rod. Before I could warn him, I climaxed. He stayed with me until I lay back on the blankets panting.

He came up to face me, his teeth gleaming in the darkness as he smiled. "Did I do it as good as Timo Bowers?"

"Timo was a thing of my boyhood. That was a thing of my manhood. I hadn't truly made love to anyone until that day in the glade on the south side of the Yanube. When you warned me what was going to happen, I almost ran away."

"Do you wish you had?"

"No. I found my man that day. An *ozuye*, a warrior who gave me the gift of wisdom about myself along with his seed."

"Hah! Now I will impart a little of my wisdom and a lot of my seed. I have enough stored away to keep you busy all night."

He turned me on my stomach and toyed with my nether regions until I quivered with anticipation. Then he moved between my legs and probed with a member slick from magic excitement fluid. I was so hungry for him that the solid bulk of his cock inside me made me feel safe. He lay motionless for a long time before moving. Slowly. Gently. Faster. Harder. As he grew wilder, the pressure of his body fired up some of my aches, but they were acceptable. I knew not what gave me the greater rush … the pleasure of his great cock stroking my insides or the knowledge this was what he desired above all else.

# # # # #

A hint of autumn rode the morning air as we rose with the coming sun to partake of a meal of *papa*, dried meat. Then it was time to meet Buffalo Leg and Touch the Clouds on the river. We packed our plunder aboard the horses and headed toward a thin column of smoke in the distance where Buffalo Leg was preparing the medicine lodge.

Touch the Clouds spread out a robe and put each of us in one of the four cardinal directions to conduct the medicine pipe ceremony. I took but a shallow pull when my turn came.

While Touch the Clouds chanted a prayer to the morning, his friend went to scoop rocks heating over a fire into the *themni*. When the tall man's voice fell silent, Buffalo Leg called to say the lodge was ready to receive us.

We stripped and entered the bark structure in proper order. Our seniors entered first, and then Matthew preceded me as the husband of our new household. My nostrils, indeed my head, seemed to open up to the medicine heat.

As Buffalo Leg sang Lakota songs, mental toxins in my brain loosened like phlegm to join poisons of the flesh flushing away in a river of sweat. Would Berglund be washed away and leave me in peace? Would guilt over my unintended complicity in Otter's and James's deaths depart, leaving me pure again — just as the Blessed Jesus promised in exchange for simple belief?

When the prayers ended, we talked of many things. My mind saw the great battles of the past — Greasy Grass, Rosebud, Powder River, Tongue River — in word pictures painted by some of the participants. During the telling, my eyes were opened. My husband was accepted as a warrior by these two veterans. My heart could scarcely contain itself.

Talk turned to the Yanube country. The two Lakota knew of the *tiospaye* in great detail and surprised us with familiar talk about Yellow Puma, Cut Hand's father, Cut Hand, himself, and Billy Strobaw. Both knew of River Otter and his fate. The talk was good.

Just before I died of suffocation, we left the lodge for a quick, cold dip in the White River. I am not sure which bothered my sore ribs and belly muscles more, hot steam or frigid water.

As we made ready to start for home, Buffalo Leg handed Bear a plain, wooden flute and advised him to play a heap of love songs to me. He also counseled Matthew to beat me only when necessary. Honest advice or sly tickling?

We thanked our two friends and turned east to catch the road, aware of how changed were our circumstances since coming this way eight days ago. Eight days. It seemed more like eight weeks. Being penned up in an iron cage distorts a man's sense of time.

On this return journey, I ignored sore belly muscles and took time to admire the beauty of the land. Had it not been for our family worrying about us, I would have dallied to explore new country. Even though Captain Hughes had promised to telegraph Fort Yanube with news of Matthew's exoneration and our release, that message would not reach Ma and Pa unless Gideon had an opportunity to visit the Mead, or Crow remembered to ask Andre to send a messenger pigeon.

Bear did not appear to share my pleasure in the travel. His headache had abated, but he withdrew within himself, causing me anxiety until he finally spilled out what was eating at him.

"We may not yet be free of trouble. Now we have to go home and deal with Raven Strongbow."

"Nay, I think not." I told him of Crow's talk with Pa.

"So the rapist is dead?"

"I don't know that. Crow just said he wouldn't be a problem from now on. That could mean he's dead, or that the scouts chased him out of the territory."

Bear pursed his lips. "I'll ask Crow when we get home."

"He'll not answer, but he'll be so positive about Raven you'll lose your long face."

"Long face? You're thinking of the long *che* I used on you this morning."

"That inchworm?" I laughed and kicked Arrow into a lope for a short distance. Behind me, I heard the shrill notes of a flute. He played it little better than I did. Nonetheless, the breathiness of the tones aroused me in my stones. Moments later, the notes faded into silence, leaving an imagined echo of death and resurrection.

Matthew caught up and gave me a mischievous glance. "You ever stop to think we're jailbirds now? Can people can tell by looking?"

"I hear tell every blood in the territory's seen the inside of a clink. So yes, they'll know."

We did not push the pace, but both Arrow and Wind were fat and anxious for exercise, so we made good time. By that afternoon, the landscape was beginning to look more like the prairie at home. Bear, riding to my left, began speculating on who he would take for his second wife. He was teasing, but the mere thought of sharing him with another soured my mood.

He saw the change in me and reached across to place a hand on my left thigh to restore my humor. He achieved his goal. He continued to look straight ahead, but he knew my yard was responding. He cupped my growing groin.

Then he crashed against me, startling Arrow and nearly unseating me. I cried aloud and almost missed the boom of a gun. Leaning low over Arrow's neck, I reversed direction. Bear lay motionless on the road, his head bloody. A panicked Wind Rider raced down the trace.

I snatched my rifle from its scabbard and threw myself out of the saddle just as the unseen weapon barked a second time. I had no clear idea of where the shots were coming from, but the jumble of rocks a hundred yards to the left was the probable ambush spot. Would the bushwhacker shoot the horses and leave us shanks mare out here to land in a shallow grave? A slap on my buckskin's hindquarters sent him down the road after Wind. Neither horse would stray far.

Realizing I was exposed, I dropped to the ground. This time my eye caught a muzzle flash in the rocks. A bullet sang through the space where I'd stood moments before. Afraid to go near Bear lest I draw fire to him, I wiggled my way to a depression on the south side of the road. As the bushwhacker loosed a rain of bullets, I tried to burrow into the earth.

Who would do this? Road agents? Hanlihan? If it was the busted sergeant, why would he hang around to take pot shots at us? Did his hate run that deep? Even if the answer was yes, it still made no sense. How did he know we'd been released? What did it matter? Matthew … Bear was what mattered. Was he dead? Unconscious? I needed to get to him, but I was penned down.

Every fiber of my being cried out to throw caution to the wind and make a run for him. But even now the ambusher probably had his sights pointed straight at where my head had disappeared. Unless he was riding down on us to finish the job. I snatched a quick look. No one was racing toward us. Neither did he shoot at me. I rolled to another small depression closer to where Bear lay. Again, no shot.

Puzzled, I risked a longer look. Nothing stirred in the rocks. Movement down the road drew my attention. Arrow was trotting back toward me. Wind followed a distance behind him.

A rider appeared at the edge of the rock pile and answered my questions. The blue-uniformed man *was* the disgraced sergeant. But the roan's heavy limp told me why Hanlihan set up the ambush near the road. He needed a healthy mount. And what would be better than a horse to a fugitive? Two horses and more weapons.

I sprawled in the depression and rested my rifle on the lip. Nervous, it was hard for me to sight. I forced myself to be calm until the sergeant was well clear of the sheltering rocks. Was Bear bleeding to death while I stalked his killer? Couldn't be helped. I quelled my rising anxiety and held to my purpose. Dead, I was of no use to Matthew.

When the limping horse was halfway down the slope on what appeared to be flat ground, I fired. The animal screamed and pitched on its side. Hanlihan was pinned. No, he pulled free. Cursing in frustration, I tossed two shots after him as he grabbed his carbine from the dirt and crawled around behind the animal's body.

While he was distracted, I raced to Bear and jerked him off the road into some bushes. He groaned, so he wasn't dead. As soon as we were in a sheltered place, I took a quick look at him. An ugly furrow cut the flesh across his forehead. A bullet strike or a concussion from a near miss? Moving him had started blood flowing again. A bandage of cloth ripped from my shirt restrained the flow somewhat.

That done, I turned my attention to the fallen pony uphill of us. No portion of Hanlihan was visible. He wasn't there any longer. He'd seen me go for Bear, and instead of trying to shoot me down, he'd moved his position. Had he gone for the horses? I muttered under my breath. By waiting to kill his mount, I'd allowed him to halve the distance between us.

Abandoning my mate for the moment, I backed down the hill and took the most sheltered route east where I'd last seen the horses. As I darted from brush to rock to the occasional tree, I expected to hear the crash of a rifle and feel the shock of a bullet. But everything was quiet except my nerves. They were jangling. I spotted Arrow and whistled to him. His head came up and his ears whipped around … but not toward me. Hanlihan! He was close.

I charged up out of the small ravine straight for Arrow and saw Hanlihan on the opposite side of the road gathering himself for a rush to the pony. The man seemed to be limping. He saw me just as he moved and threw himself sideways, raising his carbine as he went. I didn't have time to react, but his abrupt motion caused him to miss.

Both horses bolted, running between the two of us down the road toward Bear.

I dropped to the ground and caught sight of Hanlihan scrambling to get on my side of the road. I swung my rifle around and fired. The sergeant jerked sideways and rolled in the dirt. But he wasn't finished. In seconds, I was scrambling backwards into a depression as bullets sang over my head.

I backed down the ravine toward Bear and the horses, equivocating. Hell, I wasn't a warrior. I was a farmer. Maybe Hanlihan was wounded unto death, or perhaps he was only lightly injured. But my mate needed my aid.

Bear was conscious but helpless. His eyes focused when he saw me. He demonstrated some sense, but it deserted him shortly thereafter. I located the horses and gathered their reins without spooking the nervous animals. Once they were in the brush with Bear, I laid his rifle on his belly and took up a position to consider our situation. I might not be a warrior, but I was a hunter and knew how to track game.

On the other hand, if we started back for the fort where there was a medical man, Bear's wound could be treated by tomorrow morning. Not only that, we'd leave an injured Hanlihan stranded far behind without any way out except to walk. Or ambush someone else.

The sergeant made the decision for me. A bullet tore through the brush beside my head. I hugged the ground. The terrain was clear for a hundred feet, so he had to be in a depression somewhere in front of me. I fired a shot at nothing and edged backwards into the small ravine Should I try to flank him? Or wait for him to try the same maneuver? I paused and sought to suppress my labored breathing in order to hear.

I lay there — my skin crawling — as the sun dropped lower and lower in the sky. Then I heard a grunt. Hanlihan. He was in pain. Faint shuffling noises started and then stopped. Had he heard me? Intending to get a view of where the gully curved just ahead, I rolled to my right. A shot shattered the silence. His bullet plowed into the ground where I'd been a moment ago. Disoriented, I glanced up. He wasn't in the ravine. He was at the top, swaying unsteadily as he struggled to cock his weapon. He saw me throw up my rifle and reeled backward. He hit the ground hard, but I'd missed him.

I rolled to my left and aimed at the lip of the ravine expecting to see his barrel poke over the edge. Nothing happened. Had he headed for Bear and the horses? I caught movement in the gully to my right. As I tried to turn, he fired. Something punched me in the side and flipped me over. Hanlihan staggered from the cover of the ravine wall and let out a triumphant shout. His left shoulder was covered in blood, broken from the awkward way he levered the carbine.

I rolled over on my back and pulled the trigger. My bullet struck — a solid, meaty sound. He dropped the carbine and clutched his chest with both hands. Recognition lit his eyes just before they went dead. He fell forward on his face and lay still. Unwilling to risk he was still alive, I tried to get up and go to him. When I fell over, I discovered his bullet had pierced my left side.

CHAPTER 22

Bear was conscious but in a bad way when I reached him. My side was bleeding, so I took time to strip off my shirt and bind my midriff before dropping to the ground at his side. Uncertain if he was taking it all in, I fought my skittering nerves and tried to make him understand the situation.

"Hanlihan … dead?"

I told Bear we had to go back to Fort Robinson.

"No!"

"There's a doctor at the fort. You need help. And I'm shot in the side. We both need help."

"How bad?"

"I'll make it. But I need to be treated. They can do that at the fort. For both of us."

"Arrest us … killing Hanlihan."

"No, he was a deserter."

He closed his eyes, skepticism painted across his pain-filled features.

"Matthew … Bear, there's no other way. Trust me."

"'Nother way," he mumbled. "Cave. North. Near … river. Blood-Mark-Boy."

"The man who took care of you before might not even be there now."

"Take me."

Was my reluctance born of jealousy? Without committing myself, I told him he had to help me get him up on Wind.

Thank God his white man's saddle had strong stirrups. Both our horses were trained to be mounted from the near side in the American way. Bear held onto the pommel while I put his left boot in the stirrup and shoved on his butt until he was able to heave his right leg over the horse's back. He started to slide off the other side, but I steadied him. Then I had trouble getting aboard Arrow.

Because Bear was addled, I took Wind's reins and headed back down the road toward Fort Robinson. We hadn't gone a mile before he fell out of the saddle. I scrambled off Arrow and ran to him. His forehead was bleeding again. I snugged the bandage, but a head wound bleeds copiously. He roused enough to beg me to go to the river and look for a white stone rising out of the earth like a phallus.

"Then turn south to the bluffs. Look for a cave," he said between gasps.

I gave my promise and began the effort of getting him mounted again while he was still conscious. This time, all we could manage was to lay him on his belly across the saddle.

The sun was halfway over the horizon by the time I saw the line of bluffs Bear had described. It was dusk before I spotted a stone resembling an erect male member and headed south to the twenty-foot bluff. I began calling Blood-Mark-Boy's name aloud over and over again. The light was going fast. I became disoriented and started when I sensed someone at my side. A shadowy figure reached out to me. When I shrank back, a light voice spoke in Lakota.

"You called me. I am Blood-Mark-Boy."

I nodded, or at least my head flopped around. "Need help. My friend's in a bad way. He told me to come to you."

The figure scurried around to the other horse and let out an exclamation, *"Dho!"* Then he returned to me. "Can you ride? I'll lead Bear's pony."

He walked away with Wind's reins in his hand. Arrow followed without much direction from me. Just as it seemed he was going to walk straight into the cliff side, Blood-Mark-Boy halted and told me to dismount. Bear was a dead weight. It took both of us to carry him into a large, airy cave worn into the side of the rock. As soon as Bear was deposited on a bed of twigs and leaves covered with thick buffalo skins, Blood-Mark-Boy shooed me outside to take care of the horses.

Carrying Bear inside had about done me in, but the animals needed tending. I managed to unsaddle Arrow and Wind, rub them down, and put them in a large enclosure in a grassy area penned in by a system of staggered stacks of old logs. Lifting our heavy packs and dragging them into the cavern about finished me off. My side felt as if someone was jamming a red-hot poker in it.

The cave had the look of a wizard's lair. Sticks and poles holding mysterious curatives jutted from sockets in the walls. I sank to the ground beside the fire and took my first good look at Blood-Mark-Boy. He was no boy, but a diminutive, well-formed man a few years older than I ... somewhere around twenty-five or so. He wore a woman's skirt over a pair of man's leggings. His movements were graceful — perhaps excessively so.

Neither spoke as he cleansed the wound across Bear's forehead with what looked to be boiled Stone Root. Once this was done to his satisfaction, he fished a white man's steel needle and a thin sinew from a kit Ma called a "housewife" and put them in a kettle of boiling water.

He turned to me. "I need your help."

Distracted by the light voice dancing between a man's and a woman's range, I roused enough to nod. While I washed my hands in heated water, he lashed Bear's arms to his sides with an excess of rope. Then, as directed, I sat at my lover's head and cradled him in my arms.

"He might not feel nothing, or he might put up a fight. Be ready."

With that, Blood began to stitch the torn flesh on Bear's brow. My mate was deeper into the unconscious than expected and did not move a muscle while the healer worked.

Although I knew most of the healing herbs Otter had kept in his Pandora's box, this man used a few things I didn't recognize. He finished the wound treatment with a generous smear of honey to seal the cut from infection.

Then he poked Bear with his fingers and the heel of his hand while holding crushed yarrow leaves to his nostrils. "He's gotta breathe in some of the leaves so his head won't hurt so bad when he wakes up."

Blood worried Bear's flesh until he drew in an agitated breath. After that, the healer scurried around throwing things in a pot to steep some sort of tea. When garlic cloves went into the mix, I knew its intent was to strengthen the system.

Only then did he turn his attention to me. He untied my shirt from around my middle and examined the wound, mumbling more to himself than to me.

"Gunshot. Went clear through. Good. Bled a lot. Good." He got up and spread more blankets and ordered me to lie down. As he worked over me, I studied his features. Pretty … like a girl. Smooth … like a girl. Yet, there was a subtle masculinity there. A blood-red birthmark rose from his neck to curl up over his right cheek. Even so, it was a seductive face. Jealousy added to my discomfort.

His hands touched my belly and chest. "You took a beating. Who done this thing?"

So I told him the entire tale, grunting and gasping now and then as he did something painful. He worked without comment until I finished.

"You killed Hanlihan? Good."

"You knew him?"

"I helped out the surgeon at the post. I was just his clean up boy, but when he seen I knew about healing, he let me help him. That's how I know fire kills the little creatures you can't see. Germs."

"Why did you leave?"

"He got sent to a post somewhere back east and couldn't take me with him. I didn't like the new man, so I come here."

The doctor had likely seen more in Blood than a bent for healing.

"Thank you for saving Bear ... back then."

He glanced across at my lover. "Now we gotta do it again. The infection's got inside him. He's starting to sweat. You strong enough to help me keep his fever down tonight?"

"I'll make myself strong enough." Perhaps there was some fire in my voice because he looked at me.

"He dear to you?"

"He is my other heart." Blood's sudden frown frightened me, so I spoke up. "Will there be jealousy between us?"

"I protect my belongings. But maybe Bear ain't mine. Red Star, maybe. But Red Star don't exist no more. When he fucked me, he talked about someone back home called John." Blood's pretty eyes met mine. "You that John?"

I nodded. "John Strobaw. And he's Matthew Brandt in the white man's world. I've known him since I had five summers. I don't know when it turned into love."

His eyes took on a wistful look. "He is much man. Perhaps enough for both of us. But first, we gotta save him. Then we'll see how things settle out."

My hackles rose, but to rebuff Blood might make him decide it was better to let Bear walk the Western Road than cede him to me. The other side of that coin, of course, was to feed me some mixture of healing herbs with a toxin hidden among them.

"Git some sleep. I'll stay with him. He's gotta have some tea now and then. You have bait in your packs?" I nodded. "Good. You both gotta eat. Build up your strength."

Mistrust flooded my mind. Nonetheless, my body betrayed me. I fell asleep and didn't wake until Blood touched my shoulder.

"He's got the shaking fever. I gotta rest. Keep him covered, but wash his face with a wet rag. If we don't break the fever, he gonna die."

With those stark words, Blood moved to his own blankets and lay down. When I rose, I was weaker and more pain-filled than before I slept. Nonetheless, I struggled to Bear's side and was shocked by the sight of his head bathed in sweat while the blankets trembled from his shivering.

I dipped a scrap of cloth into a bowl of cool water and wiped the perspiration away. Speaking in low tones, I recounted the joys and pains of our childhood and reminded him of our first coupling. I rambled, interspersing my words with reassurances of love. I slipped my hand beneath the blankets and cupped his manhood.

The bowl of water was empty, my words had run out, and I was practically asleep while sitting at his side when I felt a pulse in his cock. I almost laughed aloud. Of course, that part of him that would come alive first. I stroked his bulb with my thumb, and it stirred again. Blood rose from his bed and started for us, so I removed my hand.

"He moved," I said.

Blood laid a hand to Bear's head. "The fever's down, but it ain't broke. Go back to your blankets. I'll watch over him."

# # # # #

We fought for Bear over the next few days, bringing the fever ravaging his body down only to see it soar again. Twice he was so hot, I was certain his heart would burn out. Had he died, I would have followed him. Not from any overt act, but from a sympathetic system. On the fourth night, I noticed the blankets no longer shook. The mound of flesh beneath my palm was warm, but not hot. It pulsed.

"Feels ... g ... good."

I lifted my head and saw his dark eyes gleaming in the firelight. "You decided a four-day sleep was enough?"

"F ... four?" I lifted his head and gave him a sip of water. "Seems like four hours. Still tired."

Blood appeared at my side. "So you come back to us."

"Blood-Mark-Boy. Glad Eagle ... found ... " He faded away, but it was sleep, not unconsciousness.

"The worst sickness is over," Blood said. "The hard part now's gonna be keeping him from going out hunting and making war before he's ready."

CHAPTER 23

We had arrived at Blood's cavern in desperate straits at the Moon of Changing Seasons. The healer's skill had spared me the infection that often comes with bullet wounds. I would regain my health, although I noticed a stiffness in my side that had not been there before.

It was not until the Moon of Falling Leaves — November in the white man's calendar — that Blood removed the stitches on Bear's forehead. Believing himself whole again, my mate was impatient to go outside, to ride, to do something besides remain in the cave. I would happily have encouraged riding straight for home, but he was still too weak for a five day trek across a chilly landscape.

If we did not leave soon, we would be forced to pass the winter in this cave, a fact brought home to me when Blood started collecting an excess of firewood. He enlisted my help, so we took the horses in aid of the effort. How Blood managed without a mount was a mystery. The pen that held Arrow and Wind and the metal water trough in it indicated he had once owned a pony.

In the time we had been with him, Blood had received several visitors seeking medications or his healing skills in exchange for supplies. Still, the cold months must be a hard time for him.

One day when we returned from a wood-gathering trek, we found Bear sitting on a rock outside the cave entrance taking in the warmth of the autumn sun. The scar on his forehead was still angry from the removal of his stitches, but in time it would not be so noticeable. In truth, even now it enhanced his masculine good looks like some tribal tattoo. His manliness almost unhinged me.

He helped with unloading the wood and took up a hand-axe to chop a log we had dragged back, but he had little stamina and soon allowed me to ply the tool. Blood stacked the rest of the wood near the entrance to the cave and disappeared inside with Bear while I hacked at the timber. A few minutes later, a quiver ran up my spine. I looked around, but perceived no danger. Both horses munched grass nearby.

I dropped the axe and entered the cave. By the light of the campfire, I saw Bear lying on his blankets, his eyes covered by one arm. Blood knelt at his side. One of the healer's hands caressed my mate's chest while the other was deep inside his trousers. I let out a gasp.

Bear sat up and shoved Blood aside as I staggered outside. Once in the sunlight, I leaned against the side of the cliff fighting a pain in my chest. A moment later, Matthew was behind me, molding his body to mine. I experienced the hardness of his male member pressing against my buttocks. It was exciting, yet shattering. Another had aroused him to that estate. I made to move away, but he held me tightly.

"Forgive me, Eagle. It was all Blood asked in payment for what he's done for me ... for us. He just asked to touch me."

I turned in his arms but could not meet his eyes. "Now I realize how much I hurt you when I let Timo put his mouth on me. I couldn't understand how angry you got. Now I do."

"You are my shadow self. If you are certain of nothing else, be sure of that. For always."

He kissed me, almost robbing me of my strength and resentment ... yet a little of each remained. But he inflamed me enough to restore some of my shriveled soul. I dropped to my knees and clawed at his britches until he was long and hard and throbbing in my hand. I took him, glorying in the taste and the warmth and the vitality of his cock. Before it was over, I touched him everywhere I could reach: hard buns, full testicles, flat, veined stomach. I was fingering his sphincter when he came.

Then he stood pressed against the cliff while I freed my cock and fucked his belly. My orgasm was as sweet as any I'd ever had. Short of breath, I told him I was going to the sutler's store tomorrow morning to buy supplies as recompense for Blood. Left unsaid was that if he had to make payment in his way, do so during my absence.

When I turned to pick up the axe, Blood disappeared into the cave. No doubt he had witnessed everything.

# # # # #

I slept little that night and rose at dawn to grab my pack and depart for Fort Robinson. We had traveled half a day from the post when Hanlihan ambushed us, but we'd ridden west a distance to find Blood-Mark-Boy's cave, so I could make the trip there and back without overnighting. Arrow needed exercise, so I set off at a decent canter. The leaves on oaks and cottonwoods had turned, and pines and firs had laid carpets of needles. Did this herald an early winter? I knew the weather patterns at home, but they were foreign to me here. Well before high sun, I approached the sutler's store on the outskirts of the fort. The merchant again showed no hesitation accepting silver from an Indian.

After purchasing the wares I wanted, we bargained for a small painted pony with a spirited look about him. Then I headed into the fort and hitched my animals before the headquarters building.

An enlisted man fetched Captain Hughes for me. The officer appeared well recovered from his shoulder wound and was not at all aggrieved when I informed him of the incident on the road. The officer likely figured I'd spared the military the trouble of hanging the deserter.

While at the post, I confirmed Hughes was aware of Blood-Mark-Boy's camp to the east of them. He admitted some troopers slipped off to take treatment from the healer on occasion. Did they seek something other than healing from him?

I took my leave and started back for the cavern sometime after noon, deep in thought over news Hughes had given me about something called the Meeker Massacre on the White River Ute Reservation. What would that uprising mean for the rest of us? It had happened over a month ago, so would be of little consequence aside from contributing to nervousness on all sides.

The autumn sun had a bite, so I held Arrow to a slower pace. I liked the cut of the paint I'd acquired. He had a spring to his step and was the right size for a man of Blood's build.

On the way to the fort I'd been worried over telling the military I'd killed a deserter who'd once been one of their own. But on the return trip, I had no such distractions after putting the news of the Meeker Massacre in its proper place. Now, images of Matthew and Blood engaging in intimacies flooded my brain. I hauled up on the reins.

When had he become Matthew to me again? When I saw him permitting Blood to take liberties. My gut went hollow imagining what had they done in my absence. Had Blood been satisfied with tonguing Matthew to orgasm, or had they fucked, as well? My skin crawled. They'd probably spent the entire day in the blankets, draining one another of strength and fluids.

My lungs could not draw in enough air. I was suffocating while sitting astride my horse. Tears welled behind my eyes, but I was determined not to be a woman about this. I was a man — a man with a bent — but a man, nonetheless. I pulled a sleeve across my eyes and drew a great breath. The burden did not lift.

How would I feel about Matthew after this? The same? How could that be? Did I still love him? Lord, yes! With my entire being. Did he still love me? The answer was less positive. So what did his liaison with

Blood matter? Nothing … everything. In some perverse way, it opened up the issue of morality. My mother believed man-love was wrong … sinful. Matthew lying with Blood seemed wrong to me, too. Sinful? Possibly. Why was it not so with Matthew and me? Self-interest? Personal indulgence? I wasn't smart enough to figure that out.

My life with Matthew, a matter of no great dispute in my grandfather's time, was now shameful. And what could I do about it? Nothing. I was who I was. Helplessly so. Hopelessly so.

I was so wrapped in misery that I tarried overlong on the road and was now south and east of the cave. I turned the horses off the road toward the bluff in the distance. Twilight smudged the air as I approached the white stone phallus from the east. Movement ahead caught my eye. Suspicious, I slipped from Arrow's back and hitched the animals. After drawing my rifle, I approached the rock at a slow, cautious pace. Halfway there, I saw Blood, holding a rifle in his arms, standing with his back to me. Using the phallus as a shield, he waited in ambush. For me.

I went into a stalk and drew within fifty feet of him before one of the horses neighed. Blood was fast. He whirled and threw up his rifle. His shot fanned my cheek. He dropped to the ground and rolled. My bullet took a chip out of the jutting rock.

I jumped to the side, expecting him to fire again. Instead, he rolled behind the stone monument. Now he had cover, and I was standing in the open. I cocked my rifle as I fell to my belly. Gambling he would circle, I aimed at the right side of the rock. I was correct, his gun barrel appeared. But he was high, not low as expected. He got off a shot. The bullet burrowed into the ground in front of me, throwing dirt into my face.

I twisted to the right, swiping my eyes as I went. As soon as I could halfway see, I aimed at the opposite side of the phallus. Last time he'd gone high. Now he'd go low. He did, and I peppered him with chips of stone. But he withdrew unhurt.

I scrambled to my feet and raced as fast as my stiff side would permit toward the stone. Flattening my back against the cold rock, I whipped my head back and forth. Which way would he come? Or would he retreat? Call it quits.

A moment later, the tip of his rifle barrel protruded around the rock at my left. He didn't know I'd moved. I grabbed the barrel and jerked. The rifle went off, and the heat of the bullet racing through the metal seared my hand. But Blood was taken by surprise and lost the weapon as he stumbled into my line of vision.

Again, he was quick. He launched himself at me, clawing for the knife at his waist as he came. I swung the stock of my Henry and caught him on the shoulder. His arm must have been near deadened, but he brought it up, lunging for my throat. I jerked back. His blade made a rasping sound on the stone. While he was off balance, I smashed the rifle barrel against his head. He dropped to the ground flat of his back. I stepped on the knife and placed the bore of the rifle against his forehead.

"Were you going to shoot me from hiding, or would you have given me warning?" My breath was labored. My legs felt leaden. Perhaps I hadn't recovered as much strength as I thought. In a hand to hand, this little man might have taken me.

"Killed you. He's mine. He ain't no farmer. He's a warrior. He oughta be free."

"He's free to do anything he wants. But I'll tell you one thing. He loves me. If you'd shot me, he'd either kill you or ride away and leave you in misery."

"Then how come he fucked me all day? We made great love. He talked fine words that went straight to my heart."

"I oughta shoot you where you lie."

"Go on and do it. I waited for Red Star all my life. I knew he'd come, and I knew he'd go, too. But my spirit told me he'd come back to me. And he done it. I oughta have let you die!"

The words came up out of his soul, and for a moment I pitied him. "You couldn't. You're a healer." I stepped away. Acting on my heart, I put my finger to the trigger, but my head prevailed. Jeremiah Berglund still visited my dreams. I didn't need another joining him. "Get up."

Hoof beats drew my attention for a moment. Wind Rider was thundering toward us at breakneck speed. In that instant, Blood moved. He grabbed his knife from the dirt and flung it at me. I managed to deflect it with the rifle barrel. Cursing, I raised my rifle as he raced for the cliff. Then I dropped the weapon to my side. I'd won. Why take his life?

Matthew must have realized what had happened because he reined Wind to the right and rode into the fleeing man, sending Blood sprawling in the dirt. I got aboard Arrow and rode out to meet them, trailing the pinto behind me.

Matthew stood over the man, muscles taut, face flushed. "I ought to kill you. I won't because I owe you. But if this man dies by your hand, you will die by mine. We will take our leave now. Because of Eagle's generosity, you have a pony and supplies. I'll leave your rifle somewhere along our trail. If you follow us after that, I will understand you are bent on harm. That would be a mistake."

Blood made himself scarce as we returned to the cliff to gather our things. As we entered the cave, I was puzzled by my own feelings. The man had tried to kill me. *Would* have killed me if I hadn't been wool-gathering and approached from the wrong direction. So why wasn't I enraged? I was angry … furious even. Yet it was because of his taunt about lying with Matthew, not for his attempt on me.

It was far too late in the afternoon to begin our journey. I was tired from my earlier trip, and my side was burning and threatening to cramp. Matthew needed another few days to recuperate, but circumstances dictated we leave. If there was a moon tonight, we could put a decent distance between this twisted shaman and ourselves.

Blood was nowhere in sight when we headed east around the end of the sandstone bluff. Unknowing if he had eyes on us, Matthew tossed the healer's rifle in the dirt and, and I released the pinto's reins as we rode on without pausing.

"You think he'll come after us?" I asked.

"I don't know. I didn't think he'd try to kill you, but he did."

We kept a careful eye on our rear all the way to the road. Cloud cover brought darkness early, but there was enough shadowed moonlight for us to continue. In the hour after what I judged to be midnight, Matthew's normally straight carriage was slouched, so I called a halt. We left the road and backtracked a good hundred paces to a small clump of trees. There, I strained my side by handling both of the heavy packs, although Matthew unsaddled his own mount. We ate from our supplies of jerky and tins without lighting a fire.

Later, as we lay in our blankets listening to the night sounds, he reached over and brushed my lips with a thumb. "What did Blood say to you?"

Resentment lurched up out of my groin and put bile in my throat. "That you'd fucked all day."

His sigh was laden with exasperation and regret. "I had a tumble with him. I won't deny that. Because of what he's done for both of us. Nothing more. But after that, I denied him, Eagle. But you aren't Eagle any more, are you? You're John."

I nodded against the thumb still resting on my lips. "Just as you are Matthew to me."

"Why?"

I was loath to answer because it might put a strain on our future. But he deserved honesty. "When you become Shambling Bear, you are something I am not a part of. You are a warrior with knowledge and skills I know nothing about. I feel safer when you are Matthew."

He was silent for so long, I feared he had taken offense. "I am who I am. My heart is a warrior's heart. Yours is a farmer's. I understand yours because I lived that way for a good part of my life. Mine is a mystery to you, which makes you fear it." He was silent again but he wasn't finished.

"This makes me worry over our future. I cannot promise something won't call me back on that road. There are troubled times coming, and warriors will be needed again. Think on the *hemblecha*. Your dream predicted great and joyous dancing, the death of an important man, and then disaster. That foretells our future. Yours and mine and our people's. We will have to play our part in it. Both of us."

He threw a leg over mine. His right hand rested on my nipple. His nose was against my cheek. "I suspect the time will come when you will ride beside me."

There was no answer to that, so I lay silent while his breath heated my neck, a comfortable feeling as the night was chilly. The hobbled horses munched grass nearby, giving occasional snorts as they moved from plant to plant. A hint of clover scented the night air. A shadow startled me as a nighthawk flew between me and the cloud-draped moon. Then I relaxed and slept.

EPILOGUE

A soak in my bathing room at Turtle Crick had never felt so good. Our four-day trek home had exposed our weakened state. Matthew had suffered more from a bullet graze than I had being shot through and through. I trembled to think how close I came to losing him.

I was not yet twenty and one, and our relationship was young. Yet it had been tested. He'd watched Timo Bowers tongue my member, and I knew he'd fucked his healer. A jealous would-be suitor of mine had denounced Matthew and sent him to the guardhouse in Fort Robinson while a covetous, one-time lover of his had sought to shoot me from the saddle.

Raven. Was he dead, or walking around out there somewhere? What of my Spirit Dream? Dancing, death, and disaster.

My attention turned to Matthew as he stepped from his tub. I dried his back, feeling the firmness of the muscles playing beneath my hands. He needed to gain back a few more pounds, but soon he'd be fit to undertake whatever he chose. I moved in front of him and met his gaze.

He smiled. "Gold-flecked hair, gold-flecked eyes. You are a wonder of nature."

I planted my tongue in the center of his chest and sank to my knees, sensitive to each part of him. He was rampant by the time I reached his rod. No need to gain more weight there ... it was weighty enough. I tongued the broad slit, and the thing jumped in my hand. I slid the foreskin back and curled my tongue around his crown. He murmured something. I moved down the underside to his full sac. He opened his stance, and I took him to the root, almost dislodging my jaws in the doing. Then I came out to the end and took a more comfortable portion of his length and girth, settling into a steady rhythm.

He cupped my head in his hands. It was getting serious. He hunched against me, sending his mighty cock deeper and deeper. Finally, he let out that special groan and spurted seed into my mouth. He came and came and came, thrusting into me even after the well was dry. Then with his spent cock still in my mouth, he tousled my hair.

"John Strobaw ... War Eagle ... Night Sky Hair, I love you all."

MARK WILDYR

A native Oklahoman, Mark Wildyr has had a lifelong interest in history, Native American cultures, and mythology. After earning an undergraduate degree in history, Mr. Wildyr served in the United States Army before pursuing a career as a businessman. He presently resides in New Mexico, the setting of many of his stories, which explore developing sexual awareness and intercultural relationships.

Over fifty of his short stories and novellas have been acquired by such houses as Alyson Publications, Arsenal Pulp, Bold Strokes Books, Cleis Press, Companion Press, Green Candy Press, Haworth Press, STARbooks Press, and *Freshmen* and *Men's* magazines. His fiction covers many genres, including mystery, adventure, fantasy, sci-fi, military, police, and sports.

The Hawk Takes Flight, a Novella (STARbooks Press) follows the adventures of two Native American trackers on the trail of drug runners along the Arizona-Mexico border.

In *Cut Hand*, his first published novel (STARbooks Press), the author indulges his passion for both history and First Nations in a 19th Century setting. *River Otter* (STARbooks Press) continues the tale and explores changes in the customs and mores of the times. This novel, *Echoes of the Flute*, is the third in the Cut Hand saga.

He is currently working on the fourth in the series, a novel entitled *Medicine Hair*.

The Victor and The Vanquished (STARbooks Press), examines the delicate path a young Native American gay man must travel in today's world.

STARbooks is bringing out another contemporary book entitled *Charley Blackbear* in the fall of 2014.

Mr. Wildyr hopes you will check his site at www.markwildyr.com. He encourages your comments, believing he learns from the reactions of readers.

aring any underwear. "Excuse me," I said, having a hard time lo

inded by that bulge in his crotch, "but don't I know you?" "May

nd of t ___ bou

with Ray ___ God

loser? ___ in?"

id. "Lik ___ s stro

ce body ___ e on

lly, he l ___ s I ev

up to t ___ any i

staking ___ ne sa

, I coul ___ ery l

ood raci ___ ne s

ng with ___ e in

we go ___ beh

ill see u ___ in p

ed?" he ___ vent

rivacy. ___ grak

hard. I

k, traci ___ t, so

ed it, ha

with m ___ bing

obing, I ___ n co

LOOKING FOR

MORE HOT STORIES?

WOULD **YOU** LIKE TO **CONTRIBUTE**
TO AN **UPCOMING ANTHOLOGY?**

VISIT
http://www.STARbooksPress.com

Hot Deals!

Subscribe to Our FREE E-mail Newsletter!

Submission Guidelines for Authors!

Buy Books and E-books Online!

VISIT
http://www.STARbooksPress.com
TODAY!

he sound of unzipping filled the small space. I don't know who's

, but before I knew it, I had his rod in my hand, and mine was in l

it to do?" he asked, his tone challenging. I knew exactly, and san

www.ingramcontent.com/pod-product-compliance
Lightning Source LLC
Chambersburg PA
CBHW051130020726
47501CB00005B/1434